KEEPING QUINN

THE NEXT GENERATION

RILEY EDWARDS

Keeping Quinn
The Next Generation
Book 6

Riley Edwards

Cover design: Lori Jackson Designs

Written by: Riley Edwards

Published by: Rebels Romance

Edited by: Rebecca Hodgkins

Proofreader: Julie Deaton and Rebecca Kendall

Keeping Quinn

Print ISBN: 978-1-951567-04-0

First edition – January 2020

Copyright © 2020 Riley Edwards

To my family - my team – my tribe.
This is for you.

1

"Brice?" I gasped.

Yes, I gasped.

And not for the normal reasons my voice got all breathy when I was in the presence of Brice Lancaster—hot guy firefighter.

No, right then my sharp inhale was caused by seeing the white bandage that started under his navy blue Station 57 t-shirt, continued down, and wrapped around Brice's bicep.

"What happened?" I continued.

"Nothing."

Brice walked past me to get to his apartment, which was next door to mine, and with my key still in the lock of my front door, I turned to watch him.

"Don't look like nothing," I pressed, noting he

had soot on his forehead and some still on his cheek. Which of course made me stare at his fabulous bone structure, something I couldn't stop myself from doing no matter how many times I've told myself to stop.

"Leave it, Quinn," he barked and my body jerked.

I wouldn't say that Brice was ever super-friendly with me, not in the six months we'd been neighbors, and not in the years since I'd met him. But he'd also never snarled at me. Not because he liked me but because he worked with my best friend, Jackson Clark, and the two of them were tight.

If I was Jackson's female best friend, Brice was his guy best friend. So that meant Brice was always pleasant if not a little standoffish. That also meant I was off-limits —which was a crying shame. The crying shame part was not reciprocated, which was down-right disappointing.

"Righty ho," I mumbled. "Hope you're okay, Brice."

I unlocked my door and scurried in. Not because Brice scared me, even if he did kinda shout at me. No, I hurried into my apartment before I could make a fool out of myself and rush to his side and help him into his apartment. Or worse, ask him if he needed any help cleaning his wounds, which would necessitate him being shirtless.

It was more than thoughtless to think about wanting to see Brice shirtless when he was injured, but there it was.

I flipped on some lights on my way to my living room and tossed my purse on the couch, needing to get out of my heels and work clothes.

I, Quinn Walker, had a desk job. Something I never in my whole life thought I'd have. But after spending the six years since high school trying to find myself and failing, I decided it was time to settle on something. Mainly because I liked my apartment and I liked to eat, which meant I needed a paycheck. Partly because I was worrying my dad. He was a hoverer and worried more than my mom that I was still wandering through life not knowing what I wanted to do with myself.

So to give my dad some peace, which I'd given him little of over the years, I accepted the job he offered me at Triple Canopy. This I knew made him extremely happy because he'd told me every day since I'd started working there three months ago. That was after I'd worked at a hair salon for three months as a receptionist-slash-wash-girl. I was trying it out in a salon to see if I wanted to go to cosmetology school to become a stylist.

I loved styling hair. I was good at it, seeing as I had long thick hair and everyone always complimented me on how I wore it. But in the three months I was at the salon, I realized that was not a job for me. It seemed fun in the beginning but then when the diva bitches came in, something I had zero patience for, I couldn't hack it. Mean people sucked. Bitchy women who bitched just because they could and were demanding on top of that, double sucked.

No, thank you.

So Triple Canopy it was. At least I got to work with family. The downside was I sat behind a desk and worked with family. I loved my dad. Adored my uncles. My cousin Carter was the bomb. But I loved them at family gatherings, where they were always nosy and in my business but I could escape them when I needed. Now, I saw them every day, therefore they were *in* my business.

Uncaring it was before seven p.m. on a Friday night, I slipped on some pjs and headed for the kitchen. This was something else that had changed, I was freaking exhausted after working all week. Gone were the days of Friday and Saturday night adventures. Not that I'd ever limited them to

Friday and Saturday nights, but the sentiment was the same. I couldn't even remember the last time I'd hit a bar with my girls. Hell, I couldn't even remember the last time I'd hit the mall with my sisters.

Adulting sucked monkey balls. Big time.

I hadn't made it to the fridge yet when there was a knock on the door and I sent up a prayer it was my mother with dinner. What could I say? I loved my mom's cooking, one of the things that had kept me living with my parents into my twenties even though all of my friends had moved out and started their lives as soon as they could. Emily Walker spoiled her family. One of the ways she did this was through food.

It wasn't often, though it wasn't rare for my mom to stop over to drop off something she'd made. Sometimes it was a casserole, other times it was a cake or cookies.

My mom rocked.

Without checking who it was, I threw the door open and my smile faded.

"You okay?"

"You didn't check the peephole," Brice grumbled.

I didn't say anything because he was right, I

hadn't—though I wasn't sure why he was bitching about it.

"And you didn't ask who it was," he continued.

Right again, I hadn't done that either, but I still wasn't sure why he was pointing it out.

"You live alone. You're the size of a ten-year-old. Don't be an idiot. Check the peephole before you open the door."

"I'm not the size of a ten-year-old," I snapped, totally affronted, and not to mention humiliated, that he thought I looked like a little girl.

"Babe, you're five-foot-nothing and weigh less than what I press."

He was right, *again*. I was the shortest out of my sisters, and maybe a little under-average than most women, something that pissed me off. But still, I did not look ten.

"Press?"

"Bench press." My confusion must have been clear because Brice sighed and explained. "Weights, Quinn. I can bench press two of you and still not break a sweat."

That was true, by the looks of him he could. Not that I knew that for a hundred percent fact, but his arms and shoulders were huge so I figured even if he was exaggerating it wasn't by much. Which made me glance at the bandage.

"Did you need something?" I asked.

"Yeah. Wanted to come over and apologize for acting like a dick."

"And you thought you'd do that by gettin' in my face about not checkin' the peephole?"

His lips pinched together before they twitched and I tried to remember the last time I'd seen him smile. I couldn't remember, but what I could and did remember was that Brice had never smiled at me.

"And not asking who was at the door," he reminded me.

"Right. We can't forget that."

He didn't miss my sarcastic reply. "You always a pain in the ass?"

"Friend, if you think this is me being a pain in the ass, then you don't know me. This is me wondering why after I've lived next door to you for six months—you never once knocking on my door—decided to do it tonight, and you do it to give me shit about not checking the peephole. Or shouting down my house asking who's standing outside."

"Told you why."

"No, you didn't. You told me not to be an idiot. And you insulted me by saying I looked like a ten-year-old. Maybe that barb will be appreciated when I'm say, *sixty-five*. But I can assure you no woman my age wants to be told she looks like a little girl."

"Wasn't trying to insult you, Quinn."

"Whatever. I'm tired. I'm hungry. And now I need to muster up some energy to cook dinner. So, if you're all right and don't need anything..."

"I could eat."

Yes, that was what Brice Lancaster said before he pushed his very large body through my door, making me step to the side or risk bodily injury as he mowed me over.

This was not good. I'd never tested this theory because I'd never been alone in a room with Brice, but I didn't think it was in my best interest to share space with a man I'd crushed on for years. Not because he knew I had said crush and not because I was afraid he'd make a play—which incidentally I would catch and enjoy every second of. No, because I was Quinn Walker and I had zero filter. Shit flew out of my mouth that should not be said.

I'd been that way my whole life and everyone said I got it from my mom. Though I cannot see sweet Emily Walker blurting shit out willy-nilly.

"Um. Brice?"

"Yeah?" he asked. Though it's worth pointing out he didn't stop his progression to my couch.

I watched as he settled his ass on my brand-new sofa. I did this for a long time thinking I liked the way he looked in my space. So much so, I knew he could not stay.

"Quinn?"

"Brice—"

"Pizza, Chinese, or Thai?"

"I don't—"

"Fuckin' starved, babe. Spent the last three hours in the ER. Help me out here."

Belatedly I noticed his phone in his hand as he waited on me to make a decision so he could order food. Still, this couldn't happen.

"Maybe—"

"Chinese it is," he decided. "Anything you don't eat?"

"What's happening?"

"I'm ordering dinner. But to do that I need to know if there's something you don't eat."

"Brice—"

"As much as I like hearing you say my name, babe, that's not helping me order dinner."

Did he just say he liked hearing me say his name? Oh, boy.

"I eat anything," I stupidly told him.

"Right. You got beer in your fridge?"

"No."

"Here." He tossed his keys in my direction which I proudly nabbed out of the air. "Do me a favor, yeah? Go to my place and grab a few."

"Your legs broken?" I snapped.

"No. But my fucking arm is on fire and sitting up feels like I got something piercing my gut. Would appreciate it if you could do me the favor so I don't have to get up, drag my carcass next door, then come back."

Shit, I felt like a bitch. He was hurt.

"Is it a good idea to drink while you're on pain meds?" I asked softly.

"Not on any."

"What? That's crazy. You need to take something."

"Not gonna happen. Have a family full of addicts that have taught me if your last name is Lancaster you should not ever take a pain pill."

Holy, *holy*, shit. I didn't know this about Brice's family. I didn't know anything about Brice really, other than he preferred hot blondes and he liked his women tall. Which was a double bummer for me because I was short and dark.

"I'll be back."

I turned to leave, and before I had my front door open, I heard the rumble of his voice ordering us dinner. I liked that a whole lot, too.

All of this was a bad idea.

I didn't need to share a meal with Brice.

I didn't need to know he had a family full of addicts.

And I really didn't need to know that he shared something personal with me straight out without prompting, telling me he was honest and easy.

Well, I knew Brice was easy, considering Jackson had told me a million times he was a man-whore.

It's just dinner, I reminded myself.

It seemed like mistake number five-million-sixty-two was getting ready to be scratched onto Quinn's List of Stupidity.

2

Sitting on her couch, I knew I was going straight to hell. All the warning signs were there but I was choosing to ignore them. I knew what I was doing was wrong, but I wasn't getting up. It had been a long time since I'd enjoyed a woman's company for something other than sex.

Not that I didn't enjoy flirting—I did. Not that I didn't enjoy the thrill of the chase—I did. Not that I didn't enjoy the fruits of my labor once I got a woman to her bed—I did, immensely. Some more than others.

But sitting back relaxing on a woman's couch sharing a meal? No. That hadn't been the description of enjoyment since probably high school.

No attachments. No relationships. No bullshit.

Those were the rules. I knew the rules. Fuck, I was the one who'd chiseled them in stone.

Yet there I was, enjoying a meal with Quinn Walker, number one on my List of Women to Avoid.

Since I knew I'd never take her to bed, I'd convinced myself I wasn't breaking my rules.

But I knew I was.

I could never have Quinn in any way other than what we were doing—relaxing, bullshitting, and watching fuckin' TV. That was all I allowed myself and it was debatable whether my best friend, Jackson, would agree. Likely, he'd kick my ass if he knew I was sitting in his childhood best friend's apartment even if it was innocent. That was because Jackson knew me. I didn't hide shit, not from him, not from anyone.

I was who I was and that was it. I loved women. I enjoyed them as frequently as I could. And I didn't hide that from Jackson, either. It wasn't that I didn't invite a woman back if we had a good time. I did. It was just that the moment bullshit crept in or they got too clingy or too close, they were done. Jackson knew that as well. So actually I knew my friend would kick my ass for being inside Quinn's apartment.

But it still hadn't stopped me.

So there I was sitting on Quinn's couch, next to

Quinn because she had no other seating, and it was fucking torture.

I lied when I told her she looked like a ten-year-old. Her tits and ass said otherwise and they spoke loudly. She had an abundance of both, and while she was short, her legs were fucking phenomenal.

The only thing that had stopped my dick from getting hard in the last few hours was the burn on my arm. The pain was constant.

"What...um...how'd you get hurt?"

I hated that Quinn stuttered her question, but from the way I'd bitten her head off out on the landing when I first got home from the ER, I couldn't blame her.

"Shit call out this afternoon."

"Anyone else hurt?"

The concern in Quinn's tone twisted my gut. I knew she was close to Jackson, therefore she'd immediately be concerned about his welfare. It wasn't jealousy I felt. It was the knowledge that there wasn't a damn person in this world who upon finding out my partner was injured would be concerned enough ask about me.

"You know he's fine because if he wasn't, your family would've called you, or the second I saw you tonight I would've told you."

She nodded then asked, "Wanna talk about what happened?"

"Nope."

"Right."

It was the easy acceptance that made me want to share. Quinn didn't push, demand, or throw a fit because I'd told her no. She simply let it go and her eyes slid back to the horrendous reality TV show she had on.

"We found a mother and daughter on the second floor of a house fire. Jackson went straight to the mother and was helping her out the bedroom door. I had the kid up, we were right behind Jack and the mom when suddenly the kid pulls out of my arms and runs back to the bed. I'm struggling with the girl, and she finally finds the fucking stuffed animal she's after. We get back to the hall and it was damn near fully-engulfed. I took my coat off, wrapped her in it, and ran. And before you say shit about me taking off my coat, I'll warn you I already got an earful from Jack and my captain. I'll tell you the same thing I told them. No way was a little girl gonna get singed while we were running through fire. Don't give the first fuck—"

"What you did was brave," Quinn whispered.

"Scary, crazy, and brave. So how bad are your burns?"

It took a moment for her words to fully sink in, and while I processed what she'd said, I took in her face. The prettiest damn jade green eyes I'd ever seen. Normally they were striking, but right then they were soft and lazy and so far beyond beautiful it wasn't funny. Being anywhere near Quinn Walker was a mistake, being in close proximity when her eyes looked like that—mammoth mistake.

"Not bad," I managed to get out. "Second degree. They'll heal in a few weeks, and if I'm lucky, the scaring will be minimal."

"Right."

Her gaze dropped to my arm and when it did I called, "Quinn." I waited for her fantastic eyes to hit mine before I continued. "I'm fine. The burns really aren't that bad. The little girl's fine. The mother's fine. So all in all it was a good day."

"But you said it was a shit call out so I know it really wasn't a good day."

"I was wrong, babe. No call is a shit call when everyone walks out breathin'. I'm just being a whiny dick because I had to sit in the ER for hours while my captain and your friend bitched at me."

"Sounds like Jackson." Her lips pursed together

and I swear to God I was fighting the urge to skim my thumb across them to see if they were as soft as they looked.

"Yeah, Jackson's a 'do as I say, not as I do' kinda man. He would've done the same thing and he knows it."

"He would've. And you would've been the one standing next to him in the ER bitching at him for doing exactly what you did. Seems to me that both of you are the 'do as I say' type of men."

Oh, honey, you have no fucking idea how right you are.

Straight. To. Hell.

The longer I spent with Quinn the worse it got. Normally when I saw her, I could flee before I started conjuring up images of her naked. But now the thoughts came freely and frequently.

Time to leave.

"Gotta go, babe. Thanks for letting me stay for dinner."

"You paid for it, so thank *you* for dinner."

I glanced at the table and wondered if I had it in me to clean up the mess and found that I did not.

"Next time I'll do the cleanup."

Jesus Christ, what was I talking about—there'd be no next time.

"Since you're hurt, I'll let you slide...this time. But don't get used to it. There's no such thing as a free ride around here. Even if you pay, you still have to clean up."

Fuck, but she was cute.

"I'll remember that."

Maybe I could control myself enough to come over, hang out, and be friends with Quinn. It would be a struggle but as I'd learned tonight, the struggle would be worth it.

Her eyes widened in shock and she jerked back.

"What's wrong?"

"Nothing. You've just never smiled at me."

"Come again?"

"Even tonight. You'd laugh at the TV. You'd laugh at something I said, doing it looking at the TV or your food. I've seen you smile of course, lots of times, but...um...never at me. You have a nice smile—always—but it's even better when you're aiming it at me."

Christ. I didn't know what I wanted to do more, kiss the fuck out of her or leave and never come back.

I chose to leave and I did it fast, mumbling, "Thanks again."

I didn't hear anything she said after that because

all I could hear was her telling me my smile was better when it was aimed at her.

No way in hell could I be friends with Quinn. It was out of the question.

———

FOR THREE WEEKS I'd successfully avoided Quinn.

In the almost seven months she'd lived next door to me, I'd seen her going or coming not a lot but still often—a few times a week. But for the last three, I'd gone to great pains to make sure I didn't see her. And in those weeks I was still thinking about what she'd said and how it made me feel.

But all of my careful avoidance came crashing down when I was walking by her apartment door one night and heard her screaming.

Without a thought, I tried her doorknob, it opened, and the door crashed against the wall as I muscled my way in.

My eyes scanned the apartment. Candles lit, lights low, but no Quinn. My gut twisted as she yelled again.

"No, no, no!"

I followed the shrieks into her bedroom—lights

off, bed made—but I could see the light on under the closed door of the master bathroom.

"Dammit!"

The door flew open, Quinn exited, and before I could stop her, she was yanking off her t-shirt and tossing it on the floor. She hadn't noticed me in her bedroom and I found my voice as her hands reached around to unclip her bra.

"Stop!"

"What the—" she screamed and stumbled back.

Her hip hit her nightstand with such force the lamp teetered before it fell over and sent her sideways. Before she could take a header, I moved as quickly as I could and hooked my arm around her waist and yanked her to me.

"Fuck, Quinn, I'm sorry."

Her knee came up, connecting with my thigh as she struggled like hell to get out of my hold.

"Stop. It's Brice."

Her body went still. So still, her ragged breaths became nonexistent.

"Let me go," she wheezed.

"You gonna try to knee me in the balls again?"

"Maybe."

"Then I'm not letting you go." The room was semi-dark, the only light came from the open bathroom door, but I didn't need the lights on to see. I could feel—every inch of her soft body was pressed against mine.

Fuck.

"Are you okay?"

"What?"

"Babe, when I walked by your door I could hear you screaming. Are you okay?"

"Let. Me. Go."

I didn't, but I did loosen my hold. Her face that had been resting against my chest tipped up. I took in her pretty face and forced myself not to move. Good God, she was gorgeous. By far the most beautiful woman I'd ever seen. Prettier than her sisters, and that was saying something because the Walker girls had it going on.

"What happened?" I tried again.

"What?"

"Why were you shouting?"

"Shit!" She shoved with all her might until my arms fell away from her and she rushed around me. "I need to call maintenance. A pipe's broken."

I remained rooted in my spot trying to get my heartrate under control. And as I was doing that, I was trying to puzzle out which had the organ pumping harder: thinking Quinn was in danger, or holding her. My palms on her silky flesh. Her tits incased in nothing but a pink bra pressed against me. Seeing the swell of her ample cleavage in said sexy-as-hell bra.

Her in danger, that had to be it. I wouldn't allow myself to think about the rest.

3

By the time I'd finished leaving a message with the maintenance guy, tossed my cell back on the counter, and went back into my bedroom, I still hadn't processed that Brice was in my apartment.

And when I peeked into my bathroom, finding him on his ass in a puddle of water, half his body under my sink, I'd yet to find a way to calm myself down.

"You scared the shit out of me, Brice."

"Back atcha."

"Seriously? *You* were in my bedroom—in the dark. How did I scare you?"

"Told you, I was walking by and heard you screaming. Thought you were hurt. Came in, saw candles lit, heard you screaming 'no', thought you had someone in your bed."

That made me feel nice and warm—he thought I was hurt so he'd rushed in to save me. But more than a little shocked he'd think I had a man in my bed.

"A man in my bed?"

He hefted his upper body out from under my sink and stared at me, soaked tampon box, toilet paper, towels, and miscellaneous crap scattered around his legs. I would've been embarrassed if there wasn't an inch of water flooding the linoleum, water which was now creeping into the carpet—the reason I'd been screaming.

"Fuck, Quinn, you're a beautiful single woman shouting 'no, no, no' from her bedroom."

"You think I'm beautiful?"

"Christ." His chocolate-brown eyes blazed with anger, something I found immensely interesting. "Put a fucking shirt on."

I belatedly remembered why I'd been rushing out of my bathroom. Yes, I'd needed to get my phone, but the silk blouse I'd worn to work was drenched, as were my slacks. I was going to change into something more appropriate to wear while I tried to stem the flow of water leaking from my broken pipe. So I was indeed standing in front of Brice with my shirt off. I was mortified, therefore I did what I always did when I was embarrassed. I lashed out.

"Sorry, does my bra offend you? I would think a man who's seen literally thousands of them would be immune."

His jaw clenched and without another word, he dipped back under the sink.

"Jeez, what's crawled up your ass?"

He didn't answer, which pissed me off. I had an older brother, an older sister, and two younger sisters, and a bunch of cousins. I wasn't big on being ignored, therefore, I'd learned young how to be persistent until I got a reaction.

"Whatever you're doing under there, you don't have to do. I called maintenance."

Nothing.

"And in the future, I'd appreciate you knocking before you barged into my house."

Still nothing.

"What if I *did* have a man in my bed and we were playing some kinky game? That would've been awkward."

Not that I actually played any sort of kinky games in bed but it sounded good. But Brice was completely ignoring my taunts.

"Besides, I thought you were avoiding me."

Gah! Nothing. My annoyance elevated to a new high.

"And I think you broke my lamp. I liked that lamp so I'm pretty pissed it's broken."

That was a semi-lie. I didn't know if it was broken. However, it was dangling by the cord in front of my nightstand.

I should've been watching what Brice was doing instead of lamenting about a Target lamp I really didn't give two shits about, because suddenly Brice was in my face and I'd completely missed him getting up.

And when I say, in my face, I mean one hand had gone into my hair tugging it back and the other around my waist hauling me close.

"Lock your motherfucking door." I was stunned into silence—hell, I was just plain stunned. "I already told you once."

"No, you didn't," I squeaked. "You told me to check the peephole."

It was then his deep, angry growl rumbled and the area between my thighs was suddenly drenched and that had nothing to do with the broken pipe.

"Not gonna warn you again."

He stared down at me, I stared up at him, heat

sizzled between us. I knew he felt it, too. There was no way he could miss it, the hissing of electricity so strong it was magnetic.

I rolled up on my toes to get closer.

Then the banging on the door started, and without warning, Brice set me aside. After that he released me and his face scrunched in utter disgust.

That hurt.

A lot.

"Put on a goddamned shirt," he ordered and left.

I jumped when my bedroom door slammed. I rushed to my dresser to find something to wear. By the time I made it to the living room, Brice was gone and in his place was a very impatient maintenance man.

It wouldn't be until hours later when the water was turned off to my bathroom, the flood had been mopped up, and the carpets had been shop-vaced, that I'd finally right the lamp on my nightstand.

It would be hours after that, lying alone in bed, exhausted but nowhere near sleep, when I allowed my mind to replay the scene with Brice. Not the scary part when he rushed into my apartment almost giving me a heart attack. Not the part where he demanded I put on a shirt. Not even the part where

I'd caught him staring at my chest. No, I was thinking about the last part.

The part where his hand was in my hair and he was looking down at me like he wanted to kiss me. Never had I felt that sort of desire. Never had I ever been handled so roughly and never, ever had I wanted a man so badly.

I tossed and turned trying to get comfortable. An hour later, I rooted through my nightstand, found my toy, and with Brice as my muse, I took care of business.

Then I slept.

"I KNOW. I know. I'm running late." I was on the phone with my best girl Paula, rushing to the front door as fast as I dared.

It wasn't like I was completely inept, I wore heels pretty much every day. But I was going out to a new club that had opened the weekend before. Paula was being Paula, therefore she was able to get us on the VIP list. I didn't ask how she accomplished this because I was afraid of her answer. So since we were going to Pulse, I decided on a new outfit—of course that included new shoes. Since I'd never worn my brand-new, hot as sin, four-inch stilettos I was being careful. The heels were pencil-thin and certainly not made to run in. Hell, they weren't meant to walk fast in. No, these shoes that were way out of my budget but when I saw them I had to have them, were meant to strut in.

They made a statement. I just wasn't sure if I was capable of carrying out what that statement said, but I was going for it.

Two weeks of lying in bed thinking about Brice with nothing but self-induced orgasms made me realize I was nearing twenty-five and I needed to go out and have some fun. Moreover, I needed to get laid. This was not my normal MO. I'd been taught to be cautious with my heart and my body. I'd always been the wild child in my family but that did not include getting laid. Going out and breaking curfew, yes. Not knowing what I wanted from my life, absolutely. But I'd been with three guys. All of them boyfriends. All of them waited until I was ready to have sex.

Tonight I was dressed to the nines, and as Paula called it, on the prowl. As she'd explained, there was nothing wrong with me 'getting me some'—her words. Bottom-line was, she was right. If men could do it, so could women. And as Brice had pointed out, I was a single woman. He'd also said I was beautiful, but I wasn't going there.

Tonight I was pushing all things Brice Lancaster out of my mind, and hopefully by the end of the night, I'd have something else to think about.

"You were supposed to be here ten minutes ago," Paula bitched in my ear, reminding me I was very late. But I needed the extra time to trick out my hair.

"I know." I grabbed my purse off the breakfast bar as I passed it and finished, "Leaving right now. Love you."

I didn't wait for her response, I'd see her in five minutes. I tossed my cell in my bag, swung open the door, flew through it, and smashed into a hard, very delicious-smelling brick wall.

"Jesus."

Strong hands went to my biceps to steady me, and as annoyed as I was that Brice was touching me because now I'd have that memory all night, I was grateful. Breaking a heel, or tearing my fabulous little black super-short very clingy dress, wouldn't do.

"Sorry. Sorry. I'm in a hurry."

When he didn't speak, I chanced a look at his

face. Oh, boy, he was pissed. His features were set in stone, his normally melty chocolate eyes blazed.

Not good.

"Seriously, Brice. I'm really sorry. I didn't mean to slam into you."

The silent treatment he often reverted to was getting old. I hated talking to someone and being ignored.

"Hello? Earth to Brice. You can let go now."

Unfortunately he did. He also stepped back and did a top-to-toe sweep. His gaze came back to mine and something had changed. He still looked angry, but there was something else there. I wanted to ask him why he was looking at me like it was the first time he'd ever seen me. Why his expression had gone from hard to hungry. And if I was reading him right, if he wanted to go into my apartment.

"Brice?" I hadn't meant for his name to come out breathy, but the way he looked at me made it hard to breathe.

His eyes focused on mine, something flashed, wordlessly he stalked to the stairs and descended without a backward glance.

That hurt.

Not that it should've, he was nothing to me. My best friend Jackson's other best friend. I'd stupidly thought that after we'd shared Chinese and a few laughs on my couch, we could be friends, too. Sure, it would've been a little awkward at first, seeing as I'd crushed on him for years. But we were both adults, and eventually I'd get over it.

But I was wrong. Apparently Brice didn't like me all that much.

And that hurt the most.

"Girl, have I told you how freaking hot you look in that dress?" Bridgett drunkenly asked.

Bridgett was one of my other girls. Paula, Bridgett, and I grew up together. Much to my father's dismay, we'd stayed close. He called us troublemakers. He wasn't wrong. When the three of us were together, if there was fun to be had—we had it. If there was trouble to find—we found it. My dad loved Paula and Bridgett—what he didn't love were the shenanigans. But he also knew there was no one more loyal than my girls. He'd seen it, the three of us had stuck together through thick and thin.

"You have," I told her, probably sounding just as inebriated as she did, considering we'd had the same amount of liquor. "About a hundred times."

"Did I mention your shoes? They're hot as shit. I'm totally borrowing them."

"Okay," I happily agreed.

We shared everything except men. That was our only rule. A rule that had kept the three of us close as sisters.

"We're here to get Quinn laid, not talk about clothes," Paula broke into the conversation much too loudly.

And I knew her voice had carried when two guys standing around the table next to us turned to look at me. Both were cute—nothing special, but cute—and both wore matching smirks. Oh, yeah, they'd heard. Now that I had their attention, I studied them, trying to figure out if I'd go home with either one. The answer was no, pretty boys did nothing for me. And both of them in their slacks and dress shirts were the definition of pretty boy.

My gaze went back to my friends; Paula was pushing another shot in my direction with a tipsy smile and Bridgett's attention was across the room.

"Smokin' hot guy at twelve o'clock. Don't look now, but his eyes are glued to Quinn's ass. I can't know for certain, but I swear I see drool," Bridgett announced. "Oh, yeah, he's hooked all right. Hurry up and shoot that so we can dance."

33

Thank God, we didn't drive to Pulse. I was well on my way to drunk and quickly decided this was my last drink. First, if I was looking for a man to go home with, I needed to be somewhat in control of myself, and secondly, I didn't want to be sloppy. There was nothing sexy about sloppy.

I took my shot; chilled vodka mixed with lemon and sugar slid down my throat and I slammed the glass back on the table and reached for Bridgett's hand.

"Let's go."

I turned, my eyes swept through the crush of bodies, and I froze.

Brice.

Bridgett crashed into the back of me and I pitched forward right into the arms of one of the pretty boy twins. I felt hands around my waist, hips pressing into mine, and smelled nauseating cologne, but my eyes hadn't unlocked from Brice's.

Therefore when his gaze dipped to where the pretty boy held me, I didn't miss it. And when it came back to mine, I didn't miss the hard set of his jaw. Damn, he was sexy. And I certainly didn't miss when he started to prowl in my direction.

He didn't twist his body as he made his way through the crowd. No, not Brice. People moved out of his way. They had no choice, it was either that or get mowed down.

I was transfixed on his powerful strides so I forgot to brace and because of that, I wasn't ready to hear his rough voice and angry demand.

"Step away."

My body jerked back to the present and I tried to do just that. Unfortunately, pretty boy didn't feel like heeding Brice's demand. I knew this because his fingers dug into my hips and pulled me closer.

"Dude, I got to her first. Back off."

Got to me first? What the hell? I tried to step back again, not liking the guy touching me. His grip tightened.

Hell no.

Hell to the no!

"Let go of me," I hissed.

"Babe—"

"Let me go!"

His smile turned smarmy and his fingers pressed harder.

"We can—"

I didn't believe in the three-strikes-you're-out rule. I believed when a woman asked you to unhand her, you complied—immediately. I'd asked the asshole twice and there wouldn't be a third time, and frankly whatever the idiot was going to say was meaningless. Mainly because he was touching me and I didn't want his hands on me.

My knee came up, made contact between his legs, his hands fell away, and Brice had me in his arms before pretty boy bent double and howled in pain.

"Lesson, asshole. The next time a woman asks you to let go, *let go*!" I shouted.

"Fuckin' tease," pretty boy grunted. "All night you've been shoving your ass in my face."

"I have not, you asshole."

"Right. You and your girls gigglin' about getting you laid. Fuck, you're practically beggin' for it."

Brice's arm around my shoulder flexed and now I had *his* fingers digging into my flesh.

"As if," Bridgett screeched. "She wouldn't fuck you with your buddy's dick, you asshole."

"Newsflash, asshole." Paula leaned in. "Women like men." Her hand shot out and swept over Brice's torso. "Real men. Not...not...whatever you are."

"Fuckin' cunt," pretty boy spat.

"Did he...did he..." Paula's big eyes turned toward me. "Call me the C-word?"

This right here was why my dad worried when I went out with Paula and Bridgett. Shit was about to get real. First, my girls were protective of me, second, they didn't take shit, and third, Paula especially was dramatic. There was no telling what she'd do. One option was she'd flounce away in a huff muttering curses as she went. The other more likely option was, she'd instigate a smackdown.

"Grab her, Bridgett!" I shouted over the music. I tried to shrug off Brice's arm. "Let me go, I need to get to Paula before she tackles him."

"You're not getting anywhere near that—"

"Seriously she's gonna hit him, Brice. Stop her."

With a sigh, he let me go, gently pushed me behind him, and stepped between my friends and the pretty boy.

"Two options," he started. "Either you turn and sit your ass back down or I put you on your ass. Actually there's a third, I step aside and let my girl's bitches put you on your ass. All of those options end with you not looking in their direction again."

"Fuck—"

"If I were you, I'd be smart, shut the fuck up, and turn around. You don't and I'll let the mouthy one at you and you'll lose more than pride tonight. Word travels fast, man, don't think you want to be known as the asshole who got his ass kicked by a woman."

"Bitch ain't worth it, Larry," pretty boy number two put in and grabbed his buddy's arm.

Larry's gaze snapped to his friend before he looked back at Brice.

"Got that right. Though the hot one might be, if she wasn't so fuckin' uptight."

"Glad you see it that way," Brice replied, cold as ice.

Pretty boys number one and two didn't go back to their table, they walked off toward the bar. And it's worth noting, both of them had to twist and turn to get through the undulating bodies. The throngs of people did not miraculously part like they did for Brice.

Brice waited until the two assholes disappeared before he turned. And just like magic when he did, our eyes once again locked and I jolted when I saw how pissed he was.

"What the fuck, Quinn?"

"What the fuck what, Brice?"

"Um. You two know each other?" Paula shrilled, and I wouldn't have been surprised if she started jumping up and down clapping, thinking I'd found my good-time guy for the night.

How wrong she was.

"He's my next door neighbor," I told her.

"I'm more than that, Quinn."

More than that? What did that mean? A shiver went up my spine thinking that I had indeed read him right that night in my bedroom when he was looking at me like he wanted to kiss me. And suddenly I had the urge to start jumping up and down. Or maybe I wanted to jump into his arms so he could carry me out to his truck.

"I'm also Jackson's best friend," he growled.

On a slow blink, my eyes drifted closed, cold replacing the sliver of excitement I'd felt moments before.

Jackson's best friend. Nothing more.

Fuck, that hurt.

Time to move on.

"Right. Well, thanks for the rescue then. Enjoy the rest of your night."

I chanced a look at my girls and it was a mistake. I knew because Bridgett's eyes were dancing and Paula was openly checking out Brice like he was a juicy peach she wanted to bite into. Not good. I'd never told either of them I'd been crushing on Brice and I never would, which meant Paula could make her move without breaking the girl code.

That would fucking suck so bad. Actually, it would more than suck, it would kill.

"You know, I don't even mind you calling me a bitch, or the mouthy one," Paula stated, not hiding the fact she was flirting. "Though my name's Paula."

Someone kill me now. Right now—quick and painless—because if Brice takes Paula home it'll be a slow, tortuous death.

4

Fuck, goddamn. Quinn Walker was going to be the death of me. Normally, the woman was gorgeous. But all made up...fucking phenomenal. Her thick black hair had a sexy wave to it that made me want to gather it up in my fist while I fucked the hell out of her, then see it splashed across my sheets as I took her slow and gentle. Her makeup was darker, sexier, her green eyes so piercing that with a single look she'd taken my breath. The dress? The fuck-me pumps? Beyond compare.

It was no secret I'd been around the block a time or two. So it wasn't lost on me that women found me attractive, but Quinn was so far out of my league it was unreal. Untouchable. And for more reasons than because she was Jackson's friend and I had my rules, or that a woman like her deserved more than I was willing to give.

The truth was, even if I was the type of man who was ready for entanglements and promises, I didn't deserve her.

No one did.

She was too beautiful.

Too smart.

Too funny.

Too sweet.

The man who finally got her would be someone far better than me. A man who came from a good, clean family. Not one like mine. I witnessed my father's embarrassment enough over the years to know I'd never expose a good woman to the bullshit my Uncle Seth, his many wives, and his asshole son brought into our lives. Rules were rules and they were put in place for a reason.

But that hadn't stopped me from dreaming about her every goddamned night since I found her shirtless. That didn't mean I hadn't fisted my cock remembering the way her tits looked in that pink bra. And that didn't mean I hadn't spent years doing everything I could to keep my distance so I wouldn't do something stupid like touch her.

All for naught because now she lived next door

and I had touched her. I had spent time with her and found that I enjoyed it. And now I was paying penance for jerking off like a creep thinking about her.

Quinn Walker was out with her girls trying to get laid.

The knowledge was like a dagger to my gut. And my chest burned at the mere thought of a man touching her. My first instinct was to drag her ass out of the nightclub and take her back to her place and safely lock her away.

She would never be mine but I didn't want her to be anyone else's.

Acutely aware her friend was flirting with me, and ever more aware Quinn didn't like it, meant I was right—about everything.

I wasn't stupid, I knew she was open to me. If I hadn't been sure before she moved in next door, she made it obvious the night we had dinner together, and blindingly clear the night her bathroom flooded and she'd rolled up on her toes getting ready to kiss me.

The fuck of it was, I was going to let her. In a moment of weakness, I couldn't fight her pull. I needed to taste her mouth just once. I needed to know what beauty tasted like. Something I'd never had and something I'd never keep. But I wanted it.

Thankfully, we were interrupted before it happened.

"Brice?" Quinn's melodious voice hit me and I felt the jolt of pain I felt every time she spoke.

Quinn wasn't mine. And thankfully I lived by a set of rules that would protect the beautiful Quinn from the type of damage I would cause.

"Paula." I jerked my chin in her direction. "You ladies enjoy your evening."

Needing one more look at Quinn, my gaze sliced to her. Fuck—perfect. Everything about her. "Good luck tonight." She stiffened, and just so she wouldn't miss my meaning, or maybe so she'd think I was the dick I was, I continued. "Be safe and glove up, babe."

I turned to leave without waiting to see her reaction and made my way back across the room where I left my buds. It took less time than I thought it would before Jarrod started in.

"Finest piece of ass here. You gonna claim that?"

I clenched my jaw, not liking Quinn being referred to as a piece of ass. "The dark one is off limits."

Jarrod looked over my shoulder before his eyes came back to me. "The blondes?"

"Have at it. But serious as fuck, the dark-haired one is a no-go."

He wasted no time and I knew why, Quinn's friends were seriously pretty. Not that they could hold a candle to her, but then no one could.

My ass had barely touched the chair when a cute redhead with a mass of curls and too much skin showing slid up next to me, her bare thigh pressed against mine, and when she leaned forward to whisper in my ear it was a goddamn miracle her tits didn't pop out of her dress.

Easy.

No commitment.

No relationship.

No promises.

My kinda woman.

"Hey, baby," she cooed. "Can I buy you a drink?"

"Nope."

"Wanna dance?"

"Nope."

"Wanna get out of here?"

"Fuck, yeah."

Her giggle filled my ears.

Easy.

When her hand went to my thigh I felt nothing.

"Your place or mine?"

Easy.

"Yours."

"Sure thing, handsome."

I stood, the redhead stepped back, I grabbed her hand, and started dragging her through the crowd. The hair on the back of my neck tingled and I looked over my shoulder. My eyes hit Quinn's wounded gaze and I knew with unadulterated clarity I was a fucking asshole. But this was who I was.

The redhead, whose name I didn't know and probably wouldn't unless for some reason she told me, squeezed my hand in an effort to get me moving.

I felt nothing. Not even a stir in my cock.

Easy.

No promises.

No commitments.

Nothing more.

Two DAYS later I saw Quinn coming up the stairs. She glanced up and looked right through me. Not a word was spoken.

Two days after that, I was coming out of my door at the same time Quinn was coming out of hers juggling three boxes wrapped in pink paper, two gift bags, her purse, and her keys. Not only were the boxes on the large side, the top one looked like it was about to topple to the ground.

"Here, let me help." I started to relieve her of the boxes when her body snapped straight.

Fuck.

"No, thanks."

"Really, Quinn, you're gonna drop them."

"Then I drop them. I don't need your help."

"Right. So you're gonna bring your niece dinged-up shit."

"How do you know about Emma?"

"I work with Jackson, babe. Emma's all he's talked about for the last week."

Jackson had also shown me pictures, pictures I didn't want to see because the Walker genes were dominant. Carter and Delaney's daughter looked just like her mother. A shock of black hair and blue eyes. The more pictures Jackson scrolled through, the harder it was to look. Each one made me wonder if Quinn's daughter would get her emerald eyes, and those thoughts sliced deep.

I had no rights to her, no claim, and I'd made it so

Quinn now hated me. But fuck, I couldn't help wondering if we had a kid if the same would be true —would the Walker genes prevail? I hoped like fuck they would, because I wanted my daughter to have gemstone eyes and dark hair.

But alas, I wasn't ever going to have children with Quinn.

"Whatever, Brice. I don't want your help."

Fuck.

I bought that, too. Her anger. The fuck of it was, she had nothing to be pissed about. I didn't take the redhead home, or rather I did, I just didn't fuck her. The truth was, I hadn't fucked a single woman in almost eight months. A goddamn record for me.

Though I wouldn't be sharing any of that with Quinn.

It was better this way. Easier. If she hated me, that meant she wouldn't let me anywhere near her. And I was too weak to keep my distance.

"Too bad. Your stubborn ass is getting help." I pulled the boxes from her arms and endured the scathing glare. I deserved it. "How'd you think you were getting down the stairs without breaking your damn neck?"

She slammed her door, checked that the knob

was locked, and bound down the stairs like the hounds of hell were on her heels.

Good.

She got to her black Honda Civic, popped the trunk, tossing the bags in, and turned to me. Just to piss her off, I took my time arranging the boxes, and when I was done I narrowly missed my arm being crushed when she slammed the trunk closed.

"You're welcome," I said to get a rise out of her.

I couldn't have her, I needed her to hate me, but that didn't mean I didn't want to talk to her.

Her eyes that never failed to touch my soul, turned cold. So fucking cold they went from emerald to frosty mint and I braced.

"You know," she whispered. "I've spent the last week, no, the last few months, wondering what it is about me that's not good enough for you. Why one second I think you're going to kiss me and how pathetic I am that I'm dying for it, and the next you shut down and can't get away fast enough. Then I try to figure out why it feels so good to be in your arms, thinking you have to feel it, too. But you walk away, *again*. Then I see you drag a redhead out of a bar and wonder why that hurts so bad I can't breathe. Since I'll never have the answers to any of that, and since it doesn't feel too good, I've decided

I don't give a shit. I've wasted years thinking about you. Wondering about you. Trying to figure out a way to get you to notice me. When none of it really matters. So next time you see me, Brice, do what you do best and pretend you don't know me. Walk away. Drag your redheads outta bars, screw easy bar flies, live your life, but do it without knowing me."

I didn't wait for the pain her words caused to score through me. I didn't need to, each one sliced as she said them. Each cut deep. Each one excruciating.

So I didn't wait, I didn't think. I stepped into her space, her back hit the side of her car, my hands went into her luscious hair, and I finally did what I'd been dying to do for years.

I kissed her.

Our lips met, my tongue surged in, and I stole everything I wanted. I tasted beauty. It was everything and nothing like I'd imagined. Quinn groaned into my mouth, the sound spurring me so I took more.

Best goddamned kiss of my life.

Bar none.

The taste of her.

The feel of her.

The way she smelled.

All of it perfect. All of it worth it. None of it mine.

I wrenched my mouth from hers, not wanting to end the kiss but knowing I needed to.

"I fucking know you, Quinn. I won't avoid you or pretend shit. And it feels so fucking, goddamned good for you to be in my arms, because that's exactly where you're meant to be. The problem with that is, it is *me* that's not good enough for you. The promise of you, so fucking spectacular, I can't live up to it. But just so you know, I didn't fuck the redhead. I dropped her off at her house, came home, and waited up like an idiot until I heard you come home. I didn't hear your bed knockin' against the wall all night, so I assumed you were alone. And if you weren't, don't ever tell me. I never want to know.

"Go see your niece, and while you're there, I want you to think real hard about what just happened. You feel like slummin' it, you know where I live. You wise up and realize I'm no good for you, which I hope like fuck you do, I'll see you around. But what I will not do, is pretend I don't know who you are."

I left Quinn in a daze against her car, knowing I'd fucked up huge. I shouldn't have kissed her, I shouldn't have offered her more. I knew better. I was not the man for her for a variety of reasons. So many I couldn't put my finger on which was the most pressing. What I did know was Quinn Walker was something special. Something so sweet, I was mesmerized.

I needed to fucking move before I took us both down.

5

I drove to my sister's house in a haze of confusion. I remember none of the fifteen-minute drive. I don't remember parking down the street because there were so many cars. I stayed in that stupor until I was at my trunk getting out baby Emma's presents and I jumped a mile when my dad approached.

"Whoa there, Quinnie." My dad put his hand on my back. "You're not paying attention to your surroundings."

My eyes lowered to the blacktop and I gritted my teeth. First Brice and his constant reprimands about my stupid door, now my dad's rebuke. I was so over the men in my life being over-protective.

"Brice kissed me," I blurted out and watched my dad flinch before the muscle in his cheek twitched.

It was not lost on me that Jasper Walker was a good-looking man. He was when he was in his twenties and he still was in his fifties. My mom had told me the story of how they met, how they struggled, and how they'd fought to get back to one another. She also told me that the moment she'd laid eyes on him, she fell in love. With all that was my dad, it would be hard not to fall in love at first sight.

"And was that kiss welcomed?"

Jeez, that was all Jasper, always going to the extreme.

"Um. Yeah, Dad. He's hot."

That declaration earned me another recoil and I wanted to smile. See the thing was, I told my dad everything. Well, almost everything. I didn't tell him when I'd lost my virginity, though my mom must've because shortly thereafter my father had a conversation with me. It wasn't uncomfortable, I was close to my dad. He didn't get into the nitty-gritty, he talked to me about respect and imparted wisdom from a man's perspective.

So even though I would always be my daddy's little girl, sharing that Brice kissed me wouldn't come as a surprise.

"You know I like Brice. Good, solid guy. But, baby—"

"I don't want to hear about his reputation. I'm well aware. Jackson has more than warned me. I'm also not stupid and I'm not going to put myself in a position to be played. I'm telling you about it, because he said something I didn't like and I need your opinion."

Dad's eyes narrowed, the over-protective beast coming to the surface, and I had to admit as annoying as it was, it felt awesome knowing my daddy loved me so much.

"What'd he say, Quinn?" His growl made me smile. Oh, yeah, my dad loved me.

"He said that he wasn't good enough for me. That I deserved better than him."

"Agreed."

"Yeah, you would, because I'm your daughter. And in your eyes no one is good enough for me, Hadley, Adalynn, or Delaney."

"So that's it? That's what's troubling you?"

"No. He also said something about me slumming it with him."

"Sweetheart—"

"No. Listen, Dad. I know who he is, I know he's got women lined up. There's no way he's missed how hot he is. Pair that with the uniform he wears...well... you know all about how women lose their minds for that. Forget that I'm your daughter, there's no way a man like him should think that any woman would be slumming it when she's at his side. I don't get it. So, I'm asking you as a man, not my dad, why would he say that about himself?"

Dad looked uncomfortable and like he was struggling to come up with the answer. There was only one reason he ever got this look, when he was thinking about his past and figuring a way to give it to me gently.

"Two things," he started. "The first is easy he'd say that to you, because you're you. Sweetie, you are gorgeous, you're sweet, you're funny, and to a man like Brice, a woman like you is untouchable. The second I can't be sure of because I don't know his story, I only know mine. But I'll tell you this; men feel used just like women do. Only we don't handle it the same way. We twist it in our heads, and as a way to protect ourselves, we lock down every emotion. We hide. Somewhere along the way, Brice was used, and probably not from one woman, from many, so to stop that feeling, he shut it down and became who he is. No promises. No relationships. Sex only."

"Were you used?" I asked, even though I wasn't sure I wanted to know the answer.

"As you said, I wore a uniform and women lose their minds over that. It didn't take long for me to understand the game they played. Never feels good to know that someone wants to warm your bed because they want that notch in their belt, not because they like *you*. Not for a woman. Not for a man."

"Sorry that happened to you."

Dad's lips twitched and I knew that if I was my brother or one of my male cousins, Dad would have a smartass retort. But me being a girl and his beloved daughter, he wouldn't dare tell me he wasn't sorry, because I was sure my dad had plenty of women before Mom who'd warmed his bed. The thought was disgusting, but nonetheless, true.

Totally gross.

"So what do I do with that comment? Talk to him about it? Pretend I didn't hear it? I hate that he thinks of himself as slumming it."

"You know Jackson might lose his ever-loving mind."

"Dad, I'm almost twenty-five. I think I'm well-past worrying what he thinks."

"You shouldn't be. Not with this. Brice and Jackson work together. Not only that, they're close.

You starting anything with Brice may put him in an uncomfortable position with Jackson."

"Dad—"

"Listen to me, Quinn. Just think about it. Can't say I'm all fired-up about my girl being with a man like Brice—"

"Uncool!"

"Sweetie, I know his reputation. I've seen it. That said, I also know he's damn good at his job, respectful to the family, and a loyal friend. I got nothing against Brice. What I have issue with is my girl getting swept up in something that's gonna make me wanna rip his head off. And straight up, sweetie, he takes you to his bed and tosses you out of it the next day, that's gonna piss me off. And know this; after I take my pound of flesh, I'll let Jackson loose and he'll take his. After that, your brother's up. So what I'm saying is, think on it. Then think on it longer."

So, it could be said, my dad was a badass—having him up in Brice's face would not be good. Having Jackson and Jason there would be worse.

"Thanks for the talk, Dad."

"Anytime. You ready to go see Emma?"

I looked at my dad's bright smile and my chest warmed. "You happy, Dad?"

"Baby girl, twenty-eight years ago, I met the woman of my dreams. Since that day, every day she's given me beauty. Every day better than the day before. So, yes, I'm happy. My girl, giving me a granddaughter, icing on an already seriously kickass cake."

"I love that you and Mom have that. That Delaney and Jason have found it."

"And one day, you will, too. The day will come when a man sweeps you off your feet. Throws your life off-course and makes you the center of his. Don't settle for anything less, Quinnie. Never take pieces of a man, demand all of him. Because you deserve nothing less than to be a man's everything."

My eyes started to prick and my nose felt funny when I told him, "You're gonna make me cry."

"Can't have that."

Dad pulled me into a tight embrace and I knew when he finally noticed all the presents for my new baby niece when he muttered, "Jesus. Am I gonna have to give you a raise so you don't go into debt spoiling Emma?"

"Might be wise," I mumbled back.

"Christ."

Seriously. I had the best dad in the world.

ME BEING ME, I did not think long and hard about my next move. I did give what my dad said consideration during my visit with baby Emma. Though not much, because my niece was seriously adorable, so it was hard to think about much else other than cuddling her and kissing her chubby baby cheeks, which were not just adorable—they were freaking perfect.

I'd also gotten lost in the new-baby smell as I'd hogged her for the two hours I visited my sister's. At first it was because I loved my niece, but it had turned into a joke because Carter was getting seriously annoyed I refused to give her back. This aunt stuff was gonna be so awesome. I couldn't wait for Jason and Mercy to start popping out babies. I wanted twenty of them to spoil rotten.

The best part of the day was watching my sister. Finally, freaking finally, she was at peace. Total serenity. After all that she and Carter had been through it was so beautiful to watch, a few times I had to swallow back the funny feeling in my throat. She was a great mom, just like we all knew she was gonna be. We had the best mom in the world, so Delaney had a great role model.

But like any good auntie who planned on spoiling her niece, I knew it was time to leave when Emma started getting fussy and rooting around for her lunch. I passed Emma off to Delaney, gave Carter a smirk—which he didn't appreciate but would get over because he loved me—said goodbye to my family, and headed home.

During the very short car ride, I didn't think harder about my dad's warning. Instead I practiced what I wanted to say to Brice when I knocked on his door. And I was totally knocking. The only thing I worried about was damage control, or more to the point, cutting off any possible damage before it happened. Most importantly, bodily damage from my dad, brother, and best friend, but coming in a close second was protecting my heart.

I had a plan.

I knew what I wanted.

I wanted Brice.

I parked my car, locked it, and went up the stairs. By the time I made it to the top, I was breathing heavy and it had nothing to do with the climb. I passed my door, went to Brice's, and knocked. And waited and knocked again.

No answer.

Damn.

I turned to go to my apartment and my breath caught when I saw Brice standing at the top of the landing, a pile of mail in his hands.

He was silent as he walked past me, opened his door, and gave nothing away as he entered. But he left the door open, so I took that as an invitation and followed.

I shut the door and hadn't turned to face him when he began.

"I see you didn't take the time with your family to wise up."

I didn't take that as an insult toward me, I took it as a dig at himself. Stupidly thinking I was better than him.

"We need to talk."

"Right."

"I thought about what you said," I started. "Then I realized it was all bullshit." Brice's eyes narrowed but undeterred I continued. "So instead I thought about how it *felt*. How I felt when I was in your arms. How it felt when you kissed me. How I've felt every time I caught a glimpse of you at the station before you tucked tail and bolted. All of that told me I needed to knock on your door. Something I plan on doing a lot. Can't say I know you, Brice, because you keep yourself locked away. What I can say is, there's no hiding the fact you enjoy a woman's company and you enjoy it frequently. So before I knock on your door I need to ask a few favors."

There was something working behind his eyes. I didn't have the experience with men in general to understand what it was but I did know it was important, so I gave him the time he needed and remained quiet. Thankfully, he didn't make me wait too long.

"Those are?"

"You treat me with respect—"

"Quinn—"

"Just listen. I'm not asking for a promise. I'm not asking for a commitment. What I'm asking for is respect, honesty, and kindness. That's all. For however long this lasts, me knocking on your door, when you're ready for that to stop, I want your honesty and kindness. All I'm asking is you talk to me, and not shut me out, ditch me, or scrape me off like a piece of trash so that we can remain friends after. I'm not asking for a ring or a promise of exclusivity. I'm asking if you take a woman home, don't come knocking on mine the same night. That shit is nasty and whacked and I will not be disrespected like that. If you're cool with all that, I'll be around tomorrow knocking on your door seeing if you're up for company."

"Quinn, you get what you're doing right now?"

"I do. I'm laying out some ground rules so I can enjoy some really great sex with my hot neighbor who also happens to be a really great guy, so I reckon he'll give me what I need since I'm not asking for a whole lot. Though, I also think he'd give me those things without me asking because again, he's a really great guy."

His lips started to curve up before they tipped down and his brown eyes became guarded.

"I'm not looking for a relationship, babe."

"Phew. That's a relief because neither am I. It'd totally suck if you fell head over heels in love with me and I'd have to break your heart and let you down easy."

"I'm being serious. Now's not the time to be a smartass."

"I beg to differ when you're talking crazy. I know you're not looking for anything. Thought I made that clear when I asked you not to take me to your bed the same day you've taken someone else."

God, that thought made me sick. Not just taking me the same night, but him having other women at all.

He was studying me and I needed to end this conversation before I started squirming and he figured out I was full of shit. I wasn't sure about any of this. I thought I could carry on an affair with Brice and keep my head on straight but I wasn't positive. But like everything else in my life, I jumped in because I was reckless. I was impulsive and I'd wanted Brice for a very long time.

And if nothing else—even if he left me broken-hearted—I was on a mission to fix him. No man as good as Brice Lancaster should ever refer to himself as slumming it. Come hell or high water, I was gonna show him he was more than what he thought he was.

Not that I had the first clue how I'd do that, but I was a Walker; when someone set a mission out in front of us, we accomplished it. We did not quit. We did not give up or back down. Dad taught us that.

"I'll leave you with this, since I see you're having second thoughts. Trust me to know myself and what I want. If you want company tomorrow, knock on my door."

"You got plans tonight?" he asked. A chill ran up my spine and sent goose bumps down my arms.

"I do. Hopefully my hot next door neighbor will be knocking on my door soon, so I have to spend some time exfoliating and moisturizing so I'm ready."

"Exfoliating?"

"And before that, shaving."

"Babe, you think I give the first fuck if your legs are prickly?"

"You might not but I certainly do."

It was then the miracle happened. Brice's head tipped back and he roared with laughter.

Damn, that felt good. So good, hope started to bloom.

It was also in that moment I realized this was going to backfire and I was going to get hurt. But if in the time between now and the heartbreak I got Brice's laughter, his smiles, and his company, I'd take it.

"See you tomorrow, Brice."

"See you tomorrow, Quinn."

I barely made it through his door and onto the landing before I let out the breath I was holding.

On wobbly legs I made it to my door.

Shit, I was doing this.

6

I didn't see Quinn the next day.

Though I did text her to tell her I'd picked up a shift at the station.

Her response was immediate: *Bummer. Shaved for no reason.* Then before I could stop chuckling from her disgruntled message, a second one came in: *Stay safe.*

Those two words showing her concern fucked me up for the rest of the night. She wasn't the first woman who'd told me to be safe while I was on the job. Though the effect of her regard wasn't something I wasn't prepared for. I hadn't expected it to feel so good.

That meant I laid in my rack at the firehouse and

tossed and turned all night. Then I did something wholly uncomfortable—I examined my life and how fucking selfish I was to drag Quinn into it. How horrifying it'd been to listen to a beautiful woman ask me not to fuck her the same day I fucked someone else. And if that wasn't fucked-up enough— and it was—told me all she required of me was respect, honesty, and kindness.

Quinn *fucking* Walker had lowered her standards to be with the likes of me.

I didn't know what to do with that. I knew what I should've done, and that was show her the door and explain again she deserved better.

But I wasn't going to. Not after I had a taste of all that was her.

<hr />

IT WAS the next evening I was passing Quinn's door on my way to my apartment in an attempt to shower before I went to her when it opened, her hand shot out, wrapped around my bicep, and she yanked me through the door.

"Saw you pull up."

That was all she said before her body collided with mine and she attacked.

Her hands went into my hair, she yanked me down, and our mouths met in the middle. Her tongue darted out and she set a frantic pace—desperate, needy, hungry. I let her take her fill, then I took mine.

Tasting nothing but beauty, but knowing I had to slow this down, I started to break the kiss but her sweet moan pulled me back in.

My hands went to her ass and I lifted her into my arms, her legs went around my waist, and swear to Christ, her arms wrapped around my shoulders like she never wanted to let go. Something I'd think long and hard about when I was alone—why I loved the feel of her holding on, doing it tight.

I shuffled us across the room, debating the couch but wanting the bed, so I moved us into her room. The lamp was on, giving the room just enough light that I'd be able to see every inch of her when I finally stripped her down.

Quinn released her legs, got to her feet, and she wasted no time yanking at my clothes.

"Baby—"

"Hurry, Brice."

"Quinn—"

"Please."

Fucking hell.

I tore my shirt off as she worked the button of my cargos, and within minutes I learned I had been wrong. Quinn Walker wasn't pretty. She wasn't beautiful. She was magnificent. Top-to-toe perfect. Curves in all the right places, but that wasn't what had my hands trembling. It was her eyes. Hot and wild, but uncertain. She was not having second thoughts. But that didn't mean that now that she stood in front of me fully nude she wasn't hesitant.

She didn't hide it. She'd started us down this path but was looking to me to guide us the rest of the way.

Nothing but trust shone, it leaked from every pore. I knew, because Quinn was not easy. She wasn't the type of woman who would meet a man in a bar and go home with him without exchanging names. The night I saw her at Pulse looked like a feeble attempt on her part and she failed to follow through with it.

There was no chance in hell she'd bare herself to me if she didn't trust me. And that feeling was so powerful, if I didn't lock it down it'd overwhelm me.

Unable to hold back another second, my hand went to her face and I ran my knuckles down the smooth skin. "You are so beautiful, baby."

Those emerald eyes flashed and I knew she liked that. Both me calling her baby and me telling her she was beautiful.

One hand skimmed her back, the other dipped from her face to her chest and skirted above the swell of her cleavage. I was afraid to look anywhere but her eyes, afraid that if I took in anymore of her I wouldn't be able to go slow and give her what she deserved. Not that I could begin to, but what she didn't needed was a quick and dirty fuck.

My lips brushed hers and suddenly my gut hollowed as the enormity of the moment hit me. There'd be no going back. From this point on, irrevocable.

"Brice?" she whispered.

"Hey, baby?"

"You okay?"

"Oh, yeah."

"You're shaking."

Fuck, yeah, I was shaking, trying my hardest to keep my body in check. Every inch of me vibrated with a need I'd never felt before and it scared the fucking shit out of me.

Quinn scared the shit out of me.

"Lie back on the bed, Quinn."

Her eyes widened and her body gave a small tremble before she scurried and did as I asked.

My hand caught her ankle before she got too far and her startled gaze snapped to mine before she relaxed and waited.

Jesus Christ. There she was—all that long thick black hair splashed across her cream-colored comforter just as I'd fantasized. Fantastic, full tits, pebbled rosy nipples. Legs so goddamned sexy, my cock jerked in appreciation.

All of it beautiful.

All of it for me.

And I wasn't the only one eating up the view—her eyes were on me, heating my skin, making me very aware she was staring.

My lips touched her calf and I smiled at the smooth silky skin.

"See you shaved again," I muttered as I made my way up her thigh.

"Of course I did. You didn't expect a cactus, did you?"

"No, I didn't, sweetheart."

My lips made it to the top of her thigh and she started to squirm and tried to close her legs.

"Stay still."

"Um..."

Over the plane of her flat stomach and mounds of her mouthwatering tits, I caught her eyes.

"Um, what?" I asked.

"Um...well...you see."

She tried again to press her legs closed but my hands on her thighs tightened, and with my thumbs splayed, I started stroking closer to her pussy. She writhed again and her trust leaned toward uncertainty.

"I see a lot of things, Quinn. All of them beautiful. All of them I'm gonna taste, some of them I'm gonna suck on and bite."

"Taste?" she whispered.

"Fuck, yeah."

"Well..."

I lowered my mouth, kissed the close-cropped triangle of hair, and inhaled.

"Christ, you smell good."

Quinn's hands flew off the bed and covered her face and her groan filled the room.

"Baby, I want you to watch when I eat you."

"Oh, God."

"I suspect you're gonna be saying that a lot tonight. But for now I need you to look at me and tell me why you're hiding from me."

Her hands remained on her face and my thumbs

moved closer to where I wanted them, finally hitting wet and dipping in.

"Jesus. So hot and wet."

"Brice," she groaned and her hips bucked.

Fuck, yeah.

"Baby, I need you to talk to me."

Finally her hands uncovered her face, now flushed with pink, which only made her sexier.

"No one's ever done that," she blurted out in a rush.

I let the shock of her statement blaze through me before I smiled. I knew it was smug and I also didn't give the first fuck. Not since my very first time, had I been anyone's first at anything. And that was mostly by design. When I was younger, I knew I didn't have it in me for that kind of responsibility. As I got older, with the women I'd chosen to spend my time with, it wasn't an option.

So hell yeah, I was a bastard but I loved that I would be the first to give her this.

"Brice," she snapped.

"Haven't gone anywhere, sweetheart."

"Why are you smiling like that? I'm embarrassed."

"I'll show you why."

Still smiling, I lowered my head, and with my

smile still firmly in place I licked her from damn near ass to clit. And if I thought her mouth was beauty, with the taste of her pussy now on my tongue I knew I was mistaken. There wasn't one part of her that was the best—she was the whole package.

Everything.

"Oh my God."

"Keep your legs wide for me."

"Um..."

"Trust me."

Her legs fell open and heat surged through me, blazing a trail of goodness in its wake and I wanted to shout in relief.

Hell. Yes.

I had a woman to please and I didn't waste another second. It took approximately two minutes before Quinn was rocking into my mouth. Two minutes after that, both of her hands were in my hair pulling me closer. I didn't need the encouragement. I licked, I sucked, I speared my tongue into her pussy and drank from her. Lapping up as much of her excitement as I could get, not wanting to miss a single drop.

Goddamned perfect.

"Brice, oh, shit," she panted.

"Give it to me, Quinn."

She bucked up into my face, I latched on to her clit, sucking it deep, and added my fingers.

Her thighs clamped tight over my ears but I couldn't miss her muffled scream as she flew apart.

Once her pussy stopped grasping my fingers, I slowly brought her back and panic set in. My body was strung so tight I thought I was going to snap. The need I had overwhelming.

Once her knees fell open again I removed my hand from between her legs and cleaned the remnants of what sounded and felt like a really great orgasm.

"Nightstand. Hurry."

I blinked in confusion and asked, "What?"

"I bought condoms. I figured we should have a stash. So nightstand. Hurry, Brice."

Sweet Quinn buying condoms, why did the thought twist my gut?

Impatient as ever, she didn't wait for me, instead she shuffled and reached for the drawer herself, in the process knocking off the same lamp that had fallen the night her bathroom flooded.

"Stupid lamp," she muttered. "I hate that ugly thing."

"Thought you liked that lamp? You said you were pissed that I broke it."

"I lied."

"You lied?" I smiled.

"Yeah. I don't like to be ignored. So I lied to get a rise out of you. But it didn't work."

Seriously as fuck, who admits that? I couldn't stop the chuckle, and when her eyes got squinty, I couldn't stop my shoulders from rocking with laughter.

"It's not funny, Brice. I don't like to be ignored so I get annoying. That way the person who's ignoring me gets annoyed and will argue with me."

"It's fucking hilarious that you're telling me that shit."

"I don't see why."

"No, baby, you wouldn't, and that's why it's funny as hell."

"Whatever," she huffed.

"No bullshit."

"What?"

"Nothing, baby. Finish what you were doing, playtime's over."

"Playtime? You consider *that* playtime?"

"*That* being me eating your pussy until you came screaming in my mouth. Oh, yeah, that's playtime. Time to get to the good stuff."

"The good stuff?" she panted.

Fuck, but this was gonna be fun.

All of it. Start to finish, all the parts in between. Not only was Quinn beautiful and sexy but she was funny as hell. If this was any indication what sex was like with her, I was in way over my head.

"Get that condom, baby, and I'll show you."

7

I'll show you.

Brice was showing me all right. And what he was showing me wasn't soft and sweet. It was hard, it was rough, it was a toe-curling experience I never wanted to end. One leg tangled with his, the other hitched high pressed against his hip. Our breaths and moans intermingled, filling the room with a sexy ballad.

I noted all of it.

How his palm felt holding my thigh where he wanted it. How his fingertips dug into my flesh. The way his other hand fisted my hair, keeping me trapped where he wanted me. How his chocolate-brown eyes bore into mine and drove hard inside of me.

I felt it all. I absorbed it. I memorized it. This

might be my only chance and I wasn't going to miss a second of it.

Brice's hand moved from my thigh, going between us, and when his thumb hit my sweet spot and electricity shot through me, every sense was heightened.

"Oh, God," I panted.

My back arched, my hips surged, and I lost what little control I had left of my body. It was his. All of it.

I couldn't stop my hands from roaming—not gentle, teasing caresses. From his firm ass, up over the muscles of his back, his shoulders—he was hard everywhere. My fingers itched to claw, scratch, and dig into his flesh. I wanted to hold him close and never let him go.

"Too much," I panted between groans.

My skin heated and prickled and my body thrashed under his. Needing more, needing to escape, needing everything and nothing at the same time.

"Let go, Quinn." The thick rasp of his voice sent me barreling toward the end.

I knew it was coming, I just didn't think I would survive. I didn't want it to be over. I wasn't ready to lose him and I knew as soon as we were done, that was it. He'd be lost to me.

It hit me without warning and I memorized that, too. The way he moved between my legs, the insane pleasure he created, the way my orgasm tore through me, the pulsing in my pussy as my body bowed to his.

"Bri...Brice..." I stammered. "Oh, God."

The bed shook with the force of his thrusts, and finally with his eyes locked on mine, hunger blazing bright, he let go.

"Christ!" he roared and planted himself as deep as he could go.

And I swear, it was the sexiest thing I'd ever seen. Better than watching his mouth work between my legs. Better than watching his eyes turn hazy when he first thrusted inside of me. Better than hearing the sounds he made as he pounded deep. Nothing was better so I decided to commit that to memory, too.

On a slow glide he started moving again, giving me gentle and sweet. Brice's head lowered and his lips brushed mine before they went to my cheek, then lower to my neck. The whole time he was placing soft kisses on my over-sensitized skin.

"Quinn," he whispered and my muscles seized.

He sounded funny.

Unsure. Strange. A hint of something I couldn't place, but I didn't like it all the same.

Shit.

"So soft," he murmured. "So sweet."

I waited for him to say more but he didn't. He nipped the side of my neck, and any other time it would've sent a thrill over me. But right then I was worried.

What now?

Did I say something?

Do something?

This was wholly new for me and I was at a loss.

"Gotta get rid of the condom, baby."

"Okay."

Brice didn't move but his body started shaking. "That means you gotta unwrap." He chuckled.

Oh. My. God. How embarrassing, he was laughing at how dumb I was.

"Sorry," I grumbled and tried to turn my face away.

"Look at me."

"Nuhuh."

"Babe, seriously. Can't tell you how much I like feeling you wrap me tight. Like it even more you don't wanna lose me."

"You're laughing—"

"I'm not laughing *at* you."

"So you're laughing at some other woman who's..." His body started shaking harder and my embarrassment turned into irritation. "Brice!"

"Quinn, you're cute as hell, how could I not laugh?"

"No woman wants to hear they're cute after fantastic sex," I educated him. "Sexy. Alluring. Beautiful. But not cute."

"You're all of those—definitely. But you're also cute, funny, and sweet."

I said, "Whatever." But what I wanted to do was sink under the weight of him and stay there awhile. A long while, basking in the warmth his big body and words had provided. However, that wasn't what I did. I unraveled my limbs and let him go.

"Be back." And with a kiss to my forehead he was gone.

But before he went, he reached to the end of my bed and grabbed the rumpled throw blanket I kept there and covered me. I thought this was sweet so I decided to go with that instead of wondering if he did it to cover the evidence of what we'd done because he felt some kind of remorse.

Brice was obviously comfortable with his nudity and probably was a practiced hand walking away from a bed with the woman he'd just ravaged still in a daze while he sauntered to the bathroom to get rid of the spent condom. The notion made my stomach churn and my chest ache.

I was not having second thoughts about having sex with Brice. I was having second, third, and forth thoughts about whether or not I was capable of handling what this was—just sex. Nothing more. No promises. Though, he had promised he would handle me with kindness. Even if he didn't commit to my request verbally, he did with action. At least I hoped him taking us to bed meant he agreed.

Gah! I was so not capable of doing this. There were too many questions. Too many landmines I didn't understand. But even if I was lying in my bed, naked, with Brice in my bathroom, and I was having a mini-freak-out, it couldn't be denied that was by and far the best sex I'd ever had in my entire life. Hence the freak-out—I wanted more. I didn't want this to be a one-time thing, and that scared me—terrified me really. I was afraid I would be ruined if I wasn't already when he ended things.

The bathroom door opened, pulling me from my crazy thoughts. My eyes landed on Brice's bare chest, down to his taut stomach, and with all my might I brought them back to his face to catch him smiling.

Damn, he had a great smile. And now that I knew his after-sex smile was even better than his normal one, I was definitely ruined. I'd never look at him the same, and that's when the realization hit and my cheeks heated that he, too, knew a few new things about me.

By the time he made his way to me, nabbed his boxer briefs off the floor, stepped into them, then sat on the bed—all of which I watched with rapt attention—I was nearly panting.

Brice Lancaster was hot, no way around it. And now after having the best sex of my life, he was sitting on the edge of my bed, brushing my hair off my face. Fortunately, my breathing was the only outward reaction to his proximity. I could've been a shivering, trembling mess.

"You okay?"

"Yeah, Brice, I'm fine."

Brice kept his gaze steady on mine and he looked like he was searching for something. Probably a way to extract himself from the situation. So when the silence slid to uncomfortable, I finally spoke.

"You hungry?"

It was with great effort I didn't flinch when the mask slammed down over his handsome face and his eyes blanked.

Shit, that hurt.

"Quinn—"

"I know what this is, Brice. I'm not asking you for dinner and conversation. I'm offering you sustenance. And just so you know it's purely selfish, I was thinking if I fed you, by the time you were done eating you'd be up for round two."

That was a cover-up of course, but when he smiled and trailed his fingertips down my arm I knew he bought it. I would've enjoyed that touch if I wasn't so relieved.

"You wanna order something?"

Yes, I was relieved.

"No. I made dinner and I always make enough for leftovers."

"You sure you're good?"

"Yeah, Brice. I'm more than good."

He knew I was better than good—he'd made that so. Therefore it was not a surprise when his grin turned into a cocky smirk.

"You don't have to be smug about it," I grouched.

"Yeah, baby, I do."

"Why's that?"

"Just is."

"Whatever."

He didn't move, not for a few long moments.

Then he finally told me he'd meet me in the kitchen and gave me some privacy to dress.

I fed Brice—we made conversation and had a few laughs. After that, he took me back into my room and round two was better than round one. I didn't think it was possible to top our first time but somehow he managed.

Then he kissed me goodbye and left.

Maybe I could do this.

If after we were done, he'd keep giving me a few minutes of sweet before he took off, I'd find a way.

8

I looked down at the text string and cringed. I hadn't
seen Quinn in three days. My work schedule was
totally jacked with two of the guys out on leave. One
had been injured and the other one's wife just had a
baby. That meant extra shifts for everyone. It seemed
I was never going to get off the three days on—one
day off rotation and it was killing me.

Normally this would not bother me. I loved my
job, liked the guys I worked with, and had no issue
with pulling extra duty. But now I was anxious to get
home and see Quinn. Which was why I was reading
over our text messages.

And everything I read told me I needed to cool
things off. There were at least fifty messages back
and forth. Something I didn't do—spend time texting

women. Not because I didn't have the time, but because it planted ideas—the wrong kind.

But damn if I didn't enjoy talking to her even in the form of texting. Most of what we texted was nonsense. Silly shit, that was truly meaningless—but really wasn't because it meant we were connecting.

Even as I stared at my phone, knowing what I needed to do, the knot in my gut growing every day, I couldn't. I didn't want to.

I wanted Quinn something fierce. I wanted to take her to bed and wring every moan I could out of her. I wanted to watch her eyes light when she got close and looked shocked it was going to happen. And, Christ, when she let go and went flying it was spectacular—and not just the way her slick pussy pulsed around my cock, not the sounds, not even the way her emerald eyes caught fire—it was the way she held on.

I'd never felt anything like it. Never had that type of closeness.

I shot off a quick text to Quinn telling her I was on my way home, and before my screen went dark I got a reply. That was something else about her, there was no bullshit. Quinn didn't play games. No wait between texts. No stupid shit like trying to make me think she was busier than she was. Straight up, no bullshit. When she was busy, she texted right away telling me so and going as far as telling me what she was doing. When she became unbusy, she messaged again. She messaged me goodnight. When I'd had to cut out of a conversation because I'd gotten a call, there'd been no bitching, just a 'stay safe'.

I really, really, needed to back off and pull away.

But when I read Quinn's message I knew I wasn't going to do that.

QUINN's front door opened and her hand shot out, but this time I was ready for her. She didn't get the chance to grab my bicep and haul me into her apartment. She was up in my arms, legs around my hips, her mouth on mine.

Christ, she could kiss. I tasted chocolate and wine but mostly I tasted her. A flavor I was quickly becoming addicted to.

We made it to her room. I set her on her feet and without delay our clothes hit her floor. One of these days I'd make her go slow, give me a show as she stripped naked. But today was not that day. It'd been three days since I'd had her and I wasn't wasting time.

"Turn around." She did as I asked, my chest hit her back and I kissed her shoulder. "You wet for me, Quinn?"

"Yes."

I bet she was but I still wanted to check. One hand went between her legs, the other went to palm her heavy breast and she melted back. Fucking perfect. I slid a finger through her folds, reached her center, and groaned when I found her not wet, but dripping. I gathered up her excitement, dragged my finger back to her clit, and circled until her hips bucked.

"Brice." The sound of her whine went straight to my cock resting on her bare ass, and as much as I wanted to make her beg, I couldn't do it.

"Lean over the side of the bed." I reached into her nightstand, found the box of condoms, and made quick work of rolling one on.

Quinn wiggled her ass in impatience, and if my dick wasn't jerking in my hand, I would've laughed, she was damn cute. I took a moment to appreciate the view of her smooth back, her silky black hair falling mostly over her shoulder, her fine ass on full display.

"You're sexy as hell bent over for me, baby."

"Hurry."

"Spread your legs a little wider." When she did, I moved in and notched the head of my dick in her opening and I didn't have to wait long—just as I hoped, Quinn pushed back, taking more of my length.

"Brice!"

"You ready for more?"

"Yes."

"You sure?" I pushed forward giving her another inch, when suddenly Quinn reared back, and fuck but that was hot as hell.

"Yes," she groaned.

Both my hands went to her hips and I ordered, "Reach between your legs and help me out."

"Huh?"

Jesus. Cute.

"Your clit, baby. This is gonna go wild and I need you with me. Reach between your legs and toy with your clit."

Her pussy convulsed, ripping a moan from my throat and necessitating I count back from ten. When I had myself under control, Quinn hadn't moved. I reached forward, grabbed her hand, and brought it where I wanted it.

"Just like this, baby." I showed her what I wanted her to do, only giving her slow, shallow thrusts that caused my balls to draw up and my spine to tingle.

With our combined fingers, I continued to tease her until she started rubbing faster.

"That's it, baby. Don't stop touching yourself."

"Okay, Brice," she panted, and not for the first time I thought about how much I liked hearing her say my name. Especially when it was breathy and coming out choppy.

"Don't stop, baby. No matter what."

I gave her a few hard thrusts and when her fingers kept working her clit, I didn't stop. I couldn't. I could feel her hand between her legs—the thought of her playing with herself, something she obviously hadn't done, or wasn't comfortable doing, yet she was doing it for me, was near enough to make me shoot off. The only thing that would've made it better was seeing her do it. I put that on the list of things to do in the future, then wiped my mind clean and rode her rough. Pulling every sound from her I could.

The room filled with grunts and groans, flesh pounding into flesh. It smelled of sex and excitement so thick I could taste it.

Fuck, but she was sexy. Everything about her—a juxtaposition—sweet but wild, sexy but shy. I didn't know what part I liked the best, and figured it wasn't one thing but all of it. All of her. She was the best dream. She tasted, smelled, and felt like happiness.

"I can't!" she shouted and her fingers slowed.

"Don't stop, Quinn."

"It's too much."

"Don't—"

"Oh, God."

"You're there, baby. I can feel it. Your pussy's so fucking tight. Just let go." A few strokes more and she detonated.

Her hips bucked, her pussy squeezed, and then she screamed her orgasm, taking me with her.

"Goddamn, Quinn." I slammed home, stayed planted, and lost all focus as my climax raced through me, making my legs weak and my hand tremble.

There was nothing like Quinn Walker. It didn't matter if she was wrapped around me or bent in front of me not touching me at all. The result was the same. And that scared the fuck out of me.

I gave us both time to come down from our high, slowly stroking, taking my time enjoying the feel of her still tight around my cock. I waited until she fully relaxed into the bed then gently pulled out. I felt the loss of her immediately, another thing that scared me.

"Up on the bed, baby."

I helped her climb on the mattress, settled her on her side, then reached for the blanket and covered her.

And when those beautiful eyes hit mine I knew, *knew*, I had to cool things down. I'd never seen eyes like hers, they said everything. Hazy with sex, absolutely. But there was something else there, something I couldn't read mainly because I wasn't allowing myself to go there, too afraid I'd get lost.

"You okay?" I asked and brushed her hair over her shoulder just because I wanted to touch it. I could spend hours combing my fingers through her midnight locks and still not believe how soft it was.

"Better than okay." I felt my mouth twitch and her eyes narrowed.

Before she could bitch about how smug I was being, I got up. "Be back."

I quickly went into the bathroom, discarded the condom, and washed my hands. What I didn't do was think about a way to pull away from Quinn. Instead I went back to where she was lying on her bed and sat back down. This was normally the part where I made my exit but I couldn't find it in myself to dress and leave.

I told myself I stayed because I'd promised her

I'd treat her with kindness, which included the respect she deserved. But sitting next to her, running my knuckles down her face, had nothing to do with any promises I made.

"You hungry?" she asked.

Yeah, I was hungry. Both for food and more of her.

"Takeout or did you make dinner?"

"Takeout."

"What do you want?"

"Pizza?" she asked hopefully.

"You stay here and relax. I'll order, run to my house, drop my bag, and grab a few beers."

"There's beer in the fridge."

My gut twisted at her announcement. Quinn didn't drink beer, she drank wine, something I learned over Chinese. That meant the beer in her fridge was there because she bought it for me. Something that sex partners do not do.

Shit.

"Be back in a few."

"Are you okay?"

Fuck, no, I wasn't okay.

"Babe, I just got the best welcome home I've ever received. I'm fuckin' great."

Why those words came out of my mouth I'll

never know. My only excuse was I was a dumb fuck and my orgasm had rendered me insane.

"Kay. I'm gonna rest a minute."

Then I did something ever stupider, I leaned forward and kissed her forehead before I left.

My stupidity didn't end there. I ordered a pizza, went back to my apartment, dropped my bag, then went back to her. And in the fifteen minutes I was gone, I had not thought about a way to pull back.

———

"Do you have any brothers or sisters?" Quinn asked from beside me. With my pizza halfway to my mouth I froze. "Um...forget I asked."

Shit. I took a bite, chewed, and swallowed as nonchalantly as I could. Knowing I should cut this conversation off and move to something safe like, say, politics or religion, I didn't. Instead I kept with the theme of the night—me being stupid—and answered.

"Two brothers. I'm the youngest, Adam's the middle, and Bryan is the eldest."

"Adam?" Quinn chuckled. "Brice and Bryan then an Adam..."

Not only did I answer but I offered more information.

"My mom's name is Bonnie. My dad is Bryan. We used to call my brother BJ until he hit junior high and started getting teased. He flatly refused to use the nickname and demanded to be called Bryan. Adam's real name is Bernard. For obvious reasons he goes by his middle name."

"Bernard? Sheesh, I would use my middle name, too." I couldn't stop the chuckle when she scrunched her face. "No offense."

"None taken. Bernard's a family name. My dad's father. Never got why they'd name their son after the mean son-of-a-bitch. But then my dad always said he was a good man when he wasn't drunk."

"The addicts," she whispered.

"Huh?"

"The night you were hurt," she started. "You said you wouldn't take pain pills because of the addicts in your family."

Shit. I hadn't remembered I'd said that, not something I normally share.

"Yeah. Most of my dad's side has issues with addiction. I've never known my grandfather not to be a drunk but Bryan does. The way he tells it, granddad used to be able to hold his liquor, then my grandmother died and he stopped trying to remain sober until at least after dinner—more like he made it his mission to be sloshed by lunch. My dad's brother, Seth, has an issue with pain pills, alcohol, and women. The pills started after a back surgery. I suspect the booze and inability to keep his dick away from women who are not his wife are because he's just an asshole. And my cousin skipped alcohol and pain meds altogether and went straight for the heroin. So with all of that, my dad might have a beer or two here and there but he's cognizant of the fact addiction runs in the family. Something he pressed upon me and my brothers. None of us are big drinkers and all of us refuse pain medication."

"Probably smart," she returned and went back to eating her pizza as if I hadn't just told her my granddad and uncle are drunks and my cousin was a junkie.

Quinn's family was damn near perfect. No issues with drugs or anything else. I'd spent a good amount of time with all of them at barbeques and other family get-togethers and I couldn't imagine any of her uncles out carousing while their wives were at home. Forget doing it with their son and nephew in attendance. But mine had. With Jackson being my best friend, I was always invited and everyone welcomed me. I shouldn't have been surprised she hadn't been judgmental or recoiled when I'd told her about my family but I still was.

"How's Emma?" I asked in an effort to change the subject.

"So damn cute I wanna steal her from Delaney and Carter. Unfortunately Carter guards the door when I'm there, probably sensing I'm trying to find a way to kidnap my niece. I told you the last time I went over to visit, Honor was there with Carson and Hudson. Hudson's getting so big, crawling everywhere and pulling himself up on everything. Don't tell Jackson, but I think Ethan and Honor are going to start trying for another one soon."

My stomach bottomed out at the mention of Jackson. Telling him I knew that Honor and Ethan were going to try for another baby would mean I'd have to tell him I gained that knowledge from Quinn over pizza in her apartment after I'd fucked her for the third time.

On top of everything else I was doing which was absolutely stupid, I was now lying to my best friend. I knew he'd lose his ever-loving mind if he found out what I was doing, something that should've stopped me dead, but didn't.

"We should talk about Jackson," I told her.

"No, we shouldn't."

"Yeah, babe. We should."

"No, Brice, there's nothing to talk about."

"He's my best friend—"

"And he's mine, too. Has been since we were babies. But what's happening between us is none of his business."

"I think he'd disagree."

"I'm sure he would. However, I'm a grown woman and *I* make the decisions about who I have sex with, not him."

Fuck, hearing her tell me she decides who she has sex with hit me with a force I was not prepared for, reminding me that that's what this was—sex. Something she hadn't forgotten. She didn't say someone she spent time with, she'd been specific. And for some unknown, godforsaken reason, that hurt.

"If he—"

"Enough about Jackson. Finish your pizza so we have time for round two, it's getting late and I have to work in the morning."

There it was, Quinn's head was screwed on straight even though mine was fucked-up.

And that didn't hurt, that fucking killed.

9

The last six weeks had been crazy.

I worked.

Brice worked.

And Brice had continued to knock on my door, then he'd come in and knock it out of the park—every time. I was now officially ruined for all other men.

Sometimes he went home first and showered before he came over, other times I met him at the door and yanked him into my apartment. We'd have sex then he'd go home.

This also meant we ate dinner together a lot. Mostly I cooked, but sometimes we ordered in. But we always ate sitting on my couch watching TV. And now that included cuddling. Something he intro-duced a week ago when I yawned during a baseball game and he pulled me close and wrapped his arm around me, ordering me to sleep and he'd wake me when the game was over. This I thought was strange —normally when that happened, he'd walk me to my room, tuck me in, and leave.

But it seemed like since he broke that particular seal, every time we watched TV, he'd yank me close and keep me there. I, of course, didn't complain. As a matter of fact, I secretly loved it. But deep down inside I knew it wasn't a good idea and it would be one more part of the heartache when this eventually ended.

During the last month and a half, I'd spent time with my family. I'd also gone out to dinner with Paula and Bridgett and we went out for drinks twice. But I didn't tell anyone about Brice, not even when Bridgett had mentioned "my hot neighbor" and asked if he was single. I stayed quiet.

I kept telling myself I wasn't lying to them. I just wanted what Brice and I shared to be between him and me. Something for ourselves that no one else got to intrude in. I didn't want advice, I didn't want to hear I was making a mistake, I wanted to live in the moment and suck up whatever time I had with him.

It would also make it easier when Brice and I went back to the way we were before the sex was introduced. There'd be no relationship postmortem. No henpecking over all the ways he messed with my head and things I should've done differently. It would be a clean break and no one would be the wiser.

It was on that thought I grabbed my phone off my desk and scrolled through my texts, landed on Brice's name, and pulled up our messages. It didn't take long for me to scroll through yesterday's conversation and find the message I was looking for.

Brice: *I need a key. I want you naked in bed when I get home.*

My heart constricted just like the first time I read the message. He wanted a key, a freaking key. Now, as a woman, my natural inclination was to dissect the message and its meaning, spending hours upon hours carefully considering each word, looking for hidden messages, twisting it a hundred times in my head until I finally came to the erroneous conclusion asking for a key meant I was the love of his life, he couldn't live without me, wanted to marry me, and make babies with me.

However, that wasn't what I did. I knew what this was and it was sex. He wanted a key because he wanted me naked in my bed so he could fuck me without wasting time getting me undressed. And

Brice would need a key because he lost his alpha-mind when I left my door unlocked.

So what did I do? I took my extra key down to the mailboxes before I left for work and slipped it in his box. I knew he was still at the firehouse and wouldn't be off shift until late. I knew this because we texted loads. This, too, shocked the hell out of me. We sent thousands of texts back and forth. It was safe to say at this point, I knew Brice well. We didn't get into flowery heart-to-hearts but we talked.

What we had felt real—more than just sex. But I knew that feeling wasn't indeed real. It was the byproduct of really awesome sex and conversation. And if I was being honest it sucked. I wanted real. I wanted Brice in a way where we didn't have to hide. But that was never going to happen and I'd never ask. He'd made all the promises he was capable of making and that had to be good enough for me.

And it was.

I'd take Brice any way he'd give himself to me.

Needing to get back to work, I sent Brice a quick message telling him where he could find the key I'd left him. Before I could toss my cell back on my desk, it vibrated.

Brice: *Perfect. Buck naked, baby. Be home after eight. Eat without me.*

Once again being a woman there was so much there to scrutinize and examine. The first shining example: he'd be *home*. Yes, we lived in an apartment building. Yes, we shared a wall. Yes, he would indeed be home in the sense he lived next door. But any woman would see those words and study them until she committed herself to believing he was referring to her home as his.

I didn't do this. I knew better.

"There a reason you're staring at your phone smiling?"

My head came up to see my dad standing in my office, his own smile beaming. Man, I loved my dad. Loved that every time he looked at me, or my sisters, and especially my mom, his expression always shone with adoration.

"There is," I told him, still smiling.

"I don't wanna know." He stopped and shook his head. "Just talked to your mom. She wanted me to ask if you'd be over for dinner tonight."

"Not tonight. I have plans."

"They the reason you're smiling?"

"Yep."

His smile faded and his face grew soft. Something else he did when he was concerned.

"You've been busy a lot the last two months."

"I have," I confirmed.

"You being safe?"

"I am." My lips twitched at the now very uncomfortable look my dad wore.

What? He asked.

"That's not what I meant, Quinn," he grouched and I giggled. "What I mean is...hell, I don't know what I mean. It is not lost on me, we had a conversation about Brice and not even a day later you're coming into work smiling—and not your normal smile. It shits me to say this because I'm your father, but I'm also a man, so the way you've been floating around here is also not lost on me. I also know Brice is not a man to—"

"He is with me," I cut him off.

I knew who Brice was, I didn't need the reminder.

"Quinn."

"Dad, you're my father so I really don't want to give you details *you* really don't want to have. We talked, I laid out some ground rules, ones I am comfortable with. I know him, I know the promises he made he will keep. That's it."

"Promises you're comfortable with?"

"Dad," I sighed. "As you pointed out, you're a man. I think you can read between the lines without me having to explain, which might be unpleasant for both of us. But I will tell you. I know what I have with Brice and I am well aware of what I don't. I'm good with what we have. We both are."

"You deserve—"

"I know what I deserve, you taught me that. And one day I'll find it. But for right now, I'm happy. Truly happy with where I'm at. If the day comes I'm no longer happy with the arrangement I agreed to, then it will end. For now you're going to have to trust me when I tell you I'm being safe in all the ways I can be."

"Okay, my sweet girl. I trust you. I believe you think you have it under control and you've locked down your heart. But, I'm your dad, and I know you —" I started to interrupt but my dad put his hand up. "Just listen. Hate I'm giving this advice to my daughter, but I feel I need to. Women and men are wired different. No two ways around it. Quinn, not only do you need to get a lock on your heart, you need to encase it in steel. Have your fun..." Dad made a choking sound and I smiled. "But know when to cut him loose. Brice is a good man, but he's a man and is capable and used to carrying on this type of relationship—and you, my sweet girl, are not."

"There is no relationship. There's fun. There's

mutual respect. There's kindness. There's more fun..." And yes, I had to throw that in because my dad was being nosy and I figured if I emphasized the fun he'd never want to have another conversation about Brice. "What there is not, is a relationship. No feelings. No hearts involved. I have a handle on it."

My dad looked wholly uncomfortable and I fought back another laugh. Sometimes I felt bad God had given Jasper Walker four girls. Then other times, when I heard the stories about him and my uncles before dad had met my mom and my uncles their wives, I thought each of them should've had only girls. Nothing like a dose of comedic karma.

"Now, if we're done talking about my sex—"

"Quinn," my dad growled.

"Yes, Daddy?" I smiled and leaned back in my seat.

"Never again say that to me."

"Well, that's what we were—"

"Payroll. I came in here to discuss payroll and the last quarter's profit and loss. We've decided to start issuing bonuses. Lenox, Levi, Clark, Carter, and myself will not draw a bonus but the rest of you will."

"I'm not taking a bonus," I told him. "But I'll run the reports."

"You—"

"How many times have you and my uncles told the rest of us, this is our legacy? That Triple Canopy was meant to be ours? For as long as I can remember," I answered for him. "In that spirit, none of us are drawing bonuses but instead rewarding the hard work of the employees. I'm family. I do not get a bonus."

"But—"

"I'm not taking a bonus," I told him firmly.

"Proud of you, Quinn. I know you had your reservations about taking the job, and when you started you looked like you'd rather have your fingernails ripped out. But you're doing an excellent job. You have great ideas, the guys all love you. Probably because you find room in the budget to buy them new gear, but they love you nonetheless. Pleased to work with you every day. But more, we know, your uncles and I, when we leave Triple Canopy we'll be handing it over to very capable hands. You and Carter and the rest when they come aboard will make what we started into something great. All of this is yours, it's your cousins'. The decisions you make today impact the future of this company and I want you to know I trust you—in all things—to make the right decisions."

At my father's proclamation, my eyes started watering and my nose stung. No girl is ever too old to hear her daddy tell her he's proud of her. But in that moment, I understood he was talking about more than just Triple Canopy.

"Means the world to me you feel that. I know I've been a pain in the ass, and you've been worried about me flitting through life. But I'm settled now and you don't have to worry anymore."

"Darlin', I'm your dad. It's my job to worry and I will until my dying breath."

"Right," I whispered, trying to control the tears now threatening to fall. "I'll get the reports you need and have them on your desk within the hour."

"'Preciate it."

"Hey." Carter joined my dad in my office and I groaned. "Laney called wanting to know if you wanted to come around and see Emma tonight."

"She's got plans," my dad informed Carter.

"More important than seeing Emma?"

"I'm thinking, yeah," my dad returned, making what sounded a lot like a gagging sound.

Which of course was the wrong thing to do because my cousin was on high-alert and I knew this when his narrowed eyes turned back to me.

"You seeing someone?" Carter growled.

Jeez, over-protective much?

"Pull up a chair, brother-in-law," I invited.

"Why?"

"Well, I figure you'd prefer to be seated when I give you all the juicy details of my very active sex life."

Carter jerked back and frowned. My father choked before his head tipped back and he roared with laughter.

When my dad finally composed himself, he announced, "That's my cue to leave."

"Yeah, mine, too," Carter agreed. "I'll just tell Laney...fuck...don't ever say that shit to me again."

Both men exited, shaking their heads in disgust. Served them right nosing around my personal life. And with the newfound knowledge the mere mention of sex would send them running, I decided to tuck that away for future use and got back to work.

I did it smiling. Not because I'd run the men off but because Brice was coming to me later. He was doing it using a key I'd left for him and he was doing it with me waiting for him in bed—buck-naked.

"Brice," I panted as he drove into me hard.

He was close, too. His rhythm was unsteady, his breaths labored, his fingertips digging into my thigh as he pushed it back.

"Fuck, baby. So damn sweet. Sweeter every time I sink into you. Let me have it."

On his demand, I shattered. His cock swelled, making my orgasm more intense. His mouth slammed down on mine and I groaned my pleasure. And just like every time he kissed me through it, he swallowed my moan and growled in ecstasy.

Brice slowed the kiss and stopped his gentle strokes. I knew what was coming. In all the weeks we'd been together, he hadn't changed. Rough and dirty sex followed by sweet and gentle. It was perfect. He'd also pull out, cover me, take care of disposing the condom, then come back to me. Predictable. Comfortable. Bliss.

"Like coming home to you naked in bed, sweetheart."

My heart squeezed and I beat back wanting to misinterpret his words. Something that was hard to do, and I had a feeling for the first time in my life I'd lied to my dad.

"Liked it, too, honey."

Brice's eyes flashed and I watched as he fought

an unknown battle within. I wanted to ask what was wrong, but I beat that back, too.

"Condom," was all he said, then he rolled out of bed.

When he came back, he did not kiss me and leave like he normally did. He pulled back the covers, got in beside me, gathered me in his arms, and silently settled in.

Wordlessly, his breaths evened out and he fell asleep.

This was new.

This was a game-changer.

I didn't think about it and forced myself to sleep.

And the next morning when I woke up in Brice's arms, I knew I'd lied to my dad.

I knew I was in too deep. I knew I loved sleeping next to Brice, I loved the way he'd held me all night, and I knew I loved waking up to him.

Therefore, I knew without a shadow of a doubt I was falling in love.

And if Brice found out, he'd gently, kindly, break things off.

I was in big trouble.

10

"Yo!" I heard Jackson call from behind me as I zipped up my backpack and my stomach clenched. "Where you off to in a hurry?"

I turned from my bunk to face my best friend and barely concealed my flinch.

I was a fucking prick and I knew it.

"Nowhere," I lied.

"Wanna stop by Lucky's and grab a drink?"

Fuck, *fuck*, fuck.

Since Jackson had found Tuesday then finally nailed her down and convinced her to marry him, I'd been ecstatic for my friend. Tuesday was a great woman and Jackson deserved nothing less than what Tuesday gave him.

However in the last three months, I'd been more

than just happy for Jackson—I'd been thankful he had a wife and someone to keep him occupied and not in my business. Not to say we weren't still close, that we didn't work the same shifts, weren't still brothers every way we could be. But that meant he didn't have a lot of time to go out—rather, he didn't make time because he had a beautiful, sweet wife at home. And I couldn't blame him—I had Quinn waiting for me, and while she wasn't my wife, wasn't even my girlfriend, I didn't want to make time for anything other than her.

I contemplated my options and quickly found it didn't matter which answer I gave—I was still a motherfucking, lying asshole. I knew Jackson would be pissed at me but what's more Quinn would take the hit.

What I should've said was yes, but that would've put me under Jackson's scrutiny for a minimum of an hour. And as the guilt about what I was doing had piled on so thick, I was genuinely worried I'd break down and come clean—which again was something I should've done. But being the selfish asshole I was, I wasn't going to admit to anything.

And in that same vein of selfishness, I should've already ended things with Quinn.

Not only was I breaking my rules, I'd also started

spending the night. Something that wasn't a rule, but it very well should've been. For over a month now, I'd been spending more nights in Quinn's bed than my own. And the nights I did force myself to leave, I'd spent lying awake wishing I was with her.

"Can't, brother, got shit to do," I answered.

"Right." He chuckled and my body seized.

What the hell? Did Quinn tell him?

"What's that mean?" I asked and braced for his ire.

"Know you're seeing someone." *Fuck. Goddamn.* I waited for him to continue. "Can't think I'm so stupid I wouldn't notice. Your fuckin' head is bent to your cell more than it's not. And you've turned down every invitation to go to the bar for at least two months."

"You keepin' tabs on me?"

"Hard to miss you smiling. Which I will say is nice to see even if I know it's temporary."

The ever-growing knot in my gut tightened and I was left without anything to say. He was right, it was only temporary, and at this point I was almost looking forward to Quinn coming to her senses and putting a stop to this madness. Something I was too weak to do myself, but I knew with each passing day she burrowed deeper and I had no defense against it.

Not only that, but I instigated the plays. I'd been the one to cuddle her on the couch. I'd been the one to spend the night without asking. Quinn silently went along, following me wherever I took us. And I fucking loved that she was.

"You good?" Jackson asked.

"Yeah, why?"

"Nothing really, you just look like you got something to say."

I did but I wasn't going to tell my best friend all the ways I was screwing up.

I needed to end this before I did something even more catastrophic and fell in love with Quinn—whatever the fuck that really meant. I was sure I wouldn't know what that felt like if someone had described it. A feeling I'd gone to great lengths to ensure I'd never feel. Love meant pain. So as a matter of self-preservation and intellect, I steered clear.

"Nothing to say, but I do have somewhere I need to be. We'll catch up on those drinks next week," I told him, praying Quinn would kick my ass out by then and I could sit next to my friend without being more of a son of a bitch than I already was.

"Right," Jackson mumbled. "Catch you later."

"Yeah, later."

I made my way to my truck, fighting the urge to go back and tell Jackson the truth and take the ass-kicking he'd dish out. I deserved nothing less.

The drive home was a blur as the anticipation of seeing Quinn grew. It'd been three days since I'd woken her up, got her into the shower so she could get ready for work, and left to start my rotation. Three days of not seeing her beautiful face or hearing her voice.

Every time I rolled into work knowing all I was going to get of Quinn was text messages was torture. I didn't ask her not to call, but she never did and I wondered if it was because she didn't want Jackson to hear us or if she knew I was busy and didn't want to bother me.

Whatever the reason, it ticked me off, though I'd never made the effort to call her. I only allowed myself the silent texts. My punishment for being a dick.

I was coming up the stairs when Quinn was coming out of her apartment and I paused to take her in.

Cute white cuffed shorts and a flowy little pink top that made her midnight hair stand out, flip-flops on her feet. Damn, she was beautiful. The outfit was simple, casual, but on her it was hot.

"Where you runnin' off to?" I asked and she jumped in surprise.

"Damn, you scared me." She turned to face me and the front of her was arguably better than the back. But only because I could see her pretty eyes. "I didn't think you'd be home for another hour. You didn't text to tell me you were on your way."

The way she said it, the cute pout on her kissable lips, made me smile. And as Jackson had pointed out, it was something I'd been doing a lot of over the last few months.

"Not an answer, babe."

"Well, I noticed we were out of...*you know*...and I thought I'd run to the store and pick some up. And as long as I was out, I'd grab us something to eat and surprise you. But now that you're home, you can tell me what you want."

"Don't need to go to the store, I have a box in my apartment," I told her and her nose scrunched.

"Two things... one, I can't get into your apartment and I wanted to be ready."

"I'll get you a key. What's the second?"

Her head tipped to the side and she gawked. "You'll give me a key?"

"I've got one to your pad, babe. Not a big deal."

"Okay," she whispered, and it belatedly hit me what I'd offered.

No woman, not even my mother, had ever had a key. And as hard as I searched for some sort of discomfort at Quinn having a key, I found none. Though the lump in the pit of my stomach made itself known—I wasn't playing this smart, keeping my distance. I was actively, willfully, and purposely trying to tie her to me.

"What's the second thing?"

"Um...well...I guess there's not really a second."

The way she paused, the shy way she'd spoken, it dawned on me what she was saying without wanting to say it.

"It's a brand new box, Quinn. Bought it after you told me you were going home to shave your legs and told me to knock the next day."

When her face showed relief, I knew I'd nailed it.

I didn't understand women, and I'd stop trying to when I was around sixteen and I watched my brother's heart get ripped out of his chest by a conniving bitch. Then I seriously stopped caring at eighteen when I saw my uncle's wife hitting on one of my father's married friends. By the time I was twenty-one I'd given up trying to understand relationships as a whole when Uncle Seth took my cousin, Elijah, and me out for a drink and the scumbag picked up a woman who was not his wife and had taken her home right in front of us. The fuck of it was Elijah hadn't cared and Seth had given his son a smile and wave as he left. That was the night my rules had been etched in stone.

Therefore, I didn't understand women, relationships, commitment, and why an unopened box of condoms would mean shit to Quinn, I only knew it did. Maybe she didn't want the reminder if I'd dipped into it to use with a woman that was not her. Who the fuck knew? But I was pleased she now looked happy.

"Okay. Well, I'll just run out and grab some food. I've got nothing to make. You've been at work for three days, I doubt you've got anything in your fridge that I'd dare eat, and I'm tired of takeout." She paused then asked, "Suggestions?"

As if my mouth had a mind of its own, I spoke—yet again I didn't think before I did it, I didn't stop myself before I said, "Give me a minute to toss my shit at my place and change my shirt. We'll hit Buckeyes."

"Buckeyes?"

"Yeah. Best freaking steaks in Georgia," I reminded her of something she likely knew.

"But takeout steaks always suck. Though their burgers are awesome."

"We're eating there."

Quinn's body jerked and I watched as her hands fisted. Yep, I was a selfish asshole. But this time it wasn't because I was pulling her in, trying to do everything I could to keep her close while lying to our best friend—it was because I'd never taken her to dinner.

She'd generously given me her body so many times I couldn't keep count. I'd taken her mouth, her pussy, her time, her beauty, and I'd given her nothing but orgasms in return.

Total dick move on my part.

"Brice. I don't—"

"I'll be out in two minutes," I cut her off and stopped to brush my lips against hers as I walked by.

I hadn't meant for the kiss to deepen, I hadn't meant to taste her, though I wasn't sorry. Especially when I broke the kiss to see her green eyes shining.

I WAS PARKING the car in front of the restaurant,

debating whether or not I should tell her about my conversation with Jackson, when she broke into my thoughts.

"Bridgett called me today and gave me shit about not going out with her the last two times she called. Now that Paula has a man, Bridgett feels left out so I agreed to dinner and drinks with her next Monday. I checked the calendar and you're on shift."

Images of the last time Quinn had gone out with her girls assaulted me, and something that felt a whole lot like jealousy mixed with a healthy dose of unease assailed me when I wanted to forbid her from going out without me.

It would be a total dick move and I had no right, but all I could picture was Quinn in her clingy, short black dress that had barely covered her sweet ass. Then of course there were the sexy-as-fuck heels she'd had on, that did the impossible and made her legs look even better. And I was not the only one who'd noticed. There hadn't been a man in the club who hadn't noticed her.

Fuck, no, I didn't want her going out with Bridgett to some bar without me there to protect her from the hungry wolves that would undoubtedly circle. But again, it wasn't my place. I had no claim over her.

And that thought killed.

"I've been selfish taking up all of your time," I started, but Quinn cut me off before I could finish.

"And I've enjoyed every minute."

"You know, you can always tell me to kick rocks or come back later. I—"

"I only get you a few days at a time. That's why I agreed to next Monday, because you're working."

I knew I'd been taking up all of Quinn's time and I had been present during one call from Bridgett where Quinn blew her off saying she was too tired to meet her for drinks, but I couldn't muster up any regret for monopolizing her time. Though I wasn't sure how to proceed. Never in my life had a woman let me in on her plans when those plans did not include me. Nor had I ever been in a situation where a woman made plans around me and what I had going on.

To say I was pleased Quinn had considered my work schedule was an understatement. The mere fact she'd jotted down the days I was on shift at the station filled me with something so huge it scared the shit out of me.

This was one of those times where I should've thought about cooling things off and backing away, but any time I started to allow my mind to go there, my stomach roiled. I didn't want to change a damn thing, except maybe to pull her in tighter.

I was completely fucked.

"Whatever you need, Quinn."

Her emerald eyes flashed, and in the dim light of the parking lot I couldn't quite make out if she was happy with my statement or if she hoped I'd say more.

"You know that goes both ways. I mean, I've been selfish, too. Most of the time I don't even wait for you to knock before I open the door. If you need—"

"Babe, I have everything I need."

That time, I couldn't miss the surprise in her eyes.

"Okay. I just...I mean...this was..."

"Quinn, trust me, I'm good. I like what we have. I like coming home and seeing you at your door. I like knowing I have something to look forward to when I leave the station. I don't need anything but what we have."

That was a partial lie. She made me happy with what she gave me, but deep down I knew I wanted more. I just had no idea what the hell to do about it.

11

I was in a total daze as Brice held my hand and walked us into the restaurant.

Held my hand—in public.

I wasn't paying a lick of attention to anything because my mind was stuck on our conversation in the car. He said he liked what we had. He liked having something to look forward to when he left the station—and that something was me.

What the hell did that mean?

As the days had slid into weeks, then into months, I'd been on pins and needles waiting for Brice to end things. But he hadn't; instead, he was now a regular in my bed. And not just for sex, he'd slept there most nights. Now we were at a restaurant, which felt a lot like a date.

This arrangement was supposed to be sex only—no commitment, no promises, complete honesty. Though Brice hadn't been with anyone else during our time together. That was something else I'd prepared for but knew it would hurt like a bitch. He'd promised he would be respectful and not come to me if he'd taken another woman. Yet, he'd never, not once, skipped my bed.

So it was with all of those thoughts jumbled in my head taking all of my attention, I didn't see what I should've before it was too late.

"Quinn?"

It's important to note that while my body locked and my lungs seized at hearing my father's voice, Brice did not let go of my hand—neither did he freeze like a deer caught in headlights.

No, he was smooth when he stopped us in front of the table my parents were dining at. I had yet to speak because I was still in absolute shock.

Brice was not. He smoothly greeted my dad.

"Jasper. Emily. Nice to see you."

My hand flexed in Brice's and I tried to jerk it away, but Brice didn't let me. Not that it mattered much—my parents already saw us holding hands.

Shit.

"Hi, guys." I tried to sound chipper but instead it came out sounding like a squeak.

Damn.

"Brice, how nice to see you." My mom smiled.

Of course she would, she was Emily Walker—polite, sweet, well-mannered—she would hide her surprise and possible hurt at my concealment I was carrying on an affair with Brice until she had me in private.

"Would you two like to join us? We haven't ordered yet," my dad offered.

Please, God, say no.

"Appreciate the offer. Quinn?"

Shit, damn, fuck it all to hell. How did I answer that? Was Brice deferring to me, hoping I'd get us out of having to sit with my parents? Or was he just being polite asking if I minded because he didn't?

I had my answer when Brice motioned to the hostess by tilting his head toward my parents' table.

"We wouldn't want to hold you up." I tried to decline.

My dad's smile broadened—he was thoroughly enjoying my discomfort—and suddenly I wanted to eat dinner with my parents so I could sit across from my father and kick him in his shin.

"Nonsense," Mom said. "Besides, you've been

working so much I hardly get to see you. Sit, have dinner with us. Seems there's a lot to catch up on."

Oh, yeah, I'd get an earful when my mom got me alone.

My dad stood, moving to the seat to my mom's right, Brice pulled out the chair to my mom's left, and waited until I sat before he and my father both took their seats.

There was a lot there. First, my father had moved so Brice and I could sit next to each other instead of across the table. Then of course there was Brice—who knew he could be a gentleman and pull out a chair for me? Not that I would know if this was normal behavior or if it was because we were in my parents' company.

Which brought me to the bigger problem—my first date with Brice would be spent with my parents.

Kill me now.

"So," my dad started and I braced. "Jackson said there were two casualties at that warehouse fire."

"There were?" I asked.

I knew there'd been a fire at a warehouse—three other houses had accompanied the 57—but Brice hadn't mentioned casualties.

"Yeah. Both male, mid-forties," Brice answered.

"Damn." My dad shook his head. "Jackson said it was bad."

"Never good when we're recovering instead of rescuing. But, yeah, it was bad."

I glanced at Brice and wondered how much more he was keeping from me and why he hadn't told me two men had died.

"How's business?" Brice asked, changing the subject.

"Good. Real good. More contracts than we can handle."

"Yeah, Quinn mentioned you were looking at hiring a few more men."

Dad's eyes cut to me and his lips curved up. I would've paid more attention to how much I liked it when my dad smiled if I wasn't still thinking about why Brice had kept something so important from me.

The conversation flowed around me but I wasn't paying attention to any of it. I was too busy trying to figure out why my feelings were so hurt. Then my heart squeezed when I remembered we weren't that —we didn't have a real relationship, not one that included heart-to-hearts and feelings.

It was the wake-up I needed, the cold, hard slap in the face that Brice's life didn't include me. Not in any real way, where he'd share how he felt about two men dying during a callout.

"Babe?" Brice tapped my knee.

"Yeah?"

"Your dad asked you if you were ready to order."

"Oh. Sorry. Yeah, I know what I want."

Brice tilted his head to study me, his look of concern unwelcome. As a matter of fact, in that moment I wished I was anywhere but in his presence. I wanted to be able to mentally berate myself in the privacy of my apartment where I could have a proper crying jag at my stupidity.

My dad warned me, told me I wasn't capable of carrying on an affair and not get my heart broken. How right he was.

"Your sister and Carter are bringing Emma over on Saturday. You should come over, we'll plan a cookout." I glanced at my mom and attempted to return her smile.

"Sure. Let me know what time."

"Brice?"

Oh, hell to the no. It was time I smartened up and started thinking straight. Brice going to my parents' house for a family dinner like he was my boyfriend or some such shit wasn't going to happen. Couldn't happen.

I needed to remember my place.

"Mom, I'm sure he's too busy. Right, Brice?"

I turned to look at Brice. His chocolate brown eyes that were normally sweet and warm when he looked at me, were angry slits.

I had no idea why he'd be upset, I was getting him off the hook. Brice had been clear from the start, but somehow everything had become murky. I wasn't sure when it happened, though if I had to guess it was the night he cuddled with me on the couch. After that, murky became muddy when he started spending the night. Now everything was screwed up.

"Actually, I'm free Saturday. I don't go back on shift until Sunday."

Brice may've been answering my mom, however his gaze never left mine.

Damn him.

"Great. Maybe we should—"

"Sweetheart," my dad cut in. "Not this time."

Oh, thank God my dad stepped in and stopped my mom before she planned a blowout family barbeque that would include all of my aunts, uncles, and cousins.

Jackson.

He would freak the hell out if he knew I was sleeping with Brice. Or rather, he'd freak the fuck out *on* Brice if he found out Brice was sleeping with *me*.

Start to finish, a really terrible idea. Beginning with Brice and me leaving the house together to go to dinner. That never should've happened. It shattered our happy bubble.

Ruined everything.

The rest of my evening turned uncomfortable. Conversation flowed easily, my parents smiled, Brice joked and laughed with them, and through it all my heart broke—just like my dad said it would.

I could pretend when it was Brice and me alone in my apartment. Nothing could touch us there. Reality didn't creep in like a cold bucket of water thrown in my face.

"You were quiet," Brice noted when we got back into the car. "Everything okay?"

"Sure. I'm just tired."

"Quinn, I've seen you tired. You do not get quiet and pull into yourself. What's wrong?"

"Don't pretend you know me, Brice. You have no idea how I behave when I'm tired."

Brice jerked back and since I was looking I saw

the muscles in his jaw tick. But if he had something to say, he locked it down and finished the drive back to the apartment in silence.

If I was being honest with myself, which I wasn't, I was firmly living in denial. That pissed me off. I wanted him to call me on my bullshit, tell me he did know me, he had paid attention over the last three months. But he didn't. Another reminder—sex only.

He parked, we walked across the parking lot and up the stairs in utter silence—it was deafening. Each step I took, way painful. Brice pulled his keys out of his pocket and used his key to open my door—that hurt, too.

Then instead of doing what I thought he'd do, which was get away from me and my foul mood as quickly as possible, he followed me in, shut the door, and locked it.

What the hell?

"What are you doing, Brice?"

He didn't answer, instead he grabbed my hand and tugged me toward my bedroom. Was he crazy? He couldn't actually think we were having sex? I'd spoken approximately a dozen words at dinner after he accepted my mother's dinner invitation and only a handful in the car.

There was no way he was so inept he missed my freeze-out.

"Seriously, I'm tired."

"Heard you the first time, Quinn."

"Then what are you doing?"

"Getting you into bed."

My blood started to heat and it became increasingly difficult not to blow my top and make a fool of myself. Though, maybe if I did, he'd go running for the hills. If I told him I'd fallen in love with him, broke the terms of our agreement, he'd end the craziness. Which was what I needed him to do. I wasn't strong enough to let him go.

"I'm not having sex with you," I blurted out.

"What the fuck?" At his angry tone, my spine snapped straight, and when I took in his posture, I took a much-needed step back.

"I don't understand why you sound so pissed. There's only ever been one reason for you to be in my bedroom. And since I'm tired and we're not going there, I don't—"

I didn't get to finish my statement. That's because Brice moved, and when he did he crowded my space, his hands went to my shirt, he yanked it over my head and unclipped my bra. And that was when my brain finally kicked in and I batted his hands away.

"What are you doing?"

"Quiet!"

He tore his shirt off. Suddenly it was over my head, and without much of a choice, I shoved my arms through the sleeves and stared at Brice in disbelief.

"Seriously, what's going on here?"

He shuffled me to the bed, knelt in front of me, pulled off my shoes and socks, then he stood and removed my jeans. The next thing I knew, I was in bed.

I was completely stunned—total loss for words— and when he undressed and climbed into bed next to me, he shocked me again.

"Brice—"

"Quiet, Quinn. You're tired and I'm unbelievably pissed. Go to sleep."

"You're pissed?" I snapped, my body going solid. "What do you have to be mad about?"

"First time I take my woman out to dinner, we find her parents are at the same restaurant. So, I'm thinking we sit with them, get that outta the way, have a nice meal. But that doesn't happen. Instead, my woman shuts the fuck down, gets quiet, and barely speaks. Then I'm treated to some bullshit about how you're tired instead of you just coming straight out and telling me what's crawled up your ass. So, yes, Quinn, I'm pissed. Now, you wanna tell me what your problem is?"

His woman?

Knife straight to the heart.

Not only had he delivered the blow, he twisted it.

"I'm not your woman," I whispered.

"You're not?"

"No."

But damn did I wish I was.

"In the last three months we've been together, you've taken another man?"

"Of course not," I snapped.

"Right. And in the last month, has it not been me waking up with you in my arms damn near every morning I'm not working?"

"That doesn't make me your woman."

"So, it's not you I talk to five hundred times a day while I'm on shift? It's not you I can't wait to come home to? It's not you who meets me at the door?"

All of that was true, with only the slight exaggeration of five hundred texts a day, though it may've been close to that. And it felt damn good to hear him say he couldn't wait to come home to me—but I knew better. He was looking forward to coming home because I was a sure thing. He knew I'd be waiting for him at the door ready to pounce on him.

"Yeah, let's talk about that—"

"Which part?" he growled, losing patience—that is to say, losing what was left of his almost nonexistent patience.

"The part about us talking five hundred times a day, or rather the things we *don't* talk about."

"Come again?"

"Two fatalities?" I reminded him.

"Yeah?"

"That's it? Just yeah?"

I sat up and glanced down at Brice lounging back on my bed like it was his, like he'd done it for years, like it was his right to be there—and that made me angry. It was irrational and dumb but it hurt to see him lying there. Which made me angry at myself for thinking I could keep him.

"Babe, I have no idea where you're taking this so you're gonna have to give me more."

"You didn't tell me two men died. You told me about the warehouse fire. You told me about five other calls you got, what the guys were up to at the station. You told me about the new kitchen appliances someone donated. You told me about the fundraiser the station was doing for the youth soccer league. But you did not tell me that two men died during a callout. Which served as a cold reminder, I am not your woman. We do not talk about important stuff, we're surface. Sex and superficial conversation. Which reminds me, you are not going to my parents' house for dinner."

"Let me get this straight. You got all of that because I didn't tell you we pulled two charred, dead bodies outta the warehouse?" I flinched at his description and my lips pinched together. "Yeah, Quinn, that right there is why I didn't say anything. I don't want to fill your head full of ugly shit that happens. Death is never pretty, but in my line of work, it's less so. What Jackson chooses to tell Tuesday is up to him. What he chooses to tell your dad and your family is up to him. But for me, I don't want to lay my shit on you when you're sitting here alone in your apartment. I don't want you worrying about me and the dangers of my job. I want you sitting here worry-free, happy, waiting for me by the door with a smile on your beautiful face."

"That's exactly my point—"

"Christ, Quinn. Because I'm trying to protect

you, you've twisted that into something that's total bullshit."

"You're not trying to protect me, Brice. You're keeping yourself away from me. You didn't tell me about the two men who died because you didn't want me to ask you questions. Uncomfortable questions like if you were all right, or how you were feeling after seeing two dead men. I get it, I really do, your feelings are not my business. So don't pretend I'm your woman. Don't sit across from my parents and act like you're something you're not. And seriously, do not try to lie to me and tell me you were trying to protect me."

After that, I laid back down and turned on my side facing away from Brice. Every part of my body ached. My heart hurt, my nose stung, and my eyes prickled with unshed tears.

The light went out but Brice made no move to roll next to me or exit the bed. So be it. If he wanted to sleep next to me, I didn't have the mental energy to argue with him.

What felt like hours later, I was finally drifting off to sleep when I felt Brice curl into my back, his arm going around my waist, holding me tight.

I should've told him to move. I should've told him he was hurting me. I should've told him I was dying inside because I'd fallen in love with him and he'd never love me back.

But I didn't. I fell asleep snuggled in Brice's arms feeling like that was where I belonged.

However, I woke up alone.

Which I knew was the beginning of the end.

12

Quinn had instigated her play and everything inside of me told me not to give it to her. To put a stop to the bullshit and force my way back in.

But that's not what I was doing. I was going to let her pull away and I was lying to myself in the process.

I hadn't seen Quinn since I'd left her sleeping in her bed three days ago. I'd called her dad to let him know I couldn't make it to dinner and gave the excuse of needing to go see my brother. To make that not an outright lie and to give Quinn what she wanted, I'd hightailed it to Jacksonville to see Bryan.

That was the second mistake I'd made, and it was arguably bigger than me letting Quinn go.

Not that she was gone completely. We'd

exchanged a handful of texts. She knew I was in Florida. I knew she was currently at her parents spending time with her niece. She even sent me a picture of her and Emma. But the messages were exactly what she'd said they were—surface shit.

And I couldn't figure out if they'd always been like that. I did know the frequency had changed. Gone were the funny memes she sent, or the two line texts telling me where she was going, or asking me if I was having a good day.

Everything had changed and I fucking *hated* it.

"You ready to tell me why you really drove your ass all the way down here?" Bryan asked.

I glanced around his backyard as if it held all the answers to my problems. Issues I'd created. Issues that I refused to face.

"You act like I never come down," I returned.

"Didn't say that," Bryan started. "I asked if you're ready to talk. Been here three days."

"And?"

"And I know you, little brother. I know when something's eating at you. Spit it out already."

"How'd you get over and move on from Lucy?" I asked the question that had been burning my gut.

"Lucy? What the fuck?"

"After what she did to you, how'd you get over it?"

Bryan studied me, not even trying to hide his confusion. And I guess he would be perplexed at me asking about his high school girlfriend.

"I'm not sure what you're asking, Brice."

"She fucked you. You were with her eight years. Engaged. Then one day she's not in love with you and breaks it off," I reminded him.

Bryan settled back in the chair as he continued to stare at me and I saw it, the exact moment light dawned and he understood my question.

"Fuck. Please do not tell me that you've been sitting on this for the last twelve years."

"Hell, yeah, I have. I was there, Bryan, I remember what she did. I remember how crushed you were. Kinda hard to forget my older brother breakin' down when the woman he loved broke his heart."

"Christ, Brice. Seriously? That's why..." He let his statement hang and he shook his head before he pinned me with his stare. "Please, for the love of God, tell me I'm wrong."

"You're not wrong," I told him.

After seeing the brother I idolized fall apart after

his bitch of a fiancée dumped him, I didn't want one thing to do with love.

"Man, I wish you would've come to me sooner with this shit. You have it all wrong."

"All wrong? She gutted all of us. All my life, the bitch was around, for as long as I can remember, then all of a sudden she doesn't love you. What the fuck, Bryan, how do I have that wrong?"

Bryan shifted in his seat and looked away.

"The break was my idea."

"What?"

"We were young, we'd only ever been with each other." He paused and smiled like he was remembering something fondly, which I have to admit was confusing as hell—why he'd smile thinking about the girl he wasted eight years on. "I remember seeing her the first day of school freshman year. 'Member Danny O'Connell? He had such a hard-on for her I wanted to beat the shit out of him. Took me a week to get the courage to ask her out. Lucy Rowe, the hottest piece in the freshman class."

"I may've been eight, but I remember she was all you talked about," I agreed.

"I was fourteen, Brice. She was my first everything. And I hate to say this because it makes me sound like a royal prick, but my senior year I was going to break up with her, play the field, can't remember what changed my mind. Then we both went to Georgia State and...shit, man, I was freaked out my first year of college. The only thing that felt normal was having Lucy. And I knew it was the same for her. We were comfortable, convenient, easy. That's why we stayed together. Then suddenly years passed. Her parents were pushing for a commitment, it seemed like the next logical step and we were going into our senior year of college."

Bryan looked back at me and his eyes drifted closed. "Really wish we'd talked about this sooner. Twelve years this shit's been fucking with your head when it shouldn't have been. You spending your life blowing through women, living fast and loose because of something you didn't understand. Fuck. I hate that for you."

The knot that had been coiling in my stomach for the last three months was suddenly getting larger by the second and my skin started to itch. I did not want to hear the rest of what my brother had to say. It didn't matter if I misunderstood what had happened between Bryan and Lucy, the fact remained that love had the power to destroy. I'd missed Lucy, too, expected her to always be a part of our lives.

"With our last year of college looming," Bryan continued, "it felt like another huge change. Soon everything would be different, and once again I was holding onto Lucy because I was scared not to have her, not because I loved her. I knew it and I felt like shit about it. I'd also spent all of high school, and nearly all of college with the same girl. A girl I was merely comfortable with, not in love with. So I started thinking about all the things I was missing out on. I suggested the break. At first she didn't want it, then she agreed. We split up, agreed we'd take a month to see what was out there, and go from there. Lucy was seriously hot, took her about one day to understand my wisdom. By the next weekend, I saw her on a date. Smiling, laughing, having fun. Two weeks later, I saw her making out hot and heavy by her car. It was a kick in the gut because I didn't expect it, but I was not broken up about it. That's when I knew, hundred percent, we didn't love each other and had no business getting married."

"You were a fucking mess at Christmas," I reminded him.

"I totally was." Bryan chuckled. "Lucy and I had officially ended things. I'd just spent weeks cramming for mid-terms. Had to think about finding a real job, start paying my student loans. And Holly Mahoney had delivered a serious wake-up call."

"Who the fuck is Holly Mahoney?"

"The first girl I slept with after Lucy. Thought we hit it off, she took me back to her place, we had some wild sex. She was younger than me by two years and the girl was wicked hot in bed—showed me shit I could not believe. Swore the next morning I was in love, and she showed me the door. Told me it was fun, and if I ever felt like fucking her again and she wasn't busy, she was game."

What the fuck? Bryan had spent the six weeks he was home for Christmas in a funk, totally moping around, foul-ass mood, slamming doors, hibernating in his room. I was sixteen, watching my big brother all but fucking cry himself to sleep every night thinking that it was Lucy's fault. That she'd torn him up. That she'd abandoned us all.

"What the hell—"

"What was I supposed to say? That I was behaving like a pussy because I was scared to go out and live in the real world? That some chick who I barely knew made me feel like a chump. That because I didn't have Lucy I was afraid I didn't even know who I was or how I was supposed to act? I had no idea you were watching me that close. You were sixteen off doing your own shit. If I had known this was eating at you, I would've taken time to explain. But I had no idea. I was twenty-two, Brice, I didn't know what the hell I was doing."

"Fuck!" I gritted my molars and rolled my shoulders trying to alleviate some of the building pressure.

"So now you wanna talk about the woman who has you all tied up and what the real issue is?"

"No."

"Too fuckin' bad, little brother. Talk!"

"I think I screwed up—huge."

"If you think you did, that means there's no doubt you did. Who is she?"

"Quinn Walker."

Bryan whistled and shook his head. He knew who Quinn was. He'd never met her but he had met Jackson and her brother Jason.

"How long has it been going on?"

"Three months."

"Jason know?"

"Nope. Neither does Jackson, but we had dinner with her parents the other night."

With very little prodding from Bryan, I laid it out. All of it. From the very beginning and how I'd been avoiding Quinn for years because I was attracted to her and knew Jackson would lose his mind, to her moving in next door, to our arrangement.

"So you're in love with her?"

"Yes."

My admission hung in the air and I waited for the panic to ensue. And it came all right, heavy and painful. I was in love with Quinn and I stupidly allowed her to pull away because I was a fucking pansy-assed fool.

"If that's the case, why are you sitting here in my backyard instead of trying to patch things up?"

"Because for years I've lived my life avoiding feelings at all costs. I don't have the first clue how to give her what she needs."

"Sure you do."

"No, really I don't. Since I was sixteen, I'd shut all of that shit off thinking I'd watched my brother take a hit that was so painful it changed him. I never wanted to experience that. Never wanted to love someone if it meant they had that kind of power over me."

Bryan flinched and guilt hit me, it wasn't his fault. It was mine, I'd done it to myself. "To clarify, I'm not blaming you. And part of me doesn't regret the way I've lived my life, but now when it matters, I have no idea how to be the man Quinn needs."

"Sounds like you've been doing it for months."

"Surface shit. That's what she called it. Told me all I give her is superficial and she's right."

"So start there. Explain to her why you were holding yourself back."

"I'm not going there. Part of that is because I'm not airing your shit, and to explain I'd have to tell her about you and Lucy."

Bryan barked out a laugh then leaned forward and rested his elbows on his knees.

"'Preciate you wanting to protect me, but I'm a grown-ass man now and I am not embarrassed about crying in my soup when I was a punk-ass kid who had no idea how to deal with an uncertain future. And that's all that was. You saw it as heartbreak but what it really was, was fear of the unknown. Explain things to her, I bet she understands."

"Maybe."

"No maybe about it. Go. Get the fuck out of my house, get in your truck, and go get your woman before she realizes she can do about hundred times better than you."

"Fuck off."

"Really, she can. If she's half as hot in real life as she is in the pictures I saw, then she is a fine piece—"

"I'm leaving." I stood and flipped Bryan the

middle finger, which only made him laugh harder. "You ever think about Uncle Seth?"

"What about him?" Bryan frowned. "The man's a dick."

"He's dad's brother."

"Yeah, what's that got to do with anything?"

"He's been married five times. Fucks around on all of them," I told him something he knew.

Uncle Seth didn't hide his extra-marital affairs, much to my mother's absolute horror and my father's anger.

"I'm not trackin', brother."

"All our lives, Dad's told us to be careful with alcohol. He'd drilled it into us that we're Lancasters —addiction runs in the family. You ever worry that other shit runs in the family, too?"

"Fuck, no. Dad has not and never would cheat on Mom. He loves her. Is that something you worry about?"

Fuck, did I worry I'd turn into cheat? Hell no, I'd never do that to Quinn.

"Forget I said anything, I don't know what I'm asking."

"Listen, Brice, Seth and his idiot son, Elijah, are a black stain. But they don't represent us as a family—"

"Don't they? Quinn's family's tight. They're a unit—all of them. Sometimes I feel so fucking guilty that Quinn's stooped so low—"

Bryan surged to his feet, eyes narrowed, arms crossed over his chest, giving me a big brother look that I'd seen a lot over the years. A look that scared the shit out of me when I was ten.

"What the fuck?" he bellowed. "Stooped low? You think that?"

"Fuck, yeah. I've got nothing to offer but a bad reputation. One I freely admit I earned and never thought I'd be uncomfortable about. But now, thinking back over all the women I've slept with I'm realizing I'm no better than Seth, the only difference is I wasn't tied to another woman while I was fucking around. But I sure as hell took what was offered, anytime it was offered, and I never thought twice about taking it."

"Uh, brother, big difference. Huge. And you said it yourself, you were not married or even in a committed relationship when you were playing the field. So by your logic any woman who's with me is stooping low, because you are not the only Lancaster who enjoys the company of a beautiful woman and enjoys it regularly. I figure one day when I find my Quinn that will end, but until then, I am not married, I am not tied down, and I'm too damn good-looking not to spread the Lancaster charm."

Ass.

"Told you I had no clue how—"

"Because you're mixing everything up. Seth has not one thing to do with you. His shit is his. It doesn't reflect on us as a family. Mom and Dad are good parents, they love each other and us. You need to untangle that, Brice. And what happened between me and Lucy I don't regret. I learned a lot from her, from loving her. It didn't last, we were kids, but that doesn't mean I'm not looking for someone to spend my life with. And your past is that—the past. We all have one. Hell, Quinn has one. Maybe not as... colorful as yours." Bryan stopped to give me a shit-eating-grin and I'd never admit it but I was happy Quinn's past didn't include as many men in her bed as mine did women. "You're a good man and she knows it. The fact that she even allowed you to enter her bedroom should tell you that. Quinn Walker isn't the type of woman who lowers her standards for any man. Remember that when you go back to Georgia and beg her to take a chance at something real."

Fuck me, Bryan was right. I should've talked to my brother sooner.

"Thanks for letting me crash at your pad."

"Anytime. Hope you know that."

"I do."

"Call me later and let me know how it goes!" he yelled as I walked to the door.

I closed the sliding glass door, leaving my brother in the hot, humid Florida sun and went to the spare room to grab my bag.

I had two hours to get my head sorted. Two hours to come up with a plan. Two hours to figure out how I was going to explain to Quinn why I'd held myself back. Then I could obliterate the distance she was putting between us.

Quinn Walker was mine.

And I wasn't letting her go.

13

"Nothing is wrong, Bridgett," I said into my phone and sighed as I heaved myself out of my car.

I was lying of course, there was something wrong.

Everything was all wrong.

I'd had four days to think about what happened with Brice. Four days of being alone. Four days of missing him.

If I'd thought our conversations before were surface stuff, I was mistaken. Now our texts weren't superficial, they were almost cursory. It sucked. Brice was pulling away—actually he wasn't *doing* anything, he'd simply done it. He hadn't even told me he was going to visit his brother in person, he sent a text *after* he was already on the road.

And that killed.

"Um...yeah, there is. I can hear it. Last week you were normal. Actually, better than normal, you sounded happy. Today not so much," Bridgett returned.

I sucked in a breath, not wanting to have this conversation. My friend was like a bloodhound, she could sniff a problem from a mile away.

I looked both ways, hitched my purse over my shoulder, and clamped it tightly between my arm and body. I was not in the best part of town, but my favorite Thai market was there nestled between a jewelry repair shop and what I thought was a nail place but looked pretty sketchy so I'd never looked too closely. The whole area was rundown and the apartment complex I had the misfortune of parking in front of gave me the willies.

"Listen, I have to hang up and pay attention before I become one of those nitwits in a bad horror movie and get jumped because I'm gabbing on the phone."

"Where are you?"

"The Thai market."

"What?" Bridgett shrieked. Yes, the area was that bad. "Why do you insist on going to that place?"

"Because it's the only place that carries the brand

of tea I like. And, hello, the name is Bang Luck Market—coolest name ever."

"You're willing to risk dying for Thai iced tea." This was not a question, it was a statement. Bridgett knew I'd risk just about anything for the creamy, sweet orange-colored tea and Bang Luck was the only place in Georgia I could buy the traditional leaves.

I rolled my eyes at her dramatics. I wasn't going to die, but there was a possibility I'd get robbed if I didn't get off the phone and start paying attention. This worked for me because it meant Bridgett couldn't continue to probe. Though I had a feeling dinner and drinks with her was not going to be fun, she'd commence a cavity search upon my arrival and wouldn't let up until I told her why I no longer sounded happy.

Shit.

"Gotta run, doll. See you tomorrow."

"I'm not new, you know."

"What does that mean?"

"It means I know you. I know when you're trying to hide something. I know when there's something making you *not* happy. We're talking about this tomorrow."

"Fine, but right now I'm hanging up."

"You're insane. Be careful."

"I will."

I disconnected and pocketed my phone, making a beeline across the street and into Bang Luck. *Seriously, how cool was that name?* Normally, I took my time perusing the aisles but I couldn't concentrate on anything other than Brice and wondering if I'd overreacted.

He hadn't made me any promises, it was my own stupid fault I'd allowed myself to develop feelings for him, and really, Brice going to my parents' for dinner wasn't that big of a deal. He'd been there before for a birthday blowout for my brother. He'd been to my Uncle Clark and Aunt Reagan's house plenty of times with Jackson for family barbeques. It wasn't like he was a stranger.

But when he called me his woman, something inside of me snapped. I had to admit—Brice confirming he hadn't slept with another woman since we'd been together made me feel great. I knew I'd agreed to an open relationship, but deep down it gave me pause. No matter what I said, I was not the kind of woman who could do no-strings sex—as evidence proved.

I paid for my tea and checked my phone when it pinged with an incoming text.

Shit on a shingle. Brice was home and wanted to talk.

Damn, damn, and more *damn*.

My reprieve was over. It was time to face the mess I'd made. Clearly, he was going to tell me our arrangement was officially done. He'd be gentle and let me down easy because that's what he'd promised. I knew it was for the best, but my heart ached. And I'd have to look for a new apartment. My lease would be up soon, and as soon as it was my ass was out of there.

There was no way I could live next door to him and know I couldn't have him. The temptation would be too great. I'd want to knock on his door, I'd wait for him to knock on mine.

I tapped out a quick message telling him I'd be home in a few hours and put my phone away. I was not exaggerating to Bridgett about needing to stay aware of my surroundings as I walked back to my car.

I had just beeped the locks when I heard it.

The unmistakable sound of someone grunting in pain. But that wasn't what had me looking at the alley next to the rundown apartment complex, it was the shouting.

Jesus! Holy shit. I fumbled my keys, dropped them on the dirty pavement. I didn't want to look back. I didn't want to witness the violence, but as I bent to pick up my keys I couldn't stop myself.

Two men beating the holy hell out of a much smaller, older man. And before I could look away— right there out in the open, right fucking *there*—one of the men pulled out a knife and plunged it in the old man's throat.

In his throat!

I may've screamed. I may've whimpered. Hell if I knew exactly what I did, but whatever it was sent the knife-wielding man's gaze slicing in my direction.

Cold, dead, angry eyes held mine, freezing the blood in my veins.

I scrambled to pick up my keys, which was really goddamned difficult because my hands shook and I couldn't break the stare. I couldn't look away. Not from the man holding a knife with blood dripping off the blade.

The man took a step in my direction and finally survival instinct took over. I snatched my keys off the ground, yanked my car door open, hit the locks, started her up, and slammed on the accelerator so hard my car shot forward and my tires squealed.

I didn't slow down as I approached the stop sign —I blew through it and broke the speed limit as I navigated through the side streets. I only pulled over when I was confident I hadn't been followed. I was trembling so bad I couldn't drive any farther.

Without thought or care, I dumped my purse on the passenger seat and found my phone. It took me three tries to unlock it and scroll to the number I needed.

"Hey, sweetheart."

"Dad! Need you," I panted.

"Where are you?"

I looked around trying to find a street name but my vision blurred as the tears I held back filled my eyes.

"Quinn! Need to know where you are."

"I...I...don't know. I was at Bang Luck. Oh my God. Dad!"

I heard my dad start his car and curse a blue streak before he gentled his voice. "Concentrate, what do you see?"

I couldn't see anything except for a man getting stabbed in the goddamned throat. There was so much blood.

"Oh my God," I whispered. "There was blood everywhere. It squirted out of his neck. I can't—"

"Whose blood, baby?"

"I don't know," I cried. "I saw. I saw it happen. He saw me, too. I'm so scared I can't drive. I can't—"

"Are you somewhere safe?"

"No! He saw me. Nowhere is safe. He saw."

"Hold on, sweetie. Gonna use my work phone. I need to get a lock on your location. Don't hang up."

"Please hurry. Please, Dad. He saw me."

"Brady." I heard my dad on his other phone. "Track Quinn's location now. Send the GPS to my phone....no, she's not okay...don't know, call you back."

"Dad, there's a check cashing place across the street," I told him.

"Are your doors locked?"

"Yeah."

"Got your location. Five minutes out. Hold tight for me."

Thank God, my dad was coming. He'd know what to do, he always did.

"I'm so scared," I whined.

"I know you are, Quinn. Be brave, my sweet girl, I'm almost there."

Five minutes felt like an eternity. And by the time I saw my dad's truck skid into the parking lot, every muscle in my body ached from strain. I couldn't stop shaking and I was lightheaded.

I unlocked my door when my dad approached and the next thing I knew I was in his arms.

"Fuck!" he roared as I sagged against his body. "I got you."

Yeah, he did. My dad always had me. The only man in my life that never let me down. Would always protect me.

14

Three goddamned days of silence.

The last text I got from Quinn, she told me she'd be home in a few hours so we could talk. I waited all fucking night for her to come home and she never did. I knew because I waited in her apartment, uncaring if that made me a crazy stalker. Three more texts and two calls went unanswered.

By the time I went into work the next morning, I was pissed she'd ghosted my ass. Now, after three days of not returning my numerous calls and messages, I was worried. Things may've gone to shit after the dinner we'd shared with her parents, but this was not Quinn. She wouldn't just ignore me.

I debated whether to call Jasper asking if he'd heard from Quinn but I didn't want her dad to think

I was a fucking lunatic. My other option was Jackson, which would cause more issues than her father thinking I was crazy.

Worry gripped my insides as I sat on my rack staring at my phone, willing the damn thing to ping with a message just like I'd been doing every damn minute of free time I'd had over the last three days.

Where the hell are you, Quinn?

"Damn, brother, who pissed in your Wheaties?"

My head snapped up to find Jackson leaning against the door frame, smiling at me.

"Hey, have you heard from Quinn?" I tried to keep my tone nonchalant but I obviously failed when Jackson squinted at me before his smile fell.

"Guess you heard, huh? Totally fucked."

Ice infused my veins and I stood, straining to keep my body's reaction to Jackson's statement in check.

"Heard what?"

"About her witnessing the stabbing."

"Come again?"

"Wait. What? If you don't know..." Jackson pushed away from the doorjamb and his worried expression turned hard. "Why the fuck are you asking me about Quinn?"

"Where is she?" I asked, ignoring his question and moving toward the door.

Jackson blocked my exit, squared his shoulders, and tried again. "Why you asking about my cousin, Brice?"

"Just tell me where the hell is she?"

"Motherfucker. You wouldn't dare—"

"Christ, just tell me where she—"

Pain bloomed in my cheek and I tasted blood. Jackson's second blow landed in my gut and with a grunt I stumbled back.

Motherfucker.

Jackson came at me again throwing a wide right hook. I easily ducked and shoved him back.

"Enough! I get I deserved that, but—"

"You get it? You're fucking my goddamned cousin!" Jackson shouted. I was honestly surprised it had taken him as long as it had to puzzle the pieces together. "I don't think you get shit, man. And really, Quinn? All the available ass and you fuck—"

"Jack, I suggest you're real careful with what you say next. I get she's your family, but you're talking about my woman."

"Your woman?" he seethed. "The fuck she is. She's your flavor of the week. And I cannot understand why you'd disrespect her like that. She's off-fucking-limits."

"Three months, Jack. I've been with her for three goddamn months."

Jackson's lip curled into a snarl. "You're telling me you've been fucking Quinn for three months while you've been—"

"There's no one else. Hasn't been anyone else since she moved in next door. Now, I understand you've got questions and you think you deserve answers. But I'm telling you, I don't give the first fuck what you think you deserve, this conversation is done."

"It's not nearly done."

"It is for now."

I strolled past him and stalked through the common area of the station. Not a single person approached though I'm sure they all heard. I found my captain in the open bay, quickly told him I had a personal family matter to take care of and I was cutting out an hour early.

With minimal argument, he agreed.

I jumped into my truck and headed to Jasper and Emily's. If Quinn wasn't there, they'd know where to find her. It might not be my smartest play but it was the only one I had.

JASPER OPENED THE DOOR, took one look at my banged-up face, and shook his head before he stepped out onto the porch.

"Jackson?" I jerked my chin in the affirmative and Jasper twisted his lips and muttered, "Fuck."

"Is she here?"

"Yeah. How much do you know?"

"Just found out," I started explaining why I hadn't been over sooner to see Quinn. "Jack said she witnessed a stabbing, but that was it before he caught on to why I was asking about her."

"I'm not sure—"

"Respect, Jasper, but I'm sure."

"My girl's been dodging your calls. She have a reason to do that?"

I clenched my jaw, not wanting to have this conversation with Jasper before I had a chance to talk to Quinn. But if I wanted into the house I had to go through her dad and there was no doubt—if Jasper didn't want me to enter, he'd break my legs without blinking.

"She *had* a reason. But things have changed." When Jasper's brow pinched I knew I had to give him more. "We've been seeing each other three months—"

"I know that. She talked to me about it the day you kissed her by her car." *Well, fuck me running. Jasper's known all along.* "Warned her not to get involved with you."

My back shot straight and my hands fisted. I wanted to be pissed-off, I wanted to ask him what his problem was, but I knew. No dad wanted their daughter wrapped up with some asshole who has a reputation of blowing through women.

"We've been exclusive," I told him, needing him to understand that I wasn't playing some fucked-up bed-hopping game with Quinn. "I didn't mean to fall in love with her. I didn't even think I had it in me *to* love anyone. I get why you'd warn her off, but this isn't that, Jasper. She's not one of them. I'm not scratching an itch and I think you know that. I think you know, I wouldn't do that to Quinn. We may've started one way but we sure as fuck aren't that way anymore. And as much as I know you love your daughter and will do anything to protect her, I hope you understand that no one, not even you, is gonna keep me from her."

Jasper stayed where he was, arms crossed over

his chest, and gave nothing away. I fought the urge to shove him aside and kick down the door to get to Quinn. He may've been her father, but in that moment he was an obstacle, the one person standing between me and the woman I loved, and I was running out of patience.

"I wondered how long it would take for you to come and get in my face to see her. I'm glad it happened sooner rather than later." I rocked back on my heels in surprise, then he continued. "She's fucked-up. Completely shaken to her core. Right after I found her, she nearly lost consciousness. The violence...fuck..." Jasper hung his head then slowly lifted it and green eyes much like his daughter's held me in place. "Knife to the throat, man. She saw the whole thing less than ten yards away."

"Fucking hell!"

"It gets worse."

Worse? How the hell did Quinn seeing someone get murdered get worse?

"The assailant saw her. Made eye contact."

There it was—worse—much fucking worse.

"Christ," I bit out. "The police catch him?"

"Not yet. Though we've been to the police station and she sat with a sketch artist. The gang task force recognized him immediately."

My head swam, completely overloaded with all of the fucked-up possibilities. Quinn could've been hurt—or worse, killed—and that wasn't a far stretch with a gang killing happening less than thirty feet away.

"Where the fuck was she?"

"Off MLK and Broadway."

"What the hell? That area is shit. Why would she be there?"

"Her favorite Thai market is there. I've asked her not to go, begged her actually, and she wouldn't listen."

"Christ!"

I hadn't realized my hands had gone into my hair until pain radiated from my scalp and I loosened my grip.

"I wanna see her."

"Know you do but—"

"No offense, but that wasn't a question. I *need* to see her. And there are things we have to talk about."

Jasper looked pensive, worn down, like a father who loved his daughter beyond reason and was trying to do what was best for her.

"She needs me, Jasper. I wouldn't be here if I wasn't positive she feels the same way about me as I feel about her. I tried to walk away, I tried to let her do the same. But it feels wrong, I can't let her go."

"Quinn's...she's gonna fight you."

"I know she is."

"You ready for that?"

"Yes."

"Don't let her push you away. She's had her phone. And with everything that happened, I've been keeping a close eye. I know how many times you've tried to call."

"Yeah?"

Jasper's jaw clenched and he looked over my shoulder. "It's the only time she cries."

Christ. I'd fucked everything up. If I hadn't been such a coward, none of this would've happened. Quinn would never have been in that hood by herself. I would've been with her or she would've been too preoccupied to go. But instead of staying and figuring out our shit, I bailed and ran to Florida like a pussy.

"She's in her old room," Jasper told me and stepped aside.

"Thank you."

"You fix my daughter, I'll be thanking you."

I gave Jasper a lift of my chin and went into the Walker family home.

I didn't stop to take in Emily's wide eyes as she caught sight of me from the kitchen. The smell of baking cookies barely registered. My mind fixed solely on Quinn and seeing with my own eyes she was safe.

15

I heard the door creak open but I didn't move. I laid on my side, staring into nothing, and I couldn't bear to roll over and face either of my parents. My mom was killing me with her worried glances and gentle coaxing. My dad looked just as worried but his stare was different, it was mixed with anger—not toward me. He was angry in general, furious I'd seen what I'd seen, and anxious there had been no arrests. I wasn't sure which of their concerns hurt me more. I didn't like that my parents were having to take care of me. I hated that they were scared, hated even more I'd been so stupid I'd put myself in that situation.

Once again I'd acted like a naïve twit going wherever I wanted to go, doing whatever I wanted to do. It was way beyond time I woke up and stopped walking through life with my head in the clouds.

Then there were my sisters, brother, cousins, aunts, and uncles. All of them had been by to check on me. All of them handled me like glass. This should've been comforting, my family rallying around me, but instead I felt like a child who couldn't get her shit together.

Hell, most of my family had been through worse. Mercy and my sister had been kidnapped and beaten. Honor had almost been killed by her crazy stepfather. Tuesday had been stalked and her house set on fire with her in it. Yet, they all pulled themselves together and moved on.

But there I was, acting like a baby, curled up in a ball on my childhood bed.

What the hell was wrong with me?

Every time I closed my eyes I saw the knife in that poor man's throat and blood spurting out. I couldn't forget the cold eyes that stared at me as I scrambled to get my keys. I couldn't think of anything else.

And the what-ifs were screwing with my head. What-if I hadn't gone to the Thai market? What-if I hadn't gotten into my car fast enough? What-if I hadn't wasted time on the phone with Bridgett?

What-if I'd just wandered around the store a little longer? One little change and I wouldn't have seen it happen. I wouldn't have watched a man get stabbed in the neck.

God. I just wanted it to stop.

The bed moved behind me and suddenly a warm, hard chest pressed against my back, and a heavy arm went around my waist, and I stiffened.

I didn't need to turn to know who was behind me. I didn't even need to look at the hand that engulfed mine. I knew the feel of him. I knew the way he smelled. I knew a lot about him, but not nearly enough.

"Why are you here?" I whispered.

"Babe."

I closed my eyes to fight the tears. For three days I'd beaten back the urge to call him, to answer the phone, message him back. Three really long, hard days. But I'd done it. I hadn't given in to the need. I'd been determined not to bother Brice with my latest crisis.

Brice nestled closer, his mouth going to the side of my neck and he kissed me there. My hair prevented his lips from hitting my flesh but I still felt it. I wanted to melt into him. I wanted to tell him all the things I couldn't tell my dad. But I couldn't.

"Why didn't you call me, Quinn?"

"Because we're not that."

"We sure as fuck are."

"No." I shook my head. "I know what we are. I may've forgotten for a while. Got caught up in the excitement. Maybe even allowed myself to believe we were more than we really were, but I remembered."

"Baby—"

"I can't do this," I interrupted him. "I lied to you."

Brice's body went solid and his hand flexed around mine.

"About what?"

"I'm not capable of doing casual. I knew it. From the start, I knew it and pretended I could because I was selfish and tried to trap you into something you didn't want. I know the type of man you are and I knew you'd never touch me unless I lied and told you I was okay with the only kind of arrangement you're comfortable with. I'm sorry. All of this is my fault."

"You have no idea the type of man I am."

Ouch! That hurt. He was right of course, I may've known him physically, but I didn't actually *know* Brice.

"You're right, I don't."

We laid there in silence for a long time. Having him that close, holding me to him, was agony. I wanted to tell him to leave. Hell, I needed him to leave before I broke down in tears. It wasn't his fault I fell in love with him. It wasn't his fault my heart shattered and I was scared it would never fit back together. It was pure torture, all of it.

"There's a lot we need to talk about." Brice broke the silence. "There're things I need to explain to you but right now's not the time."

It would never be the time. For one, we were over. For two, Brice didn't share his feelings with me.

"You don't owe me anything. I appreciate you taking the time to let me down gently, but you don't need to. I know we're over. I know—"

"The fuck we are." I jerked at the vehemence in his tone.

"Brice—"

"I'm not letting you go." And to punctuate his words, he pressed closer.

"I can't do it. I'm telling you I don't know how to have you in my bed and not have all of you."

It was on the tip of my tongue to tell him I was in love with him. That was a sure-fire way to make him run for the hills. The only thing that held me back was that I was too afraid I'd see pity in his eyes after I told him. I was already damn near broken and seeing him look at me like I was some poor, hopeless fool would gut me.

"That's part of what we need to talk about. But first we need to have a conversation about what happened, what you saw—"

"No! I'm done talking about it."

"Quinn, baby—"

"No. I'm done. All everyone wants to do is talk about it. I just want to be left alone."

"When's the last time you left the house?" He changed the subject.

I didn't answer, because I didn't want to admit that after my dad found me, drove me to and from the police station, I hadn't left the house.

"Right," he mumbled. "We're going to lunch."

Much to my surprise he loosened his hold on me and allowed me to sit up so I could turn and look at him. And when I did I was in utter shock.

"Oh my God! What happened to you?" I asked, taking in his face.

There was an angry, red cut on his lip and a bruise forming at the corner of his mouth.

"Not important."

My heart seized at his answer. It wasn't important because Brice didn't share that kind of stuff with me. He'd obviously been in a fight, I didn't think his lip would get busted up that way on the job, but what did I know? Nothing. That was what. Because Brice's personal life wasn't my business.

"You should go," I reminded him.

"Jackson," he sighed.

"Jackson?"

"You weren't answering my calls, I had no idea what was going on and had limited options to find out. Jackson came into the bunk room as I was thinking about what I was going to do next. I was well-aware of what the ramifications were gonna be by asking him, but I needed to know that you were okay."

"So...he did that?"

Damn it all to hell. Jackson and Brice were best friends. So on top of everything else, now I'd screwed up their friendship.

"Yeah, babe. I think we both knew Jackson wasn't gonna be pleased when he found out about us. I've been lying to my best friend for months. And let's not forget, he made it clear you were off-limits."

"He what? Why would he do that?"

"Same reason your dad warned you to stay away from me. They both thought I'd jack you around."

"So you told Jackson about us?"

"No, babe. I didn't have to tell him shit. He's not dumb, it took him all of two minutes after I asked about you to put two and two together. He didn't like what that equaled."

Oh, no! Jackson was going to be so mad at me. And he had a big mouth, the first call he'd make would be to my brother. If Jason got involved, shit would hit the fan. Then Jackson would rope in Ethan, Carter, and Nick and hellfire would rain down.

"I have to call Jackson," I blurted.

"No. You need to let me handle Jackson. He's rightfully pissed at me. Either he'll understand you mean something to me and he'll back off or he won't. What's not gonna happen is you getting into the middle of it, because he says one thing to you that makes you feel bad or makes you feel like you've done something wrong, him and I are gonna have bigger issues than we have now."

"But—"

"No, Quinn. I can take whatever he dishes out but *you* are not taking any of it."

"He hit you." I gestured to his face. "In the mouth."

"Yeah, he did. Again, rightfully pissed. I also allowed him to get a second swing in before I stopped him. I deserved it. He got in his licks, and now we'll deal."

"You deserved it?" I scooted to the edge of the bed and stood. "Now we'll deal?"

Brice sighed like I was totally dense for not understanding why two men I cared about deeply getting into a fistfight was okay—normal even.

"Yeah, Quinn. We'll deal. Everything's out in the open now. And honestly, if my head hadn't been shoved so far up my own ass I would've acknowledged my feelings for you and I wouldn't have hidden our relationship like a coward."

I stood unmoving and stared at Brice. My lungs burned until I finally drew in a sharp breath. I must've heard Brice wrong, nothing he was saying was making any sense. Not a single word.

"What?"

"More shit we gotta talk about. But first let's get some sunshine on your face and food in your belly."

"I think we need to talk now."

"After lunch," he volleyed.

"We're not going to lunch."

"We are. So either you put on some shoes or you go barefoot."

My hands went to my hips and my eyes

narrowed. *Since when had Brice turned into a pain in the ass?*

"And you plan on getting me out of my house how?"

"Any way necessary."

"You know my dad is probably listening at the door?"

I really hoped he wasn't but my father tended to treat me like I was fifteen and not nearing twenty-five.

God, seriously, is it any wonder he treats me like a child when I'm constantly behaving like one?

"Great. Then he can hold the door open for me when I drag your ass out of it."

"You're insane."

"Maybe. But you're not locking yourself away in this room. I understand why your parents are allowing it. They're worried about you. But, Quinn, I'm not gonna let you hide away. I'm not gonna let you sit in this room and stew. You're putting on your shoes and going to lunch with me. After that, if you're ready we'll talk about what you saw. But when we do that, we'll be at home."

"I am home."

"No. You're at your parents' house. And I get why you needed to be here. I understand you need the security and comfort. But that ends today. You're coming home with me."

He had no idea why I was hiding at my parents' house and I wasn't going to tell him. It would make me look more of a fool to admit I couldn't face him.

"No—"

The sharp knock on my bedroom door cut off my argument.

"Quinn. Brice. You're needed in the living room," my dad said from the other side of the door.

"Be right out, Jasper," Brice answered for us, then turned to me. "Shoes!"

"They're by the front door," I snapped.

"Great. Let's go."

Brice opened my bedroom door and swept his hand, motioning me to precede him. Good God, he was infuriating. Why couldn't he understand I didn't want to go anywhere with him? I wasn't ready to face what I'd done.

I walked down the hall feeling Brice following closely behind me, and when I came to the living room, I stopped dead and let out a groan.

This was not good.

This was worse than not good.

This was totally fucked-up.

Jackson stood near the couch, my dad off to the

side, but my mother was nowhere to be found—which meant Dad had warned her shit was about to get ugly. Dad would protect her from the fight that was getting ready to ensue. Normally, he'd protect me from it, too, but this was my mess.

"I can't believe you'd hit Brice." I looked at Jackson and tried not to flinch at the anger I saw. At my declaration, Brice's hand found my hip and he gently moved me to his side and Jackson's jaw clenched.

Brice was right, Jackson was pissed, but more than that he looked like I'd wounded him. We'd been best friends since we were in diapers. We'd shared everything; that was, until he met Tuesday, then he'd kept a whole lot from me. But I understood; he was falling in love and muddling his way through. But one look at Jackson told me he didn't understand why I kept Brice from him.

"And I can't believe he'd fuckin' touch you. Yet, there he is with his fuckin' hand on you."

"Seriously, Jackson, that wasn't cool."

"But it's cool you being treated like a piece of ass?"

"Jackson," my dad growled.

Brice's hand flexed on my hip, his fingertips digging in painfully.

"Warning, Jackson, that's the last time you say shit like that about Quinn. I let that shit at the station—"

"You let it? Friend, I should've kicked your ass."

"Yeah, Jackson, I let you get your shots in. But only because I knew *I* deserved it for not coming to you and straight out telling you I was dating Quinn. But Quinn not only doesn't deserve it, but right now, she doesn't need your shit. Your problem is with me. We'll handle that problem when Quinn isn't present but only after I get her sorted."

"Quinn's not your business," Jackson returned.

"The fuck she isn't," Brice growled and I knew it was time I put a stop to this.

"Why are you here, Jackson?" I asked.

My cousin's eyes sliced to me and I knew him so well, I couldn't miss his '*are you fucking kidding me*' look. Though I didn't have to wait long for him to verbalize it.

"Are you fuckin' kidding me right now? I find out you've been fucking around with him." Jackson pointed his thumb at Brice and shook his head. "And you think I wouldn't be here asking you what in the actual hell you're thinking?"

"I'm thinking it's none of your business."

This was going nowhere.

"Babe," Brice muttered and I slid my gaze from my best friend to him. "Do me a favor. Either go out to the truck and wait for me there or go back in your room for a minute, yeah?"

"I don't think—"

"Trust me. You don't need to hear this shit."

"He's right, Quinn," my dad cut in. "Go out and wait in the truck."

"What?" Jackson seethed.

I glanced at my dad and he nodded his encouragement and I turned back to Jackson.

"If he comes outside bleeding again, you and me got problems, Jackson."

Brice's hand on my hip tightened and the low rumble of laughter took me by surprise.

"Thanks for that, baby, but I think I can handle it."

"I'm sure you can," I huffed. "But it's total bullshit he hit you once. And if you get blood on my mother's carpet she's gonna lose her ever-loving mind. I'm waiting five minutes. If you're not out by then, I'm coming back in."

"Noted." Brice leaned down a fraction and kissed my forehead. "Shoes and purse. We'll come back tomorrow and pick up anything else you brought over."

I nodded and pulled away from Brice and went directly to my dad. When I got close, he tagged me around the shoulders and brought me close for a hug, then he lowered his mouth to my ear and whispered, "Everything's gonna be fine. Brice will be right out."

"Tell Mom I said I love her and I'll call her later."

"Will do."

"And I love you, too, Dad."

"Love you back."

I didn't say a word to Jackson as I walked past him to the front door. I slipped on my flip-flops and grabbed my purse before I turned around and asked Brice, "Is it unlocked?"

"Yeah, babe, and the keys are in it."

It wouldn't be until I was sitting in Brice's truck waiting for him to come out when I realized not only had Brice gotten his way, but my dad hadn't batted an eye I was going home.

I wasn't entirely sure what that meant and I was too worried about what was going inside the house to process it.

Everything was so screwed up.

16

The door clicked shut behind Quinn, and I counted to ten to make sure she was far enough away not to hear, then I faced Jackson and tried real hard to remember he was my best friend.

"We have a lot of years of friendship between us," I reminded him. "But I swear to God if you ever call Quinn a piece of ass again, I'll forget those years."

"You're fucking serious right now?" Jackson barked out a laugh. "You've been fucking my—"

"And another thing," I cut in. "I suggest you remember who else is in the room and watch your goddamned mouth."

Jackson's mouth got tight and his face turned hard. I hated what this did to him, hated he had a right to be pissed, but Quinn's dad was in the room and the last thing he needed to hear was Jackson talking about me fucking Quinn.

"That's rich coming from you, the man who nails a different woman each week. Now suddenly you're all about respect when you have no issues fuckin' whoever you want then tossin' them out on their asses when they want more."

I had nothing to say to that mainly because he was right—I never had an issue with the way I'd lived my life.

"Quinn is not *other* women," I told him.

"You're right, she's my family."

"She is."

"Yet you took her to bed."

Goddamn, I wished Jackson would stop saying that shit in front of Jasper.

"Let's focus on something else," I suggested. "Like what she means to me and how we're gonna get past this."

"There's nothing to get past, because you're gonna stay the fuck away from Quinn."

"That's not gonna happen, Jackson. I'll tell you the same thing I told her, either you're gonna get over your snit, see that she *means* something to me, and we'll move on. Or you won't. But mark this, whatever you decide doesn't change a damn thing between me and Quinn, but it will change you and Quinn. So you need to figure out a way to get over yourself because Quinn loves you. You're more than family, you're her best friend. And it would kill her if you couldn't be happy for her."

"That's a joke, right?"

"Your call." I shrugged my shoulders knowing this needed to wrap up before Quinn got impatient.

I was shocked she'd gone out to my truck in the first place but I wasn't stupid enough to think it wasn't her father's suggestion and the shock of the situation that made her agreeable.

"She staying with you tonight?" Jasper entered the conversation.

"I want her back at her place, around her stuff, comfortable in her bed. I'll stay there with her."

"When do you go back to work?"

"Three days. I figure if the asshole hasn't been locked up by then, I'll call in some vacation time so I can stay with her. Or I'll bring her back here so she's not alone."

Jasper nodded his approval, his gaze assessing, scrutinizing my every move. I didn't blame him. He'd gone out on a limb allowing me into his house. Now he was trusting me with the care of his beloved daughter.

"Please tell Emily, I'm sorry I barged in this afternoon."

Jasper's mouth curved up into a smile before he said, "Yeah, I expect you'll get an earful for not at least staying for dinner."

"Jesus," Jackson muttered. "I can't fucking believe you're okay with this shit."

"Jack, before you pass judgment on Brice, I think you need to take a minute to reflect. You know I got nothing but love for you and gratitude you've had my girl's back since you two were toddlers. If memory serves, you had more than your fair share of notches before you met Tuesday. After you think on that, I want you to cast your mind back to how you and your wife started your relationship. You and Quinn both entered into one type of relationship hoping to get something more."

"That was totally different, Uncle Jasper," Jackson protested.

"If you think that, then you're wrong. Straight up, Quinn played Brice. Not the other way around. And my suggestion to you would be to go home to your beautiful wife, calm down, and think about it. Because if I'm wrong, and you're right, and shit goes south, Quinn's gonna need you. But I don't think I'm wrong, which means Quinn's gonna need you for different reasons and one of those is gonna be you welcoming Brice to the family."

If this conversation had played out a week ago, I would've been sick, the knot in my stomach would've threatened to choke me. Now, I welcomed Jasper's approval. I'd need it as I battled it out with Quinn. The truth was, I needed Jackson, too. I'd need everyone in my corner as I convinced Quinn to give us an honest shot. As I undid the harm I'd done. I had no idea how to open up to her, I had no idea how to share feelings, I had no idea how to make her believe I was worth taking a risk on.

"You fuck her over—"

"I won't."

"You say that now but I know you. The next shiny new piece of tail struts her ass into your line of sight or Quinn wants more of you, you'll toss her aside."

That pissed me the fuck off, but what was worse, and made my gut clench was, that had been the old me, the me before I'd had Quinn.

"She gets all of me." I watched as Jackson's eyes widened and decided to give him one more thing. "She's mine, Jackson. And that means I'm hers—only hers. There's no one else and there will never be anyone else."

"Prove it."

"Plan to. Now if we're done, my woman's sitting outside in my truck, worried about her man, her best friend, and her dad, so we're done so I can go put her mind at ease." I turned back to Jasper. "I'll call you tonight after I have her settled."

"'Preciate it."

I didn't spare another glance at Jackson and headed for the door.

"I expect a call, too," Jackson demanded and I latched on to my patience.

"I'll *text* you," I grunted.

I hadn't even turned my truck over when Quinn started her rapid-fire questions.

"It's all good," I told her as I backed out of the driveway.

"That's impossible," she huffed.

"Babe, Jackson will calm down when he sees I make you happy."

"We should've talked about that before you went head-to-head with Jack and my dad."

And so it begins.

"For now let's just concentrate on what you want for lunch," I suggested.

"You know, it's super-annoying that you keep blowing me off. I know there are a lot of things that are not my business, but this isn't one of those things. This conversation is about me and what I want, so you don't get to keep putting it off with a change of topic."

"Everything's your business," I told her honestly. "I have nothing to hide from you."

"Right," she mumbled.

"I was being truthful when I told you why I didn't tell you about the DOAs. But I did leave out the part about it being hard to talk about because even after all this time knowing it's always a possibility, it guts me when we lose a victim. It feels like a failure even if they pass before we get to the call. Maybe even more so, because I can't stop thinking about response time. What did I do wrong, how did I waste time, how can I do better next time? I've never had anyone to talk to about those feelings so I didn't know how to. Didn't know if I should. I've never done this, babe. So I'm gonna need you to cut me some slack."

That was an understatement of epic proportions. I was going to need more than slack, I'd need a mile's worth.

"I know it's asking a lot," I continued when she remained silent, "but I'm asking all the same."

"What are you asking for exactly?"

"Everything."

"Everything?"

"I want all of you."

The silence was so fucking thick I was nearly gagging on it. And the longer it stretched the more irritated I became. This was not me. I was never unsure about a situation. When I set my sights on something I knew with great clarity how to get it. But Quinn was different, she was important, and I couldn't fuck this up. All of that made me uneasy.

"I can't give you that."

Her refusal snapped me out of my funk—her answer unacceptable.

She was mine. I knew it, I believed it, and soon she would, too.

I pulled up to a red light and glanced at Quinn.

So beautiful.

And if at any point in my life I'd allowed myself to think about what I wanted in a woman, she was it. Top-to-toe, she was extraordinary.

Deciding a restaurant was now out of the question I headed home. The conversation we needed would happen sooner rather than later and it would be happening in private.

"Where are we going?"

"Home. We'll order in."

Quinn remained quiet the rest of the short drive and so did I. When we pulled into the parking lot, I couldn't miss the waves of trepidation rolling off Quinn. And when I grabbed her hand to walk across the lot and up the stairs, she was stiff and distant. The last thing she wanted was me touching her, which was too fucking bad.

I unlocked her door, took her purse off her shoulder, tossed it on her kitchen table, and walked us to the couch. I wanted to take her directly to her bed and pin her under me so she couldn't escape, but she'd get the wrong idea.

Everything had changed, our relationship was no longer just about sex. It was time I set the record straight and showed her we were moving forward.

"Brice—"

"Hold on, Quinn."

I sat down and pulled her astride me, her knees pressed against my thighs, and her ass settling on my crotch. Quinn stopped squirming but she looked uncomfortable.

"Relax."

"I can't."

"We're just talking," I reminded her.

"We can talk with me sitting next to you," she snapped, and I smiled.

"I have something important I need to tell you."

"And you can't do that with me on the couch?"

"No. I need to touch you when I say it. I need to see your face. I need you close."

I picked up her hands that were resting on her thighs and threaded our fingers together.

"I went to see Bryan," I started, and Quinn's head tilted to the side at the useless piece of information she already knew. "I thought I was going there to give you space. I thought I was doing the right thing even if it felt wrong. But I went because I needed to talk to my brother. I needed to find a way to be what you deserved, be the man I want to be with you."

"I don't understand."

No, she wouldn't. She'd have no idea why I'd lived my life by a set of rules that were set in place to protect myself. And she wouldn't know because I'd never shared.

"Settle in, babe, it's a long story," I told her.

It took a while for me to tell her about Lucy and Bryan. First from my teenage perspective then to tell her what Bryan had explained.

"Brice, I feel bad your brother went through that. Lucy, too—that had to be a hard time for both of them. And I don't mean to sound bitchy, but I don't see what that has to do with you...with us."

"It has everything to do with me. Why I thought falling in love was the worst thing you could do to yourself. Why I held myself back—all my life not making promises, not wanting a relationship. I never wanted to feel what I thought my brother was feeling. He was miserable. I thought if falling in love led to that, I didn't want any part of it. It was better to not commit, keep things purely physical, than get my heart broken."

"But there're no guarantees, Brice. Falling in love can lead to heartbreak. Just because you read the situation with your brother wrong doesn't mean you weren't right. There's always a risk."

"I know, but you're worth the risk."

Quinn's eyes slowly drifted closed and this was why I wanted her on my lap. I wanted to feel her reactions. I wanted to see the swift intake of breath that made her shoulders rise. I wanted to feel her legs tighten against my thighs. I didn't want to miss a single emotion as they played across her face.

"I want more than sex, Quinn. I want the promises. I want the commitment. I want to share my day with you. I want to open up and tell you everything."

"I can't," she whispered.

"Why not?"

"Because while you thought your brother taught you about love and the ways it could hurt, that's what *you* taught me."

My body went rigid and my chest ached. *What the fuck?*

"How did I teach you that, baby?"

"How bad it hurts to love someone when they don't love you back. How it kills when the person you love holds back and refuses to let you in. You were right, Brice, it fucking kills. It hurts your heart, it eats you up, your thoughts are consumed by the other person. I can't do it anymore. None of it. Not the sex. Not you holding me while I sleep and then waking up with you. All of it hurts."

It was on the tip of my tongue to tell her I loved her, that somewhere along the way I'd fallen and I was in deep, but I didn't. I knew Quinn; she wouldn't believe me. She'd think I was using it to manipulate her.

If I needed to take sex off the table while I convinced her I loved her—then it was off the table. I could give her that but I couldn't give her the rest. I would be spending the night. I would be sleeping next to her. And I would be holding her all night. The waking up part, maybe I could give her that, too. I'd get up first and give her space.

"I want to open up. Hell, that's what I'm trying to do right now."

"Are you? Or are you making excuses for why you didn't in the past?"

"Jesus, Quinn, do you think I've ever taken the time to explain anything to anyone? Do you think, I've ever held a woman on my lap and opened myself up? The answer is, fuck, no. But for you, so you'll understand, so we can move on, so we can have a real relationship, I'm explaining."

"Brice—"

"No! You don't get to throw it back in my face because you're scared. You're not gonna sit here and tell me you love me and think for a second I'm letting you go. Not gonna happen. You have one option, to hold on. And I suggest you hold on tight, because it's gonna be bumpy. I'm gonna fuck up, you're gonna fuck up, but we're gonna figure out a way to move on —together."

"But—"

"No buts. I'm twenty-eight, Quinn, and it's no secret I've been around the block a time or two and no woman, not a single one, made me want to examine my life. But then, here you are, so fucking beautiful, so damn perfect in every way and what do I do? I finally take a look in the mirror and decide I don't like what I see, and not because I regret a single thing I've done but because I know I'm not good enough for you. I love what we have, I love spending time with you, and yes that includes the sex, but it also includes lying in your bed holding you, sleeping next to you, eating dinner with you, laughing with you, hearing about your day, watching you get ready for work. You're smart, you're funny as hell, you make me laugh and smile like no one ever has. I check my phone five-hundred times a day like an idiot waiting for your next text. And when I'm not with you, all I think about is when I get to go home to you. But, I see it now, something was missing, something big and important, something I'm gonna work my ass off to give you—give us. I want that connection with you, Quinn. I want to know everything about you and in return I want you to know me. The real me. The man I've never given to a single soul. So to get all of that, I'm keeping you, Quinn. I'm moving us forward to something more—something better."

I'd been so wrapped up pouring my heart out I'd missed it. At some point, Quinn had relaxed. Her pretty emerald eyes were soft, her mouth was slack, and it was really damn hard not to lean forward and kiss her. It had only been days but it felt like an eternity since I'd felt her lips on mine.

But as much as I wanted to capture her mouth in a scorching kiss, show her how serious I was about moving us forward, I refrained.

Quinn was now in the driver's seat. It was up to her when she wanted our physical relationship to resume.

My body hated that idea but my heart knew it was the right thing to do.

17

My head was a jumbled up mess. Serious as shit, I couldn't form a coherent sentence and I was having trouble comprehending all that Brice had said.

My heart was begging me to close up shop, lock the gate, and bar Brice from worming his way any deeper.

My body, which had reigned supreme over the last three months, was protesting my proclamation there would be no more sex with Brice.

I could trick myself into thinking I was at a crossroads—that I had a choice in the matter—but Brice wasn't going to give me the option to push him away. And I didn't know how I felt about that.

I wanted to play it safe and push him away,

demand he get out and stay out. But a bigger part of me wanted Brice to prove he thought I was worth the risk, to prove he was willing to open himself to me, to prove to me I wasn't wrong when I fell in love with him.

Suddenly we were up and moving. My legs around his waist, his hands under my ass, but it was weirdly nonsexual. It wasn't like the other times I'd wrapped myself around him as we made a lust-filled beeline to my bedroom to rip each other's clothes off. He wasn't squeezing my ass cheeks, he wasn't kissing me, he was simply walking us to my room.

"What are you doing?" I asked.

Brice placed me on my feet and stepped back to look at me. It took mere seconds for me to hate the distance he'd put between us. And I missed the way his eyes always heated when he stared at me. They weren't cold as such, but they weren't hungry, either.

"Go ahead and get comfortable. I'm gonna order some food and go back to my place and grab a few things. I'll be right back."

Relief washed over me. Which was stupid because some alone-time seemed paramount yet I didn't want it.

His hand came up and brushed my hair over my

shoulder and I fought back a shiver. He was always touching my hair, running his fingers through it, fisting it while he was inside of me, or simply brushing it off my face. I wasn't sure which way I liked the most but if I was pressed for an answer, I'd say him tugging on it while he was taking me.

Brice's lips touched my forehead before he turned and left.

And then I was alone in my room. Nothing had changed in the three days I'd been gone. My dirty clothes still littered the floor, the shoes I'd worn the night we'd had dinner with my parents were still where I'd kicked them off, never making it fully into the closet. Everything was still in its place yet something felt different.

I felt different.

Then I remembered what the detective had told me when I reported the stabbing. "Witnessing this level of violence can change a person. Don't allow it to."

Maybe that's what it was. Maybe I was just tired from the nightmares waking me up. I didn't know what it was, if it was good or bad, but something had absolutely changed.

Tears I hadn't meant to allow to spill started streaming down my cheeks. How could anyone be so cruel? How could someone so callously take a life? Over what? Money? Drugs? And he was still out there, the man with the dead eyes, he was just walking the streets living his life after he'd ended someone else's.

What if he's never caught?

And he saw me. He looked right in my eyes—no remorse, totally uncaring his knife dripped blood off the blade. The man just stared.

"Baby?"

Brice's arms wrapped around me and I buried my face in his neck, unable to stop the sob that tore from my soul.

"What do you need?" he whispered.

"I don't know. I can't stop seeing it." My voice hitched and I hated how weak I was. "I just want it to go away."

Brice shuffled me back and lifted me onto the bed. And before I could mourn the loss of his arms around me, he was next to me, covering me with his big body. Sheltering me. Protecting me.

"Tell me about it."

I shook my head; talking was the last thing I wanted to do. I wanted to forget. I wanted to get lost in something else, I needed a reprieve.

"Kiss me, Brice. Make me forget."

His eyes went half mast, but his jaw clenched and he made no move to kiss me.

"No, baby, not like that. We need—"

"I know what I need," I snapped. "I don't need to talk about it anymore. I need to *stop* talking about, *stop* thinking about it. Fucking hell, I'm so tired of talking. Do you have any idea how much it sucks when everyone around you treats you like you need to be coddled? Goddamn, I know everyone means well, I know they love me, but I feel like I'm under constant observation. I can't move on until everyone just lets me forget."

"No, Quinn." Brice's voice gentled. "You can't move on until you get it all out. Until you admit you're scared. Until you acknowledge what you saw was horrific and heinous. Baby, you can't keep it locked up."

"What do you think I've been doing for three days? You don't think I've talked to the detectives? You don't think my dad didn't listen when I told him everything I remembered—every last detail?"

"I think you've told the story, but not how it made you feel. And there's a difference."

My stomach burned and anger boiled. That was rich coming from Brice. The man who refused to tell me about how he felt when he lost two victims.

"The irony of that statement isn't lost on me," I shrieked. "Get off me."

"I felt like I'd failed," Brice said. "When I saw the first vic..." He shook his head. "Fuck, baby, it was bad. So bad I had to look away for a moment because I could taste the bile rising. When we found the second man, his leg had been trapped and I couldn't stop thinking about how hard he must've struggled. That his last moments on this earth were of him fighting to get free, scared of dying. It gnaws at my insides, every time. Every damn time we lose someone it eats at my gut until the pain is physical."

"And what do you do with the pain?"

"I bury it. I push it away and pretend it didn't happen." I opened my mouth to speak but his finger pressed against my lips. "That's how I know it's the wrong thing to do. It never goes away. The visions, the pain, they're always there. In your dreams, in the back of your mind, under your skin. One thing you have to understand, I never had anyone to give that pain to. I had no choice but to lock it down because I didn't trust anyone with it. But now I do, we both do. You can't ask me to give my thoughts and feelings to you and expect me not to want the same from you."

Did I want his thoughts and feelings? A few days ago that was a no-brainer—I wanted everything from

Brice. But now I wasn't sure I was up to the task. The risk was too great, I knew for certain he'd shred my heart.

"Tell me," he prompted when I remained quiet. I started to shake my head but stopped when he lowered his head. "Tell. Me."

"There's nothing—"

"Tell. Me. Dammit."

"What do you want to know? That just like you, I froze. That I couldn't look away when the knife was plunged into the guy's throat? That I thought I was going to throw up when blood squirted out of his neck but I couldn't even do that because I was scared to move? Jesus Christ! He just stabbed him. In a dirty alley in a shitty part of town. A man died in filth, right there, right in front of me. And I heard him, gasping. I heard it. I saw everything. I'm so scared, so fucking afraid I'm next because I saw it. And every time I close my eyes I see him—both of them. I can't unsee it. I can't stop thinking about how the man was holding a knife staring right into my eyes. Why didn't I scream? Why didn't I try to do something? Why did I just stand there and watch it? Why am I not strong like the rest of my family? Why am I always the weak one that needs to be taken care of? Why don't I ever listen? I shouldn't've been there in the first place. My dad has warned me a hundred times not to go there. And the worst part, I was on the phone with Bridgett joking about needing to get off the phone before I was mugged."

"You're far from weak, baby," he cooed. "There was nothing you could've done to stop it."

"But I should've done something."

"No, you shouldn't've. You did exactly what you should've done and that was get yourself safely out of there."

"But—"

"You did everything right. You're safe and that's what matters."

"Someone's dead so that isn't all that matters."

"Straight up, you being alive and safe is all that matters to me—to your family. Sucks someone died, but I'm not going to bullshit you. In that neighborhood, with the assailant being a gangbanger, the probability of the victim being involved in felonious activity is high."

"How can you say that? Just because the man could've been a criminal doesn't mean he deserved to die that way."

Something flashed across Brice's features and I

waited for him to hide it from me, or clear the anger from his eyes, but he didn't.

"I'm not gonna feel bad for the way I feel, Quinn. You were innocently buying fucking tea and walked up on something you should've never seen. You absolutely did the right thing staying quiet and getting the hell out of there. You also bravely reported it to the police. So, no, I cannot muster up any other feelings besides relief you are alive and breathing. That's all I've got. More relief than I can express to you. And we're gonna work on the rest, starting with you getting a good night's sleep."

The knock on the door made me jerk in surprise and instantly had me on edge.

"Fuck," Brice clipped and grabbed my hand, bringing it to his mouth, kissing my knuckles. "It's the delivery guy."

I nodded and he placed another kiss on my hand. "I'll be right back. You stay here."

He waited until I nodded again and he rolled off of me to go answer the door.

I stared up at my ceiling wondering what I should do. Brice offered me a chance at something real. Promises he'd never given anyone before. I was already in love with him. Whether it happened today or a week from now would it make a difference? Was there such a thing as different levels of love that would make it hurt worse?

Once you loved someone didn't you just love them?

So many questions swirled around in my head and unfortunately my ceiling had no answers.

18

"How is she?" Jasper asked later that night after I got Quinn settled and I called him.

I glanced at the bedroom door even though it was closed and thought about Quinn and our evening. She was a mess, jumpy as hell, and had spent a good amount of time trying to pull away from me.

Her earlier words still left a bitter sting, and for the first time in my life something that felt a lot like regret and shame burned my gut. I never should've given her space and if I hadn't been such a damn pussy she wouldn't be curled into a tight ball in her bed after crying herself to sleep. At least she'd allowed me to hold her through her tears, but not even that made me feel better.

"Did you know she's having nightmares?"

"Fuck," Jasper muttered. "I suspected she was, but she never confirmed."

"She says every time she closes her eyes she sees it—everything that happened. Though what really scares her is that the dickhead saw her."

"Detective Henderson called. They picked someone up and he wants to arrange a time in the morning for her to come in for a lineup. Hopefully after he's put in a cage, some of her worries will ease."

I felt no relief hearing about the asshole being arrested. Not a single ounce. In some ways Quinn ID-ing the man would put her in more danger. The asshole was a gangbanger, his buddies would do what they could to silence her before the trial, and after, they'd be out for retaliation. In no way did an arrest make Quinn safe.

"Jasper—"

"You don't have to say it," he growled and I knew he was feeling this—all of it—his daughter wasn't safe and right now he was powerless to make her so. "We've already thought about it. Jason, Nick, and Ethan are calling in every marker, pushing the gang task force to take down the crew. It's small in numbers, but they're trying to push for more territory, which means they've made a lot of enemies."

"What time do you need us in the morning?"

"I'll meet you at the station at nine," he returned. "Did you get your schedule worked out?"

"Yeah, Cap gave me a week off. Before I go back, we'll revaluate where Quinn's at."

There was a stretch of silence and I knew Jasper had something on his mind, but as much as I wanted to give him time, I needed to finish this conversation.

"Don't mean to rush you, Jasper, but I left my woman in her bed after she shook in my arms for damn near two hours. I don't want her waking up alone. I need to get back to her."

"This is goddamn hard," he said and I didn't miss the apprehension in his tone.

"I can imagine."

"No. You can't imagine and you won't know the burden until you're the father of a precocious, beautiful daughter. Out of all my girls, Quinn is the most independent. Always wanted to go her own way. She could never settle because she wanted to experience everything. She ate it up. She wanted to try anything and everything. Drove her mother and I crazy. But she's the most sensitive and hides it. I know she's feeling this deep. I know she's hurting. So I need to know you have this. All bullshit aside, no pretense and ego, I have to know she's safe with you. And by safe, I mean every inch of her physically and mentally."

My jaw clenched until my molars ached. I quickly tamped down my bubbling anger at being questioned and remembered this was Quinn's father.

"You know I do or you would've never allowed me in your house and you certainly wouldn't have let her leave with me if you didn't believe I'd take care of her. Never done this, Jasper. Never had a woman, therefore I've never interacted with worried fathers. But I think you get where I'm coming from—Quinn is not and never has been what Jackson accused her of being.

"I knew that from the start, going back years I kept my distance. She lived next door for six months until she wore me down. I'm not stupid, I clocked her plays the first day she moved in. We may've started out one way, but we sure as fuck aren't that way now and we stopped being that two hours after she agreed to no commitment. It just took me a while to admit it. And I'm not telling you anything you don't know, but Quinn's gonna fight this. She's already telling me she wants me to leave. She's throwing shit in my face, pushing me away one second and holding on the next. It may take a while but I'm gonna wear her down."

"Jackson will come around," Jasper told me.

"I know he will because he loves Quinn. But fair warning—while he's working through his shit and he's pissed at me, he ever infers Quinn's a piece of ass again, he'll walk away with a busted lip. I let him get his, I didn't try and stop it, and I didn't fight back. But that's all he gets. I warned him once and I'm serious. He's got issues with me, I'm a man, I can take it. But that shit does not touch Quinn. Not now, not ever."

"I'll have a word."

"'Preciate that. My attention needs to be on Quinn. Everything else can wait."

"Take care of my girl."

"Plan to."

"No, Brice, take care of her."

I took a moment to let Jasper's words penetrate. That was as close to an endorsement as I was going to get from Jasper Walker.

I glanced back at the closed door, knowing Quinn was behind it, in her bed. The bed I left her in after she'd held onto me with tears leaking from her pretty eyes. She would've crawled inside of me if she could and I wanted nothing more than to consume her hurt so she wouldn't feel it.

Our evening had not been great, it'd been filled

with anxiety and fear. But the rightness of her next to me in my arms wasn't lost on me. Quinn Walker was it for me—she was everything and I wasn't letting go.

"I'm gonna marry your daughter."

"You asking me or telling me?" He chuckled.

"I'm giving you a heads up. When the time is right, the conversation will be had face-to-face and then I'll be asking."

"I'll let you go."

"Jasper?"

"Yeah?"

"Thanks."

"You make my daughter happy, it will be me thanking you."

And with that, Jasper disconnected.

Then I sent a text to Jackson telling him Quinn was settled for the night and all was good.

My phone dinged with a message before I hit the bedroom. It may take a hot minute before Jackson came around, and he might have more to say, but bottom line, he adored Quinn, they were close, and he'd have no choice but to get over shit and accept I was going to be in Quinn's life.

Then I read the text and scowled.

I expect to be kept in the loop.

It looked like tonight was not the night he was going to get over his shit.

I made my way into Quinn's room, tossed my phone on her nightstand, and pulled off my jeans. I hit the bed, rolled Quinn to me, and tugged her close. The moment I did she melted into me. All thoughts of Jackson, her dad, and gangbangers were gone. It was just me and Quinn and her soft body wrapped around mine.

QUINN TREMBLED IN MY ARMS. I gave it a minute to see if she'd settle down and stay asleep but she gasped and jerked awake before I could make my decision.

"Shh, baby, I got you."

Her nails dug into my chest and my gut burned.

Fuck.

"I'm sorry," she whispered.

"You got nothing to be sorry for, sweetheart."

My hand on her hip flexed and her leg hitched higher as she burrowed closer. The side of her face nuzzled my chest and now my gut was burning for a different reason.

Quinn felt damn good in my arms, the only

woman who'd ever felt right, had ever made me feel and want things I didn't know existed.

"Brice?"

"Right here, baby."

"I need you."

Fucking hell.

"What do you need?"

"You."

"You have me, Quinn—all of me."

"Please make it go away."

"Baby—"

My protest died when she rolled on top of me and straddled my lap. Dawn had kissed the sky and filled the room with a soft glow. Just enough light for me to see Quinn's hands shake as she reached for the hem of my tee she'd worn to bed. Then it was gone. Her fantastic tits came into view and my cock's reaction was immediate—hard and throbbing.

Christ, all that thick black hair, tussled from sleep, most of it over her shoulder but a lock of it covering one breast, a tightly-pebbled nipple peeking through the strands. Good God, she was a wet dream perched on top of me.

Mine for the taking.

Mine to keep.

"Quinn, baby," I groaned as she glided her panty-covered pussy against my erection.

My hands went to her thighs in an effort to stop her from moving, but the second my palms hit her warm, soft skin they were itching to do the opposite.

"Need you." Her groan filled my ears as she lifted up and tugged down my boxers just enough for my cock to spring free. Then her hand wrapped around my shaft and stroked.

Fuck my life. I wanted to wait. I wanted her to be sure about us before I fucked her again. Hell, I *needed* her to be sure she wanted me and not just what we had in bed.

But I couldn't deny her.

"Take what you need," I said through gritted teeth.

And Quinn did not delay. A nanosecond later, she pulled her sexy, white lacy panties to the side and notched the head of my cock at her wet center, and on a slow glide her heat enveloped me.

"Condom," I bit out as her excitement coated my bare cock.

"Don't need one."

"Christ." My head tipped back and I fought for control. I'd never gone without a latex barrier—not once, not ever—and it must be said I was pleased beyond reason Quinn was my first.

It took a moment, four strokes to be exact and I'd counted, before I righted my head and took her in.

Green eyes stared down at me, watching me, searching, and I knew down to the deepest depths of my soul I was lost in her in a way that I'd never let her go. She was beyond compare, the best I'd ever had, the only woman who would ever own my heart.

"Lean forward and kiss me, Quinn," I demanded even though I knifed up to take her mouth.

Our lips met, her tongue brushed mine, and it wasn't like coming home, because she'd never left. Even as she tried to pull away, she couldn't, the tether that bound us together was unforgiving, unbreakable.

Quinn Walker was the sweetest thing I'd ever tasted. Past, present, and future swirled together. So fucking perfect I couldn't begin to wrap my head around how I'd gotten so lucky.

I slowed the kiss as desperation started to take over and nearly smiled at her growl of frustration. My hands on her hips limited the speed in which she could take me as she fought to move faster. Her pussy hugged my cock and without a condom I could feel everything, the tiniest spasm ricocheted through my balls and shot up my spine.

"Faster," Quinn complained.

"Slow."

"More."

"Look at me, baby."

She lifted her head, her eyes hazy and unfocused. So damn hot but I needed her with me, needed to know she understood what was happening.

"What do you see, Quinn?"

"Wh...what?"

One hand left her hip, moved up her back gathering her hair as I went, until I fisted it at the nape and held her in place.

"Tell me, baby, while you're riding my dick, looking down at me, what do you see?"

"I see you," she whispered.

"Right. When I look at you I see my future. I see the beautiful, strong woman I've fallen in love with and it takes my breath." Quinn's eyes lost the haze and then widened in shock. "And before this goes any further, and by that I mean, before I loosen my hold and let you go wild, I need you to know where I'm at. What it means to me to be inside of you. What *you* mean to me. I'm not looking to get off, I do not want a quick fuck, then you going back to a place where you think you can hide from me. This means something to me, you mean something to me. I'm laying my shit bare, Quinn, I want all of you. All the promises you can give me. I'm in deep, baby, and it would suck if you weren't there with me. But if you're not, I'll work my ass off to get you there."

"Brice—"

"Just needed you to know, baby, not looking for anything else."

Her chin dipped and I lost her eyes. But when they came back to mine, hers were glossy. I'd seen enough of her tears to last a lifetime and she'd already shed too many.

It was time to move things along. Our mid-sex discussion did nothing to calm the throbbing in my cock and if I didn't get her worked up, I'd go before her.

"I want your tits in my face, darlin', lean forward."

Her eyes flashed before she glided up and my lips captured her nipple. It would've been easier to use my hands to hold her breasts where I wanted them but that would mean I'd have to let go of her hair. There were a lot of places on Quinn's body I enjoyed. Some I liked more than others, some were downright awe-inspiring, but her long, midnight hair turned me on, and when I had a fistful of it, something I dreamt about for longer than I cared to admit, it drove me crazy feeling her silky strands.

"Brice," she moaned and arched her back and I sucked deeper. "The other one."

I did as she demanded, licking around her neglected nipple before I sucked it deep.

Wetness flooded and her hips started grinding.

"Ride me, Quinn."

She needed no further encouragement and I grunted when she used my chest for leverage and slammed down hard before she pulled up and set a fast and hard pace.

"Never using a condom again," I told her and drove my hips up to meet her thrusts. "You're always hot, tight, and wet. But, baby, this way you're on fire. You feel so goddamn good I can't take it."

My hand left her hip and found her clit. There was no slow, gentle build-up. My thumb honed in and I knew I hit the right spot when Quinn bucked and threw her head back.

From there it was a race to completion. Only I was going to lose, there was no stopping the rush of my orgasm.

"Look at me," I demanded.

Her gaze came to mine just as the first painful spurt of come shot from my cock coating her pussy.

"Goddamn," I grunted and ground my teeth as rope after rope spilled into her.

Her pussy clamped down, prolonging my orgasm, and I swear to God my vision blurred and my ears roared as she rode out her pleasure.

Quinn finally collapsed on top of me, my arms went around her, connected in every way.

And then she gave it to me with her face in my neck, hair draped across my chest and arms. A gift— the best gift I'd received.

"I love you, Brice."

"Say it again," I demanded.

"I love you."

Fuck.

"Again."

"I love you."

My eyes closed and warmth hit my chest. Best goddamned gift—ever.

"I love you, too, Quinn."

Her body twitched right before I felt the first tear leak onto my skin. I'd take these tears and soak them in. Absorb them and never forget them—not for the rest of my life.

19

Brice's hand tightened around mine as we walked across the police station parking lot. I didn't want to be here, and by the way Brice held my hand, he didn't want me to be here, either.

Then there was my dad. He stood outside the sliding glass doors in front of the station with his arms crossed against his chest, his legs shoulder-width apart, and a deep scowl completed the look. Yeah, he didn't want me to be here anymore than Brice and I wanted to be.

This morning when Brice woke me up with a kiss and the smell of brewing coffee wafting into the bedroom, this was not how I thought my day would go. I *thought* after last night he'd keep us in bed all day. I *thought* since we'd both admitted how we felt, the hard part was over and we would stay safely behind closed doors and live in our own bubble. That's how naïve I was.

And that absolutely did not happen.

The closer we got to the entrance, the more fear ticked at my spine.

"You're not alone, Quinn. Your dad and I will be with you every step."

If Brice thought that made it easier, he was mistaken. I could have him and an entire army at my back and I'd still be afraid.

"I know."

Brice sighed and stopped us in front of my dad.

"Mornin', darlin'." Dad gentled his face, and much like he'd done my whole life, he examined me closely.

I knew he saw it, how I felt about being at the police station, facing pointing out a murderer in a lineup.

"Mornin'," I grumbled.

Brice moved closer and dropped my hand, but only so he could haul me to his side and put his arm around me. That still didn't make me feel any better.

"Mom wants you and Brice over for coffee after we're done here," my dad told us.

"Fine."

My dad continued to stare, all the gentleness gone. I hated my dad looked so worried, I fucking hated that he was having to go through all of this because of me. I was so, *so*, stupid.

"Let's get this done so we can leave," Brice declared, then kissed the top of my head.

Any other day, I would love that. His arms around me, his lips touching my hair, but not today.

Today I felt like I was coming out of my skin.

My dad jerked his chin and started for the door, Brice and I wordlessly followed behind him. The station was busy, officers buzzed around, phones rang, people talked, and I ignored it all.

The first time here, I'd been so traumatized I hadn't paid a lick of attention. And this time was no different. I couldn't say what color the walls were, what the room looked like, not a single desk or chair registered. I was looking down at my shoes concentrating so hard on putting one foot in front of the other. All in an effort to stop myself from screaming in frustration.

I did not want to see the man who'd plagued my dreams, turning them into nightmares. It was selfish. It was the cowardly thing to do but I wanted to tell the detective I couldn't remember anything. That I'd been mistaken and I hadn't seen anything.

I wanted to crawl under a rock and pretend my life away.

"Mr. Walker. Miss Walker. Thank you for coming down."

I heard Detective Henderson greet my father but I didn't look up. It was rude but I also didn't care. I was still trying to figure out a way to weasel out of being there.

"Brice Lancaster." Brice introduced himself but made no move to unwrap his arm from me to shake the other man's hand. That should've been comforting, I should've felt something, but I didn't.

"Everything's ready to go. Right this way," the detective said and we were moving again.

A few moments later we stopped and Detective Henderson explained, "This should only take a moment. Firstly, no one can see you. The men will walk in, line up, they'll be instructed to face forward, then they'll turn to give you their profile, then they'll face forward again. There is no rush. You may ask any or all of the men to step closer for a better look. It doesn't matter how close they get to the glass, they cannot see you. The suspect will not be able to communicate with you. The room is soundproof, so you may speak freely. However, the accused will have an attorney present in the room with us. The attorney will be observing and listening."

"What?" I finally spoke.

"According to state and federal law, the suspect has the right to have an attorney present during the lineup," Detective Henderson clarified. "However, he is not permitted to speak to you and if he tries, I'll be right next to you and I'll put a stop to it."

"You'll be next to me? What about Brice and my dad?"

"Sorry, Quinn." The detective gentled his tone. "No one is allowed in with you."

"But—"

"Can you give us a moment," Brice cut in.

Obviously this wasn't a question—Brice didn't wait for Detective Henderson to answer before he moved us a few feet away and positioned me so my back was against the wall and he crowded my front.

"Look at me, Quinn."

I didn't. I couldn't. This was getting worse by the second. I didn't want to admit it. I didn't want to acknowledge I was so damn weak, I needed my daddy and boyfriend in the room with me or I was going to collapse.

Brice didn't ask again, both of his hands went to my face, and he softly brought my gaze to his.

"What's scaring you the most?"

"Seeing him again," I whispered.

"He cannot hurt you. He can't even *see* you. And after today he'll be locked in a fuckin' cage where he belongs."

"I'm not strong—"

"Bullshit," he snapped. "You are. You are so damn strong and brave. You can do this, Quinn. I know you can. Your dad and I will be right outside the door waiting for you."

"I want to leave. I want to lie and say I was wrong, that I didn't see anything," I admitted and my stomach roiled.

God, I was such a coward.

"That doesn't make you weak. That makes you human. Everything about this—from start to finish—is jacked. Every goddamned thing, from you not being able to go to your favorite market because the streets are filled with drugs and gangbangers, to you witnessing a murder. To you having to relive that moment. To you having to face a lineup. It's fucked-up, all of it. And if there was a way I could take it all, I would. It kills me knowing what this fucktard did haunts you. I'd like nothing more than to have five minutes alone with him. But we don't have those options. The only one we do have, the only one that will take a criminal off the streets, is you identifying him and putting him away. And, sweetheart, I know you can do it. I know you're strong enough. I know it, your dad knows it, your family knows it, and deep down you know it, too. You *know*, Quinn. You're fucking brave. Go into that room, stand strong, point out the motherfucker, and walk out with your head high knowing you did good. Don't let this asswipe scare you, he's nothing. He's a pissant who's gonna rot in jail, and he'll be there because you are goddamned *strong* and you put him there."

Brice's eyes bore into mine. No softness. He looked intimidating—almost frightening. I tried to soak up his words, tried to believe I was everything he said I was but I couldn't. There was a mental block, a picket line I couldn't cross.

"Dammit, Quinn." Brice glowered. "Dig deep and find it. It's in there, I know it is."

I caught my dad's approach out of the corner of my eye but he stopped before he reached Brice and me.

"I can do it," I lied.

"No, baby. Dig deep. Find it, Quinn. You do not walk into that room with your shoulders hunched forward like you're beaten down. You go in there fucking strong. *Strong, baby*. You got this—you're a Walker. Walkers do not ever cower from anything."

"Okay."

"Say it."

"I can do it."

"No, tell me you're strong."

"I'm strong."

Brice leaned forward, closing the small gap between us, and whispered, "Goddamned right you are. Now go in there, make your ID, and let's get the hell out of here. We got better shit to do than hang out in a police station."

I nodded but he didn't move back.

"Proud of you, Quinn."

And finally for the first time that morning since Brice told me where we were going, I wasn't frozen inside.

I had to do this.

I *could* do this.

Brice wouldn't let me crumble.

"I'm ready."

Brice's mouth curved up and he smiled. It wasn't one of his megawatt smiles that hit his eyes when I said something funny, or did something he liked a whole lot, but it was still a smile.

"Damn, but I love you."

"I love you," I whispered, wondering if I'd ever get used to hearing those words from him.

I hoped I didn't. I prayed that each time he said them, they would sizzle through me, heat me from the inside out, and make me feel exactly what I was feeling right then—special.

Jasper

Jasper Walker stood close and unapologetically listened to his daughter's man lay it out. He did this with his fists clenched and gut in a constant state of turmoil. He wasn't ready—didn't think he'd ever be ready—to hand off the care of his second-born daughter.

His Quinn. She was a handful, so much like her father, it hurt to watch her fall in love. He wanted to hate it. Wanted even more to hate the bastard who dared to take his baby girl away from him.

But he couldn't.

As a father, he wanted nothing more than for Quinn to have a strong man at her side. And Brice had proved to be that—and he had to hand it to the guy, he had balls. First, Brice showed up at his house with a busted lip and demanded to see his daughter.

Then he manned up in a big way and gave Jasper what he needed—couldn't have been easy for Brice to let his ass swing and admit he loved Quinn.

And now, Brice had his beautiful, scared daughter pressed against a wall in a goddamn police station, and he'd handled her. The perfect mix of tough and sweet.

Fuck, this was happening.

He'd known it before, but watching the two together, he really knew it. And that rumbling in his gut turned bittersweet.

Jasper followed as Brice led Quinn back to Detective Henderson. He did that thinking he'd take the bitter if that meant his girl got a lifetime of sweet.

And if Brice fell down on the job, Jasper was lucky enough to have three brothers who would not bat an eye at helping him hide a body.

But as quickly as the thought flitted through his mind, he knew Brice wouldn't fall down. He knew that look. He understood it. It was the same look Jasper had given Emily the first time he saw her, the same look Jasper still gave his wife after all these years.

Quinn was the center of Brice's world.

Yeah, Jasper Walker was fucked. And this time when he walked another daughter down the aisle, it was going to hurt like a son of a bitch—yet Jasper couldn't wait.

Emily was going to be over the moon, and Jasper loved that. Loved it so much he'd endure anything to see his woman smile.

"NUMBER THREE," I told Detective Henderson.

And for the record, I was standing tall and strong.

My voice didn't wobble. My knees didn't shake. I was scared as fuck but I was brave.

"Look one more time to be sure," the detective instructed.

I stared at the man in front of me, number three, with his dead eyes and cocky demeanor. He didn't think I'd do it, the asshole was sure he'd get away with stabbing a man in an alley because I'd be too afraid to stop him.

He was wrong.

"Number three. I'm positive."

Detective Henderson looked at the other man in the room, the accused's attorney, and smiled.

"We're done here."

"I'd like the opportunity to depose this witness," the attorney said.

"I'm sure you would and you'll be given that opportunity. However, that's not today. We're done here."

The attorney looked at me, and much like Mr. Number Three in the lineup, he had cold beady eyes. I fought the urge to cower. But Brice was right, I was a Walker.

And Walkers did not cower—ever—but especially not in front of pissants.

I was done.

Therefore, it was time to leave and get on with my day. And that did not include hanging around a police station.

20

"Babe," I called out and looked down at my watch for the fifth time in five minutes.

"One more minute," Quinn called back for the fifth time in the last five minutes.

It had taken me four days to pull Quinn out of her head after the shit at the police station. Not even taking her to her parents' house every day so she could spend time with her mom had eased Quinn's worry.

Jasper and Emily had shared more than one concerned glance with me—more like a thousand— over the three times we'd been there. Her mother and father both had had quiet words with Quinn but nothing worked.

By day four, I'd figured Quinn out. She was not a

woman you could handle with kid gloves, you couldn't wrap her in cotton like she was fragile. The more you coddled her, the more she pulled into herself.

So day four I gave it to her straight and told her to snap the fuck out of it. Straight out, those were my words. And when her emerald eyes flashed then squinted, I knew I had her—the fire returned and she let me have it, both barrels blazing.

It was beautiful to witness, my girl letting go of the fear and turning it into determination. She was damn tough, and I learned something important: when Quinn resolved to do something, she did it.

The last three days had been spent convincing her to hold off going back to work. I was not above emotional manipulation, therefore I used it. After I reminded her I'd taken seven days off work and I didn't want to spend any of those days without her, she relented.

Tomorrow morning she was going back to work and tomorrow afternoon I was, so tonight we were going out to dinner then meeting Bridgett and Paula for drinks at Pulse.

But if she didn't hurry up and finish getting ready, we'd be late for our reservation.

"Sorry, sorry, I'm ready."

The first thing I heard was her heels clicking on the hard wood, then the scent of her perfume as it filled the room with a sultry, elusive smell. Before I turned to face her, I should've braced, I should've expected it, but I didn't. Therefore when I caught sight of Quinn, I didn't guard my reaction.

"Jesus fuck!"

I took her in from top-to-toe. The woman had gorgeous hair and a lot of it. Tonight it looked fuller, she'd done something that gave it a sexy wave that made me want to muss it up and fist it. Her face was done up, way more makeup than she normally wore, most of it around her eyes, dark eyeliner that made the green pop. Lips glossed to perfection. When I finished taking in all that beauty, my gaze lowered to her dress.

"Don't move," I growled.

Those big green eyes made to look even bigger with all that shit around them widened in shock.

"What's wrong?"

"I want to look at you in that dress for a minute before you turn your fine ass around and change."

"Change?"

"You're not wearing that out."

"What?"

"No fucking way are you leaving this house in

that goddamned dress, baby. Though you'll be putting it back on as soon as we get home because I'm gonna fuck you in it with you bent over and it bunched around your hips." Now that I'd said it, I couldn't stop the images from drifting through my mind. The clingy red material against all that creamy flesh, Christ. "And the shoes stay on as well."

Quinn flashed a beaming smile that made her go from beautiful to out of this world.

"I take it you like my dress?"

"No. I'd love it if you turned around and put on jeans and a turtleneck."

"But then you wouldn't get the pleasure of sitting next to me all night in this dress while you're thinking about what's under it."

"There's not a damn thing under it, and I know, because I've been looking real hard, baby, and there's no chance you're wearing panties."

"Guess you'll have to wait until later to find out if you're right."

I knew I was right, and an elicit thrill raced through me knowing my girl wasn't wearing panties. But this was Quinn and my jealousy knew no bounds. I didn't want every asshole who caught a glimpse of her to get a fucking hard-on.

"Quinn—"

"Think of it as a time-saving effort," she said and started walking toward me. "You won't have to wait to pull it up and have your way with me."

"Quinn—"

"And just think how excited I'll be knowing you spent your night fighting the urge to drag me home."

"Baby—"

"I'm glad you like my dress," she whispered. "But you should know, it's all for you."

Sweet Jesus, she was killing me. Her hands hit my chest, and she leaned up and gave me a peck, leaving some of her gloss on my lips. Berries. God Christ, she tasted of berries, smelled like innocence, and looked like sin.

She *was* trying to kill me.

"Prettiest thing I've ever seen," I told her. "But you're gonna be the death of me. Please, Christ, do not bend over or I'll end up in the tank facing assault charges after I beat some asshole's face in."

"I won't bend over." She smiled.

"Good God, you look beautiful. I didn't think it was possible for you to be anymore stunning but I was wrong. There's nothing better than you, Quinn. No better feeling than having you on my arm, standing next to me."

Her lips started to wobble and her eyes got bright.

"I never thought I'd have this," she whispered. "I knew it was real, I've seen it happen, but I still didn't ever think I'd get my chance." Quinn took a deep breath, and her fingers still resting on my chest flexed, then she finished. "I knew it was you. The first time I saw you smile, I knew I wanted to see that every day for the rest of my life."

Fuck me. There it was—five words that rocked me to my core.

I knew it was you.

Heaviness hit my soul, our eyes locked, and the enormity of her confession nearly brought me to my knees.

"Jesus fuck." The words fell from my mouth and before I could stop myself, I decided to give her something that I knew would freak her out but I thought she should know. "I spent years running scared from you. First time I saw you, your beauty hit me so hard I had to fight to keep my feet. Then you got close and I caught sight of your eyes and the promise they held and I knew you'd knock me on my ass. Knew it, Quinn, down to my soul. I knew I'd never survive you, so I ran instead of taking you and facing the possibility of losing you. You are by and far the prettiest woman I've ever seen, and one day, all that kindness, strength, and beauty will be passed down to my kids. And I want at least three, more if you'll give 'em to me."

"I want more than three," she whispered. "Maybe four. But I want at least one girl."

Another gift.

So fucking beautiful, I knew my life couldn't get any better than holding Quinn close, while she was in a sexy dress, fuck-me shoes, all done up for a night out, all of that sexy done just for me, talking about how many kids we were going to have.

"I'll make sure you get your girl, sweetheart. But just to say, your father is in the running for sainthood, no way could I handle four of them."

Quinn's lips twitched and love shone in those green eyes. "We did give him a run for his money."

"Did?"

"Okay, maybe we still do. But Dad loves it. He'd be bored stiff if he didn't have us girls to drive him crazy. Jason was too perfect as a child. He was hard-headed for a spell, but he worked it out."

Jason hadn't turned hard-headed for a spell—her brother had gone through hell during his wife's long battle with cancer, then he lost her and lost his way. And *he* didn't work anything out—Mercy did.

"You ready to hit the road?" Quinn inquired.

"Yeah, baby, I'm ready. I want you close all night."

"Nowhere else I'd rather be."

Fuck, but I loved Quinn Walker.

ONE WOULD THINK three very pretty, very drunk women would be every man's fantasy, but they'd be wrong. Pure torture.

First, every man with a functioning dick, and even the ones that need medical help to get an erection, couldn't tear their eyes off the giggling women.

Then the topics of discussion varied and changed with a frequency that had my head spinning. The scariest part about that was the women had no issues following the free-for-all. I however got lost, only catching bits and pieces, and the pieces I did catch frightened me.

It was then I wished Jackson was behaving like a rational person because he'd never believe some of the shit that the three of them talked about. And just to say, I knew women talked about sex, I was almost certain they compared, but good Christ, nothing made a man's balls shrivel up like hearing just how far they went.

"Right, Brice?" Paula laughed.

"Say what?"

"It matters, doesn't it?"

"Woman, I'm trying my best to pretend you're not talking about whatever it is you're talking about. Pretend I'm not here."

I took a long pull from my beer and looked back over the crowd.

"But we *need* to know," Bridgett complained.

Against my better judgment, I turned back to the table. My eyes landed on Quinn first, then my gaze slid over the other two smiling women, before hitting Quinn again. She wasn't smiling, she was biting her lip in an effort not to laugh.

Good Christ, what did I get myself into?

"Need to know what?"

"Do guys like butt sex because it feels better or because it's naughty?" Bridgett asked and Quinn lost the battle and busted out laughing.

"Jesus!"

Quinn was shaking so hard when she leaned into me I, too, shook with the force of her hilarity.

"Babe? You wanna help me out?"

"I'm not a guy," she choked out. "So I can't answer that for you. Besides, I'm curious, too."

"If you're curious, how 'bout when we get home, I show you why guys like it so much?"

"No!" Paula laughed. "You can't show her, then we won't know."

"Ask your man."

"I can't. We're new, I don't know him like that."

"Are you bumping uglies?" That came from Bridgett, and serious as shit she yelled it, causing two punks walking by to stop and stare.

Before I could tell Bridgett to keep it down, Paula being near three sheets to the wind answered just as loudly.

"Um, yeah. And it's fantastic. Orgasm every time. Every. Time. Unheard of."

"Brice gives me one every time. Most of the time minimum of two. Sometimes three," Quinn added and I groaned. "And I don't even have to help." Quinn sat back and crossed her arms over her chest, which only pushed her tits higher, leaving the two assholes with a perfect view of my woman's cleavage. A smug, satisfied smile played at her kissable lips.

"Seriously?" Bridgett breathed her question and leaned in.

"And he does this thing with his tongue—"

I cupped my hand over her mouth. "Babe. You think maybe you can have this conversation with your girls when I'm not at the table?"

Quinn shrugged and Bridgett launched in.

"Take a walk, Brice. I wanna hear what you do with your tongue."

"Fuck, no."

"Come on. I'm the only one not getting any. You gotta give me something," she whined.

"I got something to give," one of the punks entered our conversation.

Tall, built, faded jeans, polo shirt, decent-looking if a woman liked her man with messy hair and a day's worth of stubble. And by the cocky way he'd barged into a private conversation and had no issue casting a line, he got laid regularly. Enough that if Bridgett didn't catch his play, he'd shrug it off knowing he'd find what he was looking for by the end of the night.

Bridgett turned her head, not hiding the fact she was checking the guy out. It was open, it was obvious, and the woman was unashamed in her perusal. I would've felt bad for the guy when Bridgett's eyes stopped on his package, if I hadn't caught him staring at my woman's tits earlier hoping for a show.

"You do?"

"Oh, yeah," the guy returned.

"You think you can do the thing Brice does with his tongue?" Bridgett asked, looking hopeful.

"Jesus Christ," I muttered. "Please tell me this isn't happening."

"It's happening." Quinn giggled. "Bridgett's the bomb."

The guy hadn't taken his eyes off Quinn's friend, and for a second I felt the need to end this. Bridgett had slid past tipsy and was doing her damnedest to skip straight to trashed.

"Don't know the man. Got no clue what he does, don't wanna know. But I'd be more than happy to show you what *I* can do—but what's more, *you'll* be damn happy and that's a guarantee."

The need to roll my eyes was damn near overwhelming, and it must've been obvious because Quinn's hand covered my mouth.

"All right, player." Bridgett slid off the high-top stool and stood. "We'll start with a dance and go from there."

I grabbed Quinn's wrist, kissed her palm, and pulled it away.

"Not out of my sight," I growled, unable to hold back.

"Right." The guy jerked his chin and led Bridgett to the dance floor.

His buddy peeled off, probably going to find some action of his own, but I kept my eyes on Bridgett. The woman's heels were higher than Quinn's—how they walked in those things sober I had no clue. Tipsy? It was a miracle. But Bridgett did it.

"Holy hell, he's hot," Paula announced.

"Eh. He was all right. Though he had nice hands. They looked rough," Quinn added.

What the fuck?

"Oh. I missed the hands. He has a nice—"

"Done!" I announced and both women looked at me. "Time to finish up your drinks."

"Aren't you in a hurry?" Paula laughed.

"Damn right."

"He likes my dress," Quinn told her. "He wants to get me home and do naughty things to me in it. He likes my shoes, too."

"Of course he does. You look hot in that dress. I'm a little surprised he let you out of the house in that number." Paula checked her phone and looked back up. "Jeremy's clocking out."

I had learned that Jeremy was Paula's new man, and he was also a bouncer at Pulse. I'd met him briefly at the door when he let us in. He wore a deep scowl until he saw Paula. Then I'd heard the women swooning—yes, they used the word "swooning" —over the way Jeremy had dropped the tough guy persona and smiled at Paula.

There were a lot of things I didn't understand about women. Most of the things were due to the fact I'd never cared to learn them. If it wasn't something that directly pertained to giving and receiving pleasure, I had never been interested.

So needless to say, the night had been eye-opening.

"Finish your drink," Quinn instructed. "We'll watch out for Bridgett."

"Thanks." Paula sucked back her drink, opened the smallest purse I'd ever seen, swiped gloss over her lips, then stood, pulling down her very short dress. "Do I look okay?"

"You look great," Quinn happily told her.

"Brice?" Paula's eyes came to mine and all the drunken bravado disappeared. She cared enough about what Jeremy thought to ask me.

Interesting. Another tidbit of information into the mind of a woman.

"Yeah, darlin', you look beautiful."

Paula's face changed, and I noted if she gave Jeremy that look, soft and warm, no pretense, the man was fucked. Paula was pretty, but when she smiled sweetly it ratcheted up that pretty considerably.

"You guys are the best. Have fun tonight." Paula winked at Quinn and strutted across the room in a pair of heels that I knew would be put to good use when Jeremy got her home.

"You okay?" Quinn asked.

"Why do you ask?"

"Well, you had to sit and endure girl talk. And by the by, you were a good sport about it."

"That shit normal?"

"No. They were laying it on thick."

"Right." I leaned closer to Quinn and whispered, "So...you like that thing I do with my tongue?"

"Oh, yeah."

Before I could tell her exactly what I planned on doing with my tongue and what she'd be doing while I was giving her what she liked, Bridgett and her man walked back to the table.

"See you tomorrow," the guy said and kissed Bridgett's forehead.

"Tomorrow, Chris." Bridgett smiled.

Jesus.

"Later." The guy called Chris waved as he left.

"What happened?" Quinn launched in.

"We're going out tomorrow."

"Tomorrow?"

"Yeah, he said he'd show me all the things he does with his tongue, but he'd be showing me when I was sober. He gave me his number and told me to call him in the morning."

Okay, so maybe this Chris guy wasn't such a douche.

"You gonna call?" Quinn whispered.

"Fuck, yeah. Did you see him? And I got a nice preview when he—"

"And, we're done," I told the women. "Let's roll."

"Someone's in a hurry," Bridgett grumbled.

I didn't feel the need to explain why I wanted to get my woman home. And by the way both of them laughed, I figured it wasn't necessary either.

"You're a lucky bitch." Bridgett smiled.

"Yeah, I am." Quinn returned the grin before she looked up at me and her grin turned into a smile.

Simply breathtaking.

21

My phone pinged and it took all my willpower to finish typing out the email that needed to be sent to my dad and uncles in the next five minutes.

I was back to work and my family was hovering. But I didn't let it bother me. This was what they did.

I clicked send and reached for my phone, swiped to unlock it, and smiled when I saw the text from Brice.

Brice: *Just checkin' in, beautiful. How's your day?*

My day was shit, that's how it was. I hadn't seen Brice in over twenty-four hours, and earlier the district attorney, Mrs. Peacock, had called to inform me Kenneth Allen's trial was coming up and she needed me to come in so they could start prepping me. Mrs. Peacock also reminded me Kenneth's attorney would be reaching out soon to depose me.

I was not looking forward to speaking to Kenneth's attorney but I didn't have a choice. I had to be strong.

Me: *DA called. She needs me to come in for trial prep.*

I tossed in a few grimacing face emojis and then a few red-horned angry faces for good measure.

Suddenly my phone rang and I smiled when Brice's name appeared.

"Hey," I greeted. "You didn't have to call."

"Babe." One word that warmed me to my core. "When do you need to go in?"

There it was, he'd have my back. I knew it by the way he asked he wouldn't let me go at it alone.

"I told her I'd call her back after I talked to you and my dad."

"Perfect. If your dad can't do it on one of my days off let me know and I'll take a vacation day."

See? Totally had my back.

"You've already taken enough vacation. We'll work it around your schedule."

"I'm not—"

"Well, I am. I don't want you wasting anymore

days on this. Vacation days are supposed to be used for fun."

"All right, sweetheart. You work it out. What else did she say?"

I took a deep breath and tried to sound as brave as I could. "She reminded me Kenneth's attorney would be in touch soon."

"Fuck," Brice snapped.

"It's okay. You'll be there."

"Damn right, I will be. Still pisses me off he has the right to speak to you. I don't even want the fucker to look at you."

"It'll just be his attorney," I reminded him.

"Right, an attorney who is defending that asshole."

"You know I love it when you get all growly and protective, right?"

"Don't get cute when I'm pissed," he warned.

"Kinda hard not to be cute when you have me squirming in my chair."

"Now you're turning me on when I'm pissed, at work, and won't get to do something about it for another two days."

"You *could* do something about it."

"Using my fist in the shower isn't the same and you fuckin' know it."

My eyes widened in shock and my face heated. "Do you...do you... um... do that?" I whispered. *Thank God, Brice wasn't there to see my blush.*

"Fuck, yeah."

"Oh."

"How 'bout tonight when you're not at work, I tell you about it?"

Yes, please.

I squeezed my thighs together and tried to alleviate some of the ache thinking about him jerking off had created.

"You're on."

"Good. Gotta get back to work. You good?"

"Yeah, I'm good."

"Call you tonight."

"Okay."

Brice rang off and I put my phone on the desk, smiling. Something to look forward to.

Damn, I missed him. I missed sleeping next to him, I missed waking up next to him, I missed him kissing me, I missed everything.

"Now that's what I like to see," my Uncle Levi said from the doorway.

I glanced up and smiled at my uncle. "Figured you were next up on rotation."

My uncle's face gentled and he walked farther into my office.

"Actually, I'm not here to check on you." Levi sat in one of the two chairs in front of my desk. "But now that you mention it, how are you holding up?"

"I didn't mention it."

Levi's lips tipped up and his golden eyes lit with humor.

"Have you talked to Jackson?" he asked.

"No. I've called once and texted twice, he's ignoring me."

"Give him a minute, he'll get over it."

"Right," I muttered, not wanting to think about Jackson and how badly he was hurting me.

We'd been friends our whole lives and I knew when I started things with Brice it would piss him off. I knew he was protective of me, I knew Jackson would take it personally when I didn't confide in him, so I knew he had a right to be mad. But, that didn't excuse what he said at my parents' house and it didn't make it okay he was now ignoring me.

"So, Brice," my uncle drawled.

"He makes me happy."

"Good."

My head tilted and I studied Levi—he looked like he meant that, which was good but suspect.

"That's it?"

"Yeah, sweetheart, that's it. If he makes you happy that's all that matters."

"You're not gonna warn me off? Tell me I'm crazy? Remind me about his past?"

"Way I see it, you're smart enough to know your mind and your heart. Not my place to warn you about anything. We all got a past, Quinn. And I am in no place to judge a man who's taken the options that were available to him. But I am a man who knows that when the woman who you're meant to spend your life with brings you to your knees, those options cease to exist. And not because they're not still available, you simply don't care that they are."

"And that's what you think? I'm the one to bring him to his knees?"

"Quinn, I think no man is going to go head-to-head with your father unless that's exactly who you are to him. Brice isn't stupid. He knew the obstacles and he was well-aware that Jackson would be the least of his worries. Brice has been around enough to know your dad. And the way Jasper told it, Brice has got some brass balls showing up at the house with a busted lip demanding to see you. That said, your dad's far from stupid, so he knows what you mean to Brice, and if he didn't believe it, your ass would be sleeping in your bedroom under his roof and not next to your man. And you know that's the truth."

I did know that to be true. When Jasper Walker wanted something, he got it, even if what he wanted was his adult daughter moving back in.

"You're right."

"I know I am." Uncle Levi smiled and leaned forward. "Hope you know if you ever need to talk I'm always around."

"I know."

"Good. Now we got training schedules to go over."

"Okay. Sock it to me."

Over the next hour, Uncle Levi went over everything I needed to know about setting up the schedules, a new responsibility I was taking over at Triple Canopy. And all throughout that hour my other uncles and my dad popped their heads in. I didn't frown or get annoyed. I was damn lucky four big, strong men loved me as much as they did. I was one lucky girl.

"He did what?" I seethed.

I was sitting on my couch still in my work clothes

having just gotten home when Brice called to tell me about his day.

And what he told me, pissed me off.

"Babe, not telling you this shit to work you up. I just thought you'd want to know."

What Brice thought I'd want to know was Jackson had asked the captain to switch his shifts opposite of Brice's so they'd no longer work together. It was stupid and over the top.

"He's acting like a child."

"He's acting like a man who's been wronged by two people he cares about. We have to give him some time."

It wasn't in my nature to give anyone time. I wasn't like my sister, Delaney, who could hold a mean grudge. I knew growing up that my family thought it was a two-way street, she and I bickering then not speaking to each other for weeks, but it wasn't. Delaney was the one who'd perfected the silent treatment, it had driven me crazy—still did. I hated being ignored.

"It's annoying when you're right. Because now that he's acting like a baby I want to call him repeatedly until he picks up his phone. Or better yet, I want to call Tuesday so she can kick his ass."

"Not a good idea. You need to let me handle him."

"What? Why?"

"Because if he mouths off to you and hurts your feelings I'm gonna get pissed. He says shit to me, as long as it isn't putting you down, I'll get over it. We just need to ride this out."

"For how long?"

Brice paused and I heard him blow out a breath.

"Fucking sucks I gotta say this to you, but it may take a while. He's known me a long time, and what he knows...he's not feeling all that fired-up about his best friend being with a man like me."

"That's stupid, Brice. He knows the kind of man you are, therefore he should know you're a good man and everyone has a past," I pointed out, repeating what Uncle Levi had told me earlier.

"A past that includes Jackson. A past he had a front row seat to. A past he's not happy about when someone he cares about is my future."

Damn, that felt good. It also felt like a dream, like I couldn't believe that Brice was planning a future with me, that he'd been the one to demand commitment and push for promises.

"That's dumb. And if he'd call me back, he'd know

that I don't give a flying rat's ass about your past. And let's not forget, I know about *his* past. I know who he was before he met Tuesday. I know *he* went trolling with you and I know *he* picked up more than his share of women. I also lived through his high school years and *he* nailed anything in a skirt. So it's pretty shitty, this double standard he's got going on. But more than all of that, Jackson is my best friend, he should be happy for me. He should be by my side supporting me just like I did when he started with Tuesday. And let's also not forget that he started his relationship with Tuesday the same way we started ours. Sex. No strings. Hell, she kicked his ass out of her house as soon as they were done. I know this because he shared and I was a good friend and listened."

"Babe—"

"No, Brice, just no. The more I think on this, the less I'm mad he's being a dick to you and the more hurt I am that he's doing this to me. He should be happy for me."

"You're right, baby, and I'm sorry he's not. But you have to know, this is about me—not you. His love and concern for you runs deep. I should've handled this differently."

"I disagree. We should've been allowed to handle

our business however we wanted to handle it. He's being an ass."

A very loud siren sounded in the background, so loud in fact I had to pull my phone from my ear.

"Fuck, Quinn, I gotta roll. Call you when I'm back."

"Be safe."

"Always."

Brice disconnected and my heart jumped into my throat. That was not the first time he'd had to cut a conversation short because of an emergency call, but it was the first time I'd heard it. And for some reason hearing the alarm was worse. I wasn't new—Jackson being a firefighter meant I had lots of experience loving someone who had a dangerous occupation. Hell, all of the men and my cousin, Liberty, all had jobs where they put their lives in danger, but there was a difference.

I couldn't explain what that difference was because I loved and cared for them all, but Brice going out on a call had me wound up in a different way. Before I could process the whys and wherefores of my newfound panic, there was a knock at my door and another sort of anxiety crept in.

It hit me so hard, I had to remind myself that Kenneth Allen—the murderer—was behind bars. I'd thought learning the man's name would ease some of my fear, that having a name would make him more human than scary monster, but it didn't. Now he was simply a monster with a name.

It took me a second to gather myself before I walked to the door and looked out the peephole.

Hadley.

I quickly unlocked my door and opened it wide. "Hey!"

My sister pushed her way in, a scowl on her face. *Oh, shit.*

"What's wrong?" I asked and shut the door.

"What's wrong? *What's wrong?* I'll tell you what's wrong."

I waited and waited and waited some more but apparently my sister wasn't ready to share because she didn't continue.

"Well? You gonna spit it out?"

"I cannot believe you."

Oh, shit. Hadley was in a snit. Out of the four of us girls, she was the one who was most inclined to drama. This was undisputed. When Hadley had an issue, everyone better brace because the girl let it rip. It started when she was three, and twenty years later, the attitude had not waned.

Brice. Shit.

"I'm sorry. I wanted to tell you. I was gonna tell you. As a matter of fact, I was getting ready to call you."

That was only an itsy-bitsy lie. Hadley was on my list of people to call, I just wasn't sure if I'd get to make that tonight.

"Right. Mom and Dad know. The uncles know. Delaney knows. Jackson knows which means Tuesday does, too. Bridgett and Paula know. But you know who didn't know? Who had to hear that her big sister finally landed Brice Lancaster from *Paula?* Me."

Damn, but Paula had a big freaking mouth.

"I'm sorry. So sorry. You're right. I should've called you."

"Damn right, I'm right."

"I said I was sorry, what else do you want me to say?"

Hadley dumped her bag on my kitchen table and walked through my small apartment until she plopped down on my couch and crossed her arms.

"I want details," she demanded.

"Details?"

"Yes. Start from the beginning and don't you dare leave a single thing out. You don't think I remember how long you've been drooling over Brice, you're wrong. I want all the deets."

"I haven't been drooling," I denied.

"Sister, the first time he came to a barbeque at Uncle Lenox and Aunt Lily's house and he took off his shirt to jump in the pool." Hadley stopped to shake her head. "Your jaw about hit the ground. Not that I blamed you, the man is smokin' hot. I wasn't sure what I wanted to look at first—his abs, his chest, or his tattoo."

"That's still not drooling," I defended, though I couldn't refute the fact I had stared at Brice. Though my sister was correct, there was a lot to look at, so much so your eyes didn't know where to start or what to focus on.

"Whatever. Stop playing word games and tell me."

"How much do you want to know?"

Hadley smiled huge. Drama over.

"Everything!"

It took a while but I told my sister everything. Well, almost everything. There were a few details I left out, mainly the sexy fun times. But she knew everything else. Including that Brice had discussed having children with me. Something that was so insanely crazy I still couldn't wrap my head around it.

"He wants kids?" she breathed.

Not surprising she'd picked that topic to henpeck out of everything I told her.

"That's what he said."

"Shit. You better not let Dad in on that little nugget. So far he seems to like him. Or at least that's what Mom said when I called her. She likes him, too."

I'd talked briefly to my mom about Brice and she'd said the same thing, that she liked him but wanted to get to know him better.

"It's good Mom and Dad are giving him a chance, unlike Jackson," I told Hadley.

"You need to cut Jack some slack."

"Why the hell does everyone keep telling me that?"

My sister's face changed in a way I didn't like, one I'd seen before. This was not her drama face—those were easy to read—this look told me she was going to tell me something I wasn't going to like.

"Because we all know Jackson."

"But—"

"Let me finish," Hadley cut me off. "He's a guy. He's protective. He's chased away all of our boyfriends. Delaney, Adalynn, Liberty, and I know what we mean to him. He's always been a big-brother type. But you're different. You and him were inseparable. You used to play fire trucks with him. He confided in you about *everything*. You are more than a little sister or cousin, you are his best, *best* friend. He's hurt you kept a secret from him."

"He kept Tuesday a secret, too," I lamely retorted.

"Quinn. That's different. Brice is also his friend. And I hate to remind you of this, but Jackson did tell Brice you were off-limits. And think about why that was."

"You know," I blurted out and stood, "I'm really fucking sick and tired of everyone judging Brice because he slept around. Who in the actual fuck cares how many women he's had? I wasn't a virgin the first time he took me to bed. If I don't care then I don't see why the hell anyone else should. I mean, serious as fuck, we're not living in the eighteen-eighties anymore."

"Girl, I can see you're all fired up to take your man's back but I was not talking about the notches in his belt. I was talking about if shit goes bad. Think about where that puts Jackson. His beloved Quinn or his closest bud Brice. Jackson would be smack in the middle faced with the impossible choice of choosing one knowing he was going to lose the other."

I froze and suddenly I understood. I hadn't thought about that. Well, I guess I kind of had, when Brice and I were keeping our relationship a secret. But I'd only thought about it in a way that meant when Brice was done with me, Jackson would never know, therefore he'd never have anything to be mad at his friend about.

Shit.

"Damn," I muttered.

"So give Jackson time. He's a big boy, and when he sees how happy you are, he'll come around."

"I hope you're right, Hadley. Jackson shutting me out is killing me."

"I know, big sis, but he is not Delaney, he doesn't possess the skills necessary to execute a months' long silent treatment." She chuckled.

I hoped she was right but feared she was wrong.

"Enough about me," I told her, still reeling from what my baby sister had explained. "What's new with you?"

"Same old shit," she complained.

"And, um, does Brady have to do with any of this shit?" I asked and watched the color drain from my sister's face. "Seems I'm not the only one who's been holding on to top-secret information."

"It's not like that," she lied.

"Liar."

"No, really. We're just friends. He's teaching me how to shoot."

"Shoot? Girl, try that shit with someone who doesn't know you've been shooting since you were five."

"Not handguns. He's been taking me to the rifle range. He's teaching me long range shooting."

"Right...because that is a skill a librarian needs to know. Unless you've decided on a new career path as a sniper."

"We're just friends," she protested.

"Okay." I shrugged my shoulders, not believing her in the tiniest bit.

"Please do not tell Dad. Or the uncles. Or Delaney. Or Adalynn. Or anyone."

"Tell them what? That two buds are paling around shooting guns? Wouldn't dream of it."

Hadley looked visibly relieved. "Thanks."

"He's a good guy, I like him," I told her.

"He's twenty-nine."

"So?"

"So, he says he's too old and too damaged."

"Show him he's not."

"I'm trying." Hadley smiled.

"I think this calls for a bottle of wine and a pizza. I'll call it in. You pop the cork."

And I spent the rest of my night shooting the shit with my little sister while simultaneously worrying about Brice.

It was after nine when Hadley left.

It was nearing eleven when Brice called to tell me they'd just rolled into the station and all was well. It took him thirty minutes to tell me about the multi-alarm apartment building fire. Luckily everyone got out safely and no firefighters were injured. What didn't get to happen, because he was wiped and called me as soon as he'd got back to the station before he'd even taken a shower, was him taking the time to tell me about what he did while in said shower.

Then I drifted off to sleep in my bed alone, wishing Brice was next to me.

22

This shit had gone on long enough. It had been a month and Jackson was still shutting Quinn out. I had no issue with him acting like a dick to me, but it was hurting Quinn and that was going to end. My shift was over ten minutes ago and I was itching to get home to my woman but determined to set Jackson's ass straight so I was standing in the parking lot next to my truck waiting for him to pull in.

Five minutes later, Jackson was parking and I was stalking to him. I knew the asshole saw me waiting, so it wasn't a surprise when he slammed his door harder than necessary and had his arms crossed against his chest when I arrived.

"I got nothing to say to you."

"Well, that's good, 'cause I got shit to say to you

and you keeping quiet will save time. Stop fucking with Quinn and call her."

"Got nothing to say to her, either."

I jerked at the venom in his tone.

"The fuck? Seriously, think about what you just said. You got nothing to say to the woman who you claim to care about? Nothing to say to the woman who's had your back since she was old enough to form a coherent sentence? Nothing to say to your friend who's been to the DA's office twice and has been deposed by a dick that's defending the fucktard who murdered someone right in front of her? That's fucked and you know it."

"No, what's fucked is the two of you going behind my back. What's even more jacked is you fucking my cousin after I told you to stay the hell away from her."

"You're gonna have to find a way over that shit. What's done is done. There's no going back and even if there was a way, I wouldn't change a damn thing."

"Why would you? You got a hot piece of ass warming your bed. A sure thing anytime you feel like nailing her."

I stepped back and counted to ten. I should've tried harder, maybe recited the alphabet, or maybe if I was smarter I would've walked away. But I didn't do any of those things which meant I didn't check my temper.

In two strides I was nose-to-nose with Jackson.

"I fucking warned you about talking this shit about Quinn, motherfucker. Warned you. The woman you're calling a piece of ass is *Quinn*. Something I never thought I'd have to say to you, but twice now I've had to. My woman is not tail I'm nailing. And if you'd get your motherfucking head out of your ass, you'd see it. But you're all fired up to see this to the bitter end and you have no idea what you're doing to your friend, to your family.

"They're all watching and while they're doing that they're coming to the same conclusion. Quinn's happy, she's being cared for, she's loved, and she's protected. The only person who is clueless is you. You wanna fuck up the friendship you have with me, whatever, at this point I'm realizing you're not the man I thought you were. But you're fucking with my woman's head and that's unacceptable.

"And one last thing, the only reason I'm not gonna beat your ass right now, is because I know one day, the guilt you're gonna feel over what you've said is gonna weigh so heavy in your gut it's gonna eat you alive. And that's something you're gonna have to live with. So you can fuck off with your bullshit about the two of us lying to you. If you can't see what Quinn means to me and trust I'd never do anything to hurt her, then fuck you."

I stepped back and started walking away, but was no more than five strides when Jackson spoke.

"But *you* are hurting her," he sneered. "You drove the wedge. It's because of you, she's lost me."

I stopped and looked over my shoulder. "Grow the hell up, Jackson. I'm not the one giving her an ultimatum."

"You're gonna rip her apart when you get bored. I know you. I know as soon as you're done you're heartless. You'll walk away and find the next one and she'll be left broken."

"If you think that then you've been paying less attention than I thought. I'm gonna marry her, Jackson. But if you're so worried about me leaving her broken then why haven't you glued yourself to her side? Why haven't you stood by her so she knows you have her back? All you've done is let her swing. And that's fucked."

"Marry her?" Jackson's body locked and even from the distance where I stood I could see the vein in his neck throbbing.

"And it's gonna be soon, so I suggest you fix this

shit now, or you'll be sitting in the nose bleed seats when I slip my ring on her finger."

I didn't wait for him to say more. I was done. My patience was gone and it'd been two days since I'd seen Quinn. Jackson would sort his shit or he wouldn't. At least I could say I tried.

"Enough," I groaned.

Quinn was leaning over my lap with her mouth latched around my cock, one hand rolling my balls, the other one on my hip steading herself.

Heaven.

Sweet Christ, the woman could give a blowjob. Perfect amount of licking and suction. She knew when to tease the head and when to take me deep. She'd been at it less than five minutes and I was going to explode.

"Quinn," I warned. "I finish inside of you."

"Just another minute." Her hand came off my hip but not my sac and she started to stroke.

"No, baby, in another minute I'm gonna come in your mouth."

Goddamn if it wasn't the sexiest fucking thing I'd

ever seen. Her working my shaft while her lips still on the tip of my cock tipped up into a smile.

"I don't mind." With her mouth so close I felt the vibration shoot down my dick and forced myself still. "I get to come on your tongue."

"You do. But I still get to fuck you after. I come in your mouth, we're done for at least ten minutes. And, baby, I do not want to wait ten more seconds."

She was obviously done with the conversation when her tongue came out and licked around my head before she swallowed my cock whole.

I waited for her to slide back up, then reached down and plucked her off my dick, flipped her over and drove home.

Christ.

"Brice," she moaned and wrapped her legs around my waist. "No fair."

I shoved my face into her neck and smiled. "If you'd quit bitchin' I could get down to business and I promise you, baby, you'll forget all about what's not fair."

"Fine," she grumbled.

Five seconds later, Quinn was no longer complaining, she was panting. And five minutes after that, her pussy clenched my cock as her first orgasm hit—she didn't say, though I'd reckoned she'd forgot all about what was fair.

"We don't have to go," Quinn told me even though we'd already talked about it and both of us were dressed and ready.

"Babe, I've been around your family plenty. I'm not worried."

"I know. But you go back to work tonight."

Something warm hit my chest and started spreading until I felt like I was going to burst at the seams.

I tagged Quinn's hand and pulled her to my chest. "You don't wanna share our time," I mumbled, loving that she felt that way.

"I only get you three days at a time."

That was true, which meant I only got her three days at a time. But it also meant I only worked twelve to fourteen days a month.

"Do you want me to see if I can go on twenty-fours? It will mean more shifts a month but I'll only be gone one day instead of two."

Quinn stared up at me and smiled. "No. I'm just

being a cry baby because I'm getting ready to lose you for forty-eight hours. But thank you."

I nodded then remembered I had something to tell her. "My parents' anniversary is coming up. Every year they do this huge thing down in Savannah. My mom asked if you were coming. I thought if you wanted, we could make a weekend out of it."

"Meet your family?"

She looked so hopeful I wanted to kick my own ass for not thinking about introducing her earlier.

"Should've already taken you to meet them. But at least this way, no one will bitch about who got to meet you first."

"I'd love to go."

"It's in two weeks. We'll head down on Friday, the party's Saturday, then we'll come home late Sunday."

"'Kay."

Quinn gazed up at me like I'd hung the moon, and that warm feeling I'd had turned into a blaze. No one had ever looked at me that way, no one had ever come close to making me feel what I felt. No other woman had ever captured my attention, my mind, my heart, or my soul.

Just Quinn.

Only her.

My throat clogged and there was so much I wanted to tell her, things that would have to wait a few more weeks.

QUINN STOOD on the other side of her parents' living room blowing raspberries on Emma's cheek, making the baby squeal in delight. A picture-perfect sight. Images of her doing the same thing to our baby filled my head and I couldn't stop the smile.

"Fuck," someone growled next to me, and I knew Jasper had joined the huddle of men I'd been talking to.

Jason chuckled and Clark outright roared with laughter.

Jasper wasn't stupid, he knew it was coming but he didn't know just how soon.

I tore my gaze from the beauty standing across the room and faced Jasper.

"I think it's about time for that conversation," I told him.

"Figured as much," he grumbled, not looking happy.

Jason and Clark stopped their snickering and it didn't escape my notice Levi had moved in.

"That gonna be an issue?"

"And if it was? Don't suppose that would change much."

"Not a goddamned thing, though it would suck if I didn't have your blessing."

"Any chance I can postpone this for, say, another thirty years?"

I wasn't a father so I couldn't say I knew what he felt—though by the sound of it, it was painful.

"You got until the Friday after next."

Jasper stood straight and every muscle tensed.

"Maybe you should slow this down," he suggested.

"Respect, Jasper, but do I strike you as a man who would fuck around when he's found what he wants?"

"Not sure—"

"Never loved another woman, Jasper. Never not once have I felt anything close to what I feel for Quinn. Never thought about taking a wife. Never thought about having kids. But when I look at her, I know she's it for me. Every time I see her smile, I know with absolute certainty I'm waking up to that smile every morning for the rest of my life. And when she turns those eyes my way, and she stares at me like she's seeing me for the first time, it hits me so hard I have to fight to keep standing because I want to fall to my knees and beg her to never stop loving me."

"Fuck," Jasper whispered and looked at his feet. It took a moment for him to gather himself before he raised his head and offered me his hand. "Welcome to the family."

I exhaled the breath I didn't realize I was holding and took his hand in a firm shake.

"You have my word I'll make her happy."

Jasper gave me a jaw lift and a bone-jarring smack on the back before he strode away.

"Brass balls," Levi muttered before he and Clark followed Jasper, leaving me with Quinn's brother.

He didn't make me wait before he started, "Waited a long time to see my sister settled. That girl flitted through life jumping from one thing to the next. Drove our dad up the wall. Mercy told me Quinn was just trying to find herself. At the time I had no clue what Mercy was talking about. But it seems she was right." I was a little lost and I wasn't sure the point Jason was trying to make, but luckily he continued. "I'm happy to see Quinn's found herself, and in doing that, she's found herself a good man."

"'Preciate that."

Jason nodded and looked over my shoulder. "Jack's here."

Shit. Not good timing. I had to leave for work which meant leaving Quinn unprotected.

"Do me a favor when I leave and watch that situation?"

"Will do."

Jason clapped his hand on my shoulder, thankfully not as hard as Jasper had, though he wasn't a father trying to make a point.

I started to make my way to Quinn when Jackson called out. Fucking hell, I did not want to do this in front of the family. It was bad enough we'd already had words in front of Jasper.

"Let me say goodbye to Quinn and we'll talk out front."

Jackson wordlessly headed to the door and I went to Quinn. She still had Emma in her arms when I got to her.

"Everything okay?" she asked.

"Yeah, I'm just coming over to say goodbye, I gotta head out."

Her smile fell into an adorable pout and I loved the look so much I didn't even try to stop myself. I leaned forward, careful not to jostle the baby in her arms, and kissed her.

"I'll walk you out."

"No, baby, you stay and enjoy your Emma fix. I know you've been missing her."

"I have but I can give her up for a few minutes."

"Jackson wants to talk to me," I sighed.

"Brice—"

"Quinn, stay inside with your family and let me deal with it."

"But—"

I brushed a lock of hair away from her face and tucked it behind her ear. "Have I told you, you're the prettiest girl I've ever seen?"

"Yes," she whispered.

"Have I told you how much I love you?"

"Yes."

"Have I told you how much I'm gonna miss you while I'm at work?" Quinn nodded. "Good. Now trust me to handle Jackson. I want you in the house enjoying your family worry-free. Jason's gonna be watching; if there're any issues, he'll step in."

Her cute frown was set to stubborn so she surprised me when she gave in.

"Okay."

"Thank you."

"Love you. Be safe."

"Always. Now kiss me so I can go."

Quinn rolled her eyes but lifted her mouth so *I* could kiss her.

"Love you."

When I made it outside, Jackson was leaning up against my truck with a face full-on angry.

Not a good sign and not the way I wanted to leave.

"Thought about what you said," he started. "I'm still pissed as fuck at you. But you were right about Quinn. Thought you'd want to know I'm gonna talk to her."

"That'd be good."

Jackson hadn't moved so obviously he had more to say. I was running short on time but since he'd been my closest friend for a lot of years, I figured I owed it to him.

"Just have one question."

"What's that?"

"Is she worth all this?"

"She's worth everything."

"Worth the end of our friendship?" Jackson continued and I ground down on my molars fighting for patience.

"You're my best friend so you have to know it fucking pains me to say this, but, brother, she is not only worth it, but if you're standing here asking me to choose between her and you I'd pick her every day of the goddamned week and I'd do it pissed as shit at you for making me. But make no mistake—I pick Quinn. Now I gotta get to work."

Jackson pushed off my truck angrier than he was before, which made my gut churn knowing I was leaving Quinn to that.

"One last thing." I looked back to Jackson and saw Jasper, Levi, Lenox, and Jackson's dad, Clark, standing not too far away. *Fucking perfect.* So much for the warm welcome into the family. "I think it goes without saying, but while you're having your chat with my woman, you'll check your fucking anger toward me and you'll remember who you're talking to."

"Don't need the reminder," he snapped.

"I think you do, because the last two times we've spoken about her you seemed to have forgotten. And I suppose I was right about that, too. It's eatin' at your gut. Quinn loves you, she's devastated that you've shut her out and I hope you mend that. Be as pissed as you want at me, but she doesn't deserve to be served up a bunch of shit when she's done nothing wrong."

"She lied—"

"No, she didn't. Her not telling you that she and

I started something up isn't lying. We were figuring our shit out, something that both of us deserved to do in private. We've figured it out. Everyone knows. Neither of us are hiding a damn thing from anyone."

Jackson's jaw got tight. His stubborn ass was fighting a losing corner and he knew it. My gaze moved beyond Jackson to the four men standing behind him, and with jerk of my chin I swung into my truck.

I made it to the stop sign at the end of the street before I pulled out my phone and sent a text to Quinn.

Me: *Love you, baby. Call me after you talk to Jackson.*

Quinn: *Will do.*

It took the rest of the drive to work for me to stop being pissed at Jackson and even longer to stop being mad at myself. All of this was my fuck-up, I should've handled it differently. And at the end of the day I was to blame.

If Jackson couldn't forgive me, it was going to suck to lose him as a friend.

23

"Happy looks good on my girl."

I turned from the sink full of dishes and looked at my mom.

"Thanks, Mama."

"I like the way he talks to you. But more I like the way he looks at you—like he's never seen a more beautiful girl. Or maybe he can't believe you're his."

"He's...he's..."

"He's what, sweets?"

"Everything."

"If that's the case, why do you look so scared?"

I wasn't surprised my mom had picked up on my fear. Emily Walker could read her children. If my dad was the protector of the family's physical wellbeing, mom was all things emotional.

"Because I am."

"Why?"

"Because it seems too good to be true. Everything's perfect and when I say that, I mean *perfect*. We just click. We fell into this comfortable relationship. It was easy. I don't know, then we had dinner with you and Dad and suddenly I realized there was something missing, and what was missing was a deeper connection and I wasn't sure I could continue as things were. But Brice wasted no time fixing it. He came straight out he wanted that connection, too, why he'd held back, then he told me he'd fallen in love with me and bam, we were back to easy, comfortable, and perfect."

My mom was smiling like a loon yet at the same time she shook her head like I was nuts.

"And I take it you've shared with him that you love him."

"Yes," I whispered.

"So you're scared because you think it's too easy?"

"Yes," I hissed. "It's happening so fast. It's like I'm waiting for a shoe to drop or some big drama. What if he changes his mind? Or what if he decides—"

"Quinn, falling in love *is* the easy part. It's fun

and exciting and scary. It should make your heart race, leave you breathless, and make all of the common sense you thought you had fly out the window. It's all the rest that's hard. But, sweetheart, sometimes perfect is just perfect. There's no such thing as falling too fast when two people are right for each other. The first time I saw your father he stole my breath, my common sense, and my heart."

I loved that my mom found that with my dad, and even after all these years, she still got a dreamy faraway look when she spoke about him. I also knew they hadn't had it easy. The falling in love part—maybe—but they'd had to fight for the rest.

"So you don't think I'm crazy? I mean, for falling for him so quickly?"

"Sweet girl, I think your whole life you've done things your way at your speed. You were my wild child—fearless and determined to suck every last drop out of life. Why would I think when you finally fell in love it would be any different?"

"So you think I'm crazy," I surmised.

"No. I think you're you and you're perfect. But what matters is what you think, what you feel, and what you know to be true. I'm going to give you one piece of advice—when in doubt, listen to your heart. Your head can be telling you one thing, logical things, but in this case, when it comes to Brice—listen to your heart."

"Thanks."

My mom pulled me into a hug and gave me a squeeze. "You never have to thank me for loving you. I'm happy for you, really, *really* happy."

"Sorry to interrupt, but may I speak to Quinn a minute?"

My body froze hearing Jackson's question and my mom gave me another reassuring tight embrace.

"Sure. Go on. I'll finish the dishes."

Jackson headed to the back door and trepidation hit. I didn't want to argue with him but I did want to clear the air. I hated he was mad, but more hurt he couldn't be happy for me. I followed Jackson out to my parents' patio, and when I shut the door, five men stared at us—none of them hiding the fact they were studiously watching. My brother made his way to the window, no doubt to watch. Brice had warned me Jason would be sticking close and he was.

Damn, I loved my big brother.

"Just let me get this out," Jackson started and I immediately went on the defensive.

"I'm not sure I want to—"

"Please, Quinn. Just let me say what I have to say."

"Fine."

Jackson's posture was stiff and his features set to hard, a look I'd never seen directed my way. And now that it was it didn't feel so good.

"Sorry. I'm being bitchy and rude."

"Nothing I didn't expect." Jackson's lips twitched and my eyes narrowed.

"Are you calling me bitchy?" I snapped.

"No." Jackson grinned and relaxed. "But I do know you. I knew you weren't going to let me apologize without giving me some sort of attitude."

"Say what?"

"I'm sorry I was a dick."

Speechless.

Jackson chuckled and continued, "I'm not gonna make excuses but I need to give you an explanation. The truth is, Brice is a good guy, my best friend, the only person other than you I confide in. I'm not saying I'm happy how shit started between the two of you, but that's because you mean a lot to me, and it burns my gut thinking about all the ways that could've gone bad and you could've been hurt. Then where did that leave me? Right in the middle. Took me a minute but I realize that way of thinking is selfish, but there it is. I can't lose either of you. There's nothing I want more than to see both of you happy. Fuck, for years I've watched Brice hoping—waiting—for him to pull his head out of his ass and realize not all women are like his brother's ex bitch—"

"It turns out what Brice thought had happened between Bryan and Lucy, didn't really happen."

Jackson jolted before he smiled. "He told you about Lucy?"

"Yeah. Things got a little twisted between us." Jackson's smile faded and I reconsidered sharing. "Can you handle hearing this? I won't lie to you. I'll tell you everything, but bottom line is I'm happy, so if my sharing changes that apology into an 'I told you so', I might punch you in the gut."

"I wanna know everything," he told me.

"Then take a seat because we have a lot to catch up on."

Jackson didn't smile, not outright. But I did see a hint of a grin before he sat and I launched into the story about how I landed Brice Lancaster—reformed hot guy firefighter and reformed man-whore.

"Damn. Your dad was right—you played Brice." Jackson smiled at his feet.

"I didn't play him," I denied.

"Quinn. You totally did. And it was the only way you were ever going to break through. Part of why I was mad was because Brice never made promises, he didn't do exclusive."

"He hasn't been with anyone else," I defended.

"I know he hasn't. And it makes me want to gag a little as I say this, but Brice may've been screwed up when it came to women, but he's not dumb. He knew what he had in his bed waiting for him and there was no way he was going to fuck that up. Not with you."

"Thanks, jerk."

"I'm not talking about sex. You're not gonna talk about sex. No one's gonna ever talk about sex. I'm talking about you—just you—having you to come home to. Giving him time to get his head sorted without pushing. No hassle. No bullshit."

That wasn't entirely true. Brice was coming home to some really awesome sex but I did give him some hassle.

"I think you're forgetting about the part where I got in his face about needing more and him taking off."

"You played that right, too," Jackson told me. "He needed the kick in the ass."

"You don't think he came back to me because he was tweaked I saw that guy get murdered and I was—"

"No. Get this shit out of your head. When I saw

Brice at the station, he looked torn up and he had no idea what had happened." Jackson went silent for a minute before his eyes locked onto mine, and much like when Hadley had her words with me, I braced. "If Brice says he loves you—he loves you—and you can believe that to be the God's honest truth. I've known him a long time. And when I say I confide in him, he confides in me as well. And never has he been in love, which means he's never said those words to another woman."

So Hadley had been right—Jackson was upset and worried about being forced to choose a side if shit went bad between Brice and me.

And my mom was right—sometimes perfect is just perfect.

The fear started to ease.

"So, are we good?" I asked Jackson.

"I am if you are."

"I'm good." I hesitated to bring it up but I had to. "And you and Brice?"

"As long as he keeps making you happy we'll get there."

That wasn't exactly what I wanted to hear, but it was something. And really I wasn't worried, I knew Brice would continue to make me happy, therefore I knew everything would work out between the two of them but I still needed to say something.

"He needs you, Jackson. Please remember that."

"Right," Jack mumbled and looked over his shoulder into the house before he squinted and turned back to me. "What the fuck is going on with Hadley and Brady?"

Oh, shit.

I pinched my lips as tight as I could but it was no use—the giggle bubbled up until it broke free and I had to hold my stomach I was shaking so hard with laughter.

Damn, that felt good.

Just like old times.

24

The vibe in the truck couldn't be ignored. The closer we got to our destination the tenser Quinn became.

"What's on your mind, babe?"

Quinn let out a sigh and I squeezed her thigh.

"Sorry. I have a lot on my mind."

"I hope you're not worried about my family. They're gonna love you."

"I'm a little nervous but I'm thinking more about the trial starting."

I was still annoyed the call had come that afternoon right before we'd loaded the truck up to head to Savannah. The judge had denied Allen's latest attempt to postpone, so the trial was set to start next week. Thankfully it started on my day off so I didn't need to take a vacation to attend. The DA had been clear; Quinn's attendance was only necessary one day and she'd only be called back to testify if the jury or the judge needed further clarification.

"It will only be a few hours of your day then you're done and you can put it behind you."

"I know you're right. But I've stopped dreaming about him and I'm scared that seeing him will make the nightmares start again."

I was glad Quinn confirmed what I thought I knew. She hadn't woken up with another nightmare since the week of the lineup, and part of me had been worried she was keeping them a secret. Or worse, she was struggling to sleep when I was on shift. Something I never asked about because I didn't want to draw attention to it. But now I wondered if I'd fucked up by not mentioning it.

"You don't talk about it and I wasn't sure if I should push," I told her honestly.

"I'm glad you're not. My family's doing what they do and that's hovering. Which I get and I love them for it. But sometimes it feels like everyone's making too big of a deal about it."

"Babe—"

"Seriously, Brice. I saw something horrible. But it didn't happen to me, I didn't get hurt. I'm not the one dead. I feel bad for the man's family, they're the ones going through something hard. Every day lots of people see bad things. At first I was shocked and scared. Then when I had to do the lineup, I was even more scared because I didn't want to see him. But now, I'm fine. I'm dealing with it and I'm okay. I'd be able to move on faster if everyone wasn't up in my face about it reminding me I acted like a baby when it happened."

"First, no one thinks you acted like a baby. Cut yourself some slack, you didn't see a mugging—you watched a murder. I don't give the first fuck what other people see or go through, and that's not me being a heartless prick, that's me only being concerned with what you're going through. Talking about it doesn't make you weak. Admitting you're scared doesn't make you a baby. And processing what happened doesn't make you anything other than you. You taking time to sort your head so you can move on. There's no rush, no time limit. But what you need to remember is, there are a bunch of people around you who love you and have all the time in the world to listen when you need to vent. Use us, Quinn."

"You know why I'm not struggling?" I felt Quinn shift in her seat and I wished I wasn't driving so I could give her my full attention.

"Why, baby?"

"Because I have you. Because I know I'm not alone. Because I know that when I feel like I want to crawl under the covers and not come out, you're there. You won't let me fall. Just like at the police station, I wanted to leave, but you reminded me I'm strong. And lastly, I know when I don't have the strength, that's okay, because you'll let me borrow yours. I swear, Brice, I'm fine. The trial's gonna suck. I admit I'm not looking forward to it, but you will be there so I know I'll get through it."

I couldn't speak as a familiar burn clogged my throat and the best kind of fire seared through me.

Another gift.

One that was possibly better than her telling me she loved me.

"Christ," the curse tore from my soul. "Fucking Christ."

"I'm—"

"Every night I fall asleep knowing. Each morning I wake up and I know. But then you say something like that and I realize I don't have the first clue."

"What don't you know?" she whispered.

"How much I fuckin' love you. How deep it runs. How it blazes through me when I least expect it. Then I wonder if I'll ever really know and I hope I don't. I hope that in thirty years from now it will still sneak up on me and I'll never stop being surprised. And I pray I'm man enough to give that same thing back to you."

"You just did."

"Fuck. I really wish we weren't still ten minutes from the hotel."

"It's only ten minutes, honey." Quinn giggled, the sound doing nothing to calm my need for her.

"That's a lot of minutes when I want to rip your clothes off and bury myself inside of you."

"Lucky for you, we're down to nine minutes then."

"You sitting over there being cute when my dick's throbbing isn't helping."

"Well, what would help?"

"In nine minutes I'll show you."

"I like it when you show me stuff."

A memory of the first time I went down on Quinn played in my mind. The look of embarrassment before it morphed into excitement. Her sweet moans as she came on my tongue. Then a vision I'd never forget— the first time I fisted her shiny midnight hair and slid inside of her. I'd memorized every second. The feel of her pussy clutching my cock, her sounds, the way she bucked and begged for more. All of it outstanding, so goddamned good I could get off just thinking about it. But it was her eyes—the way she looked at me—forget the hunger, the lust, it was more. Even then, that first time she stared up at me with love.

And I missed it. Too damn stupid to realize what she was giving me.

But never again would it escape me.

"Finally!"

I turned to see my brother Adam strolling across the hotel lobby and I groaned.

Quinn laughed beside me when I tried to keep walking.

"Stop, you're being rude."

"Babe."

"Damn, brother, I've been..." Adam trailed off when he caught sight of Quinn.

I fought the urge to punch my middle brother in the face as he was clearly checking her out.

"She has eyes, brother," I grunted.

"Yeah, she does. Jesus." I started to move Quinn

behind me when my idiot brother continued. "Hey, I'm Adam."

"Nice to meet you, I'm Quinn."

"I know. I've heard a lot about you. Mom and Dad can't shut up about meeting you."

Quinn went solid next to me and her hand flexed in mine.

"Don't be an ass," I warned.

"What? You didn't think they'd be anxious to meet the first woman you've ever been willing to introduce to the family?"

"Now you're being a dick."

"Why—"

"Well, I can't wait to meet them," Quinn cut in. "How was your drive from West Virginia?"

It took me a moment to remember I'd given her a rundown about my family when we left the apartment.

Adam's eyes cut to mine, shocked I'd shared, clearly not understanding what Quinn meant to me. But then that wasn't surprising considering I hadn't talked to Adam about her, thinking it was best to just let them see.

However, the way Adam sized Quinn up, I saw the error in my thinking. No doubt Quinn was beautiful—I should've expected my brother to all but drool over my woman, but it didn't mean I liked it.

"Long," he complained. "But it's an easy drive."

"Right, well, then we'll let you get to your room so you can rest up before dinner."

Quinn started giggling again and Adam barked out a laugh.

"Loud and clear, brother. See you later." Then Adam glanced at Quinn and smiled. "Nice meeting you."

"You, too."

I yanked Quinn toward the elevator, uncaring my brother's hilarity echoed through the lobby.

"In a hurry?" Quinn squeaked when I pulled her into the waiting lift.

I didn't answer her silly question, there was no need.

"Stop fucking around, Quinn." My hands on her hips tightened and my gaze zeroed in on her ass —and what a fine ass she had.

Black hair tumbled down her back, the tips of the long strands swaying against her lower back as she rode me.

Quinn's hands gripped my ankles as she arched her back, giving me a better view of my cock dipping into her wet. Christ, the sight was enough to make me lose my mind.

"Touch yourself, baby," I demanded. "I'm close."

Quinn's hand went between us, but she didn't play with her clit like I asked. Instead she cupped my balls and rolled.

"Quinn." The half-growl, half-groan that was meant to be a warning only spurred her on.

"I like riding you this way," she panted, slamming down on my cock.

I had to agree, her riding me reverse cowgirl was sexy as fuck. My hands moved from her hips to her ass cheeks, massaging and spreading her until the visual was too much to take.

"You take me there without you, baby, I'm leaving you hanging until after dinner. You'll sit all night squirming in your seat with my come inside of you, unsatisfied. And when we get back, I'll edge you close until you're begging."

"You wouldn't."

"Try me." I bucked my hips and closed my eyes.

Too fucking close.

Quinn's hand left my balls and she ground down before she started rubbing her clit.

Her sexy moans became loud groans and her pussy tightened.

Thank fuck.

"Christ," I grunted. "Ride it out, baby, don't stop."

I SHOULD'VE KNOWN Quinn would pull out all the stops, and when she walked out of the hotel bathroom I should've been prepared.

But I wasn't.

She left her hair down, but once again she'd curled it into sexy waves. Her makeup wasn't as heavy as the night we'd gone out with her friends, but she was wearing more than she normally did. Thankfully, her dress was long and flowy covering her gorgeous legs, but when my gaze dropped to her feet she was wearing another pair of sexy high heels.

It was going to be a long night.

A hint of cleavage that left just enough to the imagination, that would leave a man wondering, wanting—no, needing—to know what she was hiding.

"Good Christ, you're beautiful."

"You look mighty sharp in a suit," Quinn returned.

Her accompanying smile made my chest ache.

All mine.

Top to toe. Heart and soul. And all the places between—mine.

"Come on. The sooner we get to dinner the sooner it will be over and I can strip you out of that dress."

"Why is it you're always trying to get me undressed?"

She smirked and strutted to the dresser to pick up her miniscule purse. My ponderings of the ridiculousness of having such a small pocketbook were cut short when I saw the back of her dress—or lack thereof.

"Quinn."

"Yeah, honey?" She glanced over her shoulder, her lips twitching into a playful grin.

The words caught in my throat. There I stood, speechless.

"Cat got your tongue?" she cooed.

"There'll be payback for that dress."

"Looking forward to it."

"Christ," I mumbled. "You're trying to kill me."

"Is it working?"

"Like a charm."

"Good."

———

EVERY YEAR my parents had their anniversary celebration at the same hotel. My dad asked my mom to marry him in the very restaurant where they held the party. When they still had three boys to feed, it was just the two of them out to dinner. But in the years since my brothers and I moved out on our own, the party now included so many guests they rented out the back room.

The food was excellent and most years, when my dad's brother Seth didn't show, the company was better. Unfortunately this year, Uncle Seth and wife number five were in attendance, and as usual, he was sloshed.

Quinn was in the middle of an animated conversation with my mom, one that I would've put a stop to, however having my arm around my woman and feeling her shake with hilarity as my mother droned on about some embarrassing teenage antics felt so damn good I was willing to take the hit.

I was too busy enjoying the feel of Quinn pressed against my side, therefore I missed it. That was, until Quinn stiffened in my arms and my mother frowned.

"My nephew always did know how to pick 'em," Seth slurred, and suddenly Quinn's body jolted forward as the resounding sound of a slap echoed over the crowd.

Embarrassment and rage battled in my chest as memories flooded of my uncle's filthy hands smacking some skanky barfly's ass. Years ago, Seth had done the same thing to the woman right before he'd turned her and shoved his tongue in the woman's mouth. Elijah and I had watched from across the room. Me with disgust. But Elijah was looking at his dad like he was proud—like he was thinking his father was *the man*, and one day, he, too, would have a wife at home and a piece on the side.

I could take no more.

"Please tell me he didn't just put his hand on my woman," I growled.

"Son," my mom murmured.

"Oh, fuck, no." I pulled Quinn closer before I moved her behind me and suddenly my brothers were there flanking my sides.

"Fine woman you got there. Juicy ass."

My hand shot out and I grabbed my uncle by his shirt and brought him closer.

"Don't you ever put your goddamn hands on my woman, you piece of shit. You think because the women who marry you allow you to cheat and you live in some fucked-up dysfunction that you can walk up to my woman and disrespect her—you got another thing coming."

"You know how it is," Seth mumbled.

"Brice." My mom tried again to get my attention.

"Dad." I pinned my dad with a furious look and with a nod of understanding he guided my mother away.

"Brice," Quinn whispered and her hand went to my bicep.

I ignored Quinn calling my name. I couldn't bear to look at her. White hot rage pulsed through me, thinking about my own fucking uncle disrespecting my woman. A man she should've been safe with.

Piece of shit.

"No, Seth, I don't know how it is. Never did. And knowing what I know now, I've realized I will never understand nor do I want to. What I do know is that you're a sad excuse for a man. But worse, I allowed your shit to consume me for years."

"Shit, boy, I see you didn't pay attention at all. Bitch has her claws into you—"

"Not another word." I silenced my uncle and turned to Quinn. "Babe, stay here with my parents."

"But—"

"Quinn, I need you to go over to my parents."

Without further protest she did as I asked.

"Eyes on me, fucker," I growled when I noticed where Seth's eyes had gone.

"Outside," Bryan barked.

We stepped out of the hotel lobby and the cool night air did nothing to calm my anger. Seth stumbled and Adam caught the drunk fool before he could take a header.

"What's your problem, boy?" my uncle asked belligerently.

"Shut the fuck up." My ire bubbled higher.

"Not like you're gonna remember her name tomorrow. Besides, she was asking for it."

The fuck?

"Old man, be smart and shut your mouth," Adam entered the conversation.

"Valet ordered a cab," Bryan said, joining the huddle.

"I'm not leaving, we haven't even had dinner."

"You're leaving," I told him.

"Shit. Don't know where the three of you get off, but I'm not leaving."

"I see you're too drunk, probably too high, and just plain too stupid so you're not understanding this." Bryan pushed his way closer to Seth. "But I wouldn't push Brice anymore than you have. There's only so much me and Adam can do before he unleashes on your sorry ass."

"The bitch—"

"Last warning, Seth. Each time you open your filthy mouth, I'm finding it harder and harder to remember your age. That *bitch* you're talking about is my woman. A woman you put your fucking hands on. A woman who should be safe with my family—always. You disrespected her, you embarrassed her, and you fucking violated her. So this is your last warning, keep your fucking trap closed—one more word about Quinn and you'll be eating your teeth. And if you think my brothers will stop me, you're wrong. And if you think *your* brother will give two shits—you're not only stupid but you're fucking dumb. You're a damn disgrace to this family. But after the shit you pulled tonight, it's doubtful you'll be welcomed back. But what's set in stone is, I will never lay eyes on you again."

A cab pulled up and I shoved my uncle away from me and stepped back.

"Get his ass in the car," I growled, not caring which brother helped a swaying Seth.

The tight grip on my control slipped the longer I was in my uncle's presence.

Piece of shit.

My molars ground down so hard my jaw ached.

Goddamn.

"He's gone," Adam unnecessarily told me as the cab started to drive away.

"Motherfucker," I grunted. "My own fucking uncle..."

Bryan came back, his eyes sliding from Adam to me and he was smiling huge.

"I don't see one fucking thing worth smiling about," I told him.

"No, you wouldn't, brother. And I'm sorry the fuckstick touched Quinn, but that fire blazing in your eyes is good to see."

Adam started chuckling and I tensed, if there was nothing to smile about there really wasn't anything to laugh about.

"Never thought I'd see it," Adam interjected. "But I'm pleased as hell it's happened."

"What the fuck are the two of you talking about?"

"You, brother—in love," Bryan muttered. "Glad it worked out."

"Out of the three of us, never thought it would be you that'd be the first to fall. But I'm mighty happy." Adam clapped me on the shoulder.

"I need to go find Quinn."

"Bet you do." Bryan's burst of laughter followed me as I stalked back into the hotel.

I may've been pissed as fuck at my uncle, annoyed by my brothers' comments, but it felt fucking great both of them were happy for me.

25

"Maybe I should go check on Brice," I suggested, still trembling.

Now that the shock of being smacked on my ass had worn off, I worried about what Brice would do.

And really, it wasn't even the pat on the ass that shocked me, it was that *his uncle* did the patting—that was troublesome. I smelled him come up next to me, the booze seeped from his pores.

"No, darlin', you should stay here," Brice's dad urged.

"Quinn, we are so sorry." Bonnie looked stricken.

Brice's mom no longer smiled and I seriously disliked Seth for taking away her happiness. I'd been enjoying their company before the drunk uncle joined us. Mr. and Mrs. Lancaster were both easy-going and friendly and they'd immediately welcomed me to the party. Now, Bonnie looked like she fought bursting into tears of embarrassment.

"Mrs. Lancaster, please don't apologize for Seth. Brice told me he has issues with substance abuse. Please don't take this the wrong way, he wasn't being disparaging. But knowing that, and well, respectfully, smelling the amount of alcohol he'd consumed, he probably won't even remember what happened. He didn't hurt me. I was just surprised. Please don't let this ruin your night, I would feel terrible."

I reached out and grabbed Bonnie's hand and gave her a reassuring squeeze.

"That's very gracious of you, Quinn. And I promise not to let him ruin our night if you promise to come to dinner next week. Just the four of us so we can spend time with you without all the interruptions."

"Deal."

"Deal," Bonnie returned, smiling.

Mr. Lancaster stepped closer to his wife, hooking her around the waist, and kissed the top of her head. A gesture so familiar I couldn't stop smiling.

My eyes left the couple in front of me and I scanned the room until I saw Brice walking back into the private dining room. He stopped and looked around, his gaze searching, and a thrill raced up my spine knowing he was looking for me. I saw it—the moment he found me, his hard features softened and he gave me a half-grin as he made his way to us.

Out of the corner of my eye, I caught sight of a very pretty redhead checking out my man. She didn't just glance at him with friendly curiosity, the bitch stared, openly hungry. She was also bearing down on him. Not that Brice had noticed, he never broke stride in his quest to get to me.

And then he was at my side and Brice didn't disappoint, he wrapped his arms around me and held me so tight I could barely breathe. He did this for a long time until his stiff muscles relaxed and he pulled back just far enough to lock eyes.

"You okay?" I whispered.

"No. But are you?"

"Yes. I'm great. Your parents and I were talking. Depending on your schedule, we're going to their house next week for dinner," I told him.

He rewarded me with a smile. Not one of Brice's cocky grins. Not even one of his tender ones. No, this one was different, contentment was clear but it was more; he looked happy—truly happy.

"Sounds good, baby," he murmured and continued to stare down at me.

I really wanted to press for details about what had happened outside, but now that Brice was smiling, I didn't want to ask and ruin his good mood. I was curious about what he said to his uncle, but more than that, I wanted to make sure he was really okay. Something I'd do later when we had privacy.

"Thank you for always taking care of me," I whispered, but regretted it when his smile fell.

"Always." Brice's fierce declaration tingled over me and my toes curled.

Not even *I* was naïve enough to miss his meaning.

THE SIX OF us squeezed around one table but we made it work. All of the guests were seated and enjoying their meal, the feel of the room joyous and upbeat. Every once in a while, one of Bryan and Bonnie's friends would stop by the table and congratulate them on their years of marital bliss.

"So, Quinn, you have a big family, right?" Adam asked.

"God, yes. There are so many of us, I've lost count."

"That's lovely," Mrs. Lancaster beamed. "You

have three sisters and a brother, is that correct?"

"Yes. Jason is the oldest and he's married to Mercy. My older sister Delaney is married to Carter and they just had baby Emma. Then there's the twins, Hadley and Adalynn. They're the youngest."

"I was happy when we had three healthy children," Mr. Lancaster started. "But when they hit their teenage years, I was mighty pleased God had seen fit to give me boys."

"There's a running joke with my uncles, that my dad was strapped with four girls because...well... before my mom, he was a bit of a ladies' man. The way they tell it, four girls was karma. Though my mom says that God gave him four girls because my dad was a born protector."

"Dude, you are so screwed." Bryan chuckled. "I only see baby girls in your future, brother."

"Bryan," Bonnie gasped.

"Seriously, Ma."

"Yes, seriously, Bryan." Bonnie scowled and I wouldn't have been surprised if Bryan shrank down and slid under the table. The woman's eyes blazed.

"Good thing I like girls then," I said. "I have a brother and I'm surrounded by male cousins, I, too, remember the teenage years. If they weren't fighting with each other, they were fighting with someone else. And the revolving door of underdressed girls that came to family picnics was enough to make your head spin."

Brice's hand on my knee tightened and I felt him shaking beside me.

"What? It's true. My dad would've lost his mind if me or my sisters had left the house looking like that."

"Tell me about it," Bonnie commiserated. "I'm normally a rational woman, but jeez-Louise, there were times I wished we owned a shotgun."

Bryan and Adam were both chuckling and I wasn't seeing what was funny.

"Well, my dad owns more than one shotgun and it was hard getting a date," I grumbled.

Brice lost the battle of keeping his laughter under wraps. "Bet that was hell, babe."

"It was. Ask Delaney, she didn't have a date to the senior prom."

I crossed my arms over my chest and glared at Brice.

"You're cute when you're all riled up."

"You keep saying that, but you're wrong."

I felt two weighty stares and looked over to see Mr. and Mrs. Lancaster leaning into each other smiling. Much like when Brice gave me the same contented look, I took a moment to enjoy the warm glow as it washed over me.

DINNER WAS DELICIOUS.

Brice's family, awesome.

And the whole meet-the-parents thing went better than I'd hoped, in spite of Uncle Seth.

Bryan and Bonnie left the table to go mingle with their friends, leaving me and the Lancaster brothers alone to shoot the shit. It was easy to see the brothers were close even though they lived in three different states. They kept in touch and stayed involved in each other's lives.

I was so relaxed enjoying listening to the banter, I wasn't prepared when the redhead from earlier stopped at our table. At first I thought she was a guest, then I noticed she wore a name tag and the same white button-down blouse, which was a size too small if the straining buttons were anything to go by, and black slacks that, again, she could've gone up a size the way they hugged her ass and hips.

"Brice," the woman drawled.

Yes, she drew out his name and laid on a thick Southern accent that sickened me. I'd lived in

Georgia my whole life, and never had I heard the inflection.

Her hand went to Brice's shoulder, and not only did he jerk but his body went tight. I had Brice in profile so I wasn't sure, but from where I sat next to him, it looked as if he was scowling.

"Long time, sweetheart. You staying here for the night?"

Silence ensued and gone was the mellow mood.

I glanced at Brice's brothers to see neither of them was pleased at the intrusion.

"Is she trying to hit on my man, right in front of me?" I mock-whispered.

Bryan's gaze cut to me and he smiled so huge his eyes crinkled at the corners.

"It would seem so." Bryan chuckled.

"Who does that?" I asked.

"Apparently she does."

Adam's chuckle brought my gaze to him just in time to see him shaking his head.

"Don't look at me, sis." Adam shrugged, still smiling.

I glanced back to Brice as uncomfortable waves rolled off him. I'd been joking, my way of trying to keep my cool, but seeing her red-tipped talons resting on my man's shoulder made me snap.

"I suggest you take your hand off Brice if you like it attached to your arm," I warned.

Her glossed lips curved up into a smile and I braced. "Oh, that's cute, honey. But Brice and I go way back."

It's worth noting Brice went from stiff to pissed-off.

"That may be so, but see, we're in the here and now and you most certainly need to step back."

"If you think that, you don't know Brice. He likes my hands on him."

Fucking bitch.

"Mindy," Brice barked.

"Wendy," she corrected, and I burst out laughing.

"Damn, sounds to me you weren't even memorable enough he remembers your name," I said through my hilarity. "Now, *Wendy,* be a doll and get us another round."

Adam and Bryan nearly busted a gut but Brice hadn't moved, and suddenly I felt bad for making light of a clearly uncomfortable situation.

"Honey," I called and Brice turned to look at me, his eyes furious. "Two minutes ago you didn't remember she existed, and two seconds after she leaves we'll all forget her name. But if you want me to kick her ass for touching you, I will. But it'd really suck if I broke a heel. I know you were looking forward to seeing them later and they're the only pair I brought. Your call, happy to do it, but just to add— getting blood out of this material is a bitch and it would totally ruin you bunching it up around my hips." I lifted my shoulders like it was all the same to me and Brice's lips twitched as some of the anger slipped away.

"Yeah, baby, that would totally suck. Been looking forward to that all night."

"Problem solved. Wendy will scuttle off, get us a round, we'll talk about what a bitch she is for inter- rupting our night, then we'll drink, forget her name, and later you can enjoy a bloodstain-free dress."

"Damn, but I like how your woman thinks," Adam grunted. "I need to find one of those. Your sisters single?"

"My baby sisters are full of drama, nothing like me. Hadley would've wrestled the bitch to the ground without a thought and Adalynn would've been on her feet screaming the place down."

"That'd totally work for me," Adam told me, but my eyes never left Brice's. Therefore I didn't miss the amusement. What I did miss was Wendy leaving the table.

But I knew she had when Brice took a breath and relaxed.

"Totally fuckin' cute when you're riled."

I rolled my eyes at Brice. "If I wasn't worried about making a bad impression with your parents, I would've wrestled her to the ground."

"Ma would've cheered you on," Bryan told me. "But it would've sucked if Brice missed out on your heels and dress."

My cheeks heated with embarrassment and I was already regretting my outburst.

"Sorry about that," Brice mumbled.

"You have nothing to be sorry for. I figure that won't be the last time I'll have a run-in with one of your *friends*."

"Friends," Adam choked. "Woman, you are cute."

And just like I said, two seconds later Wendy was forgotten.

I WAS RUNNING late and jogging down the stairs trying to dash to my car so I could speed to work.

The night of Brice's parents' anniversary party, he'd been energetic. And he had not lied, he loved my dress and my sexy sandals and paid homage to both by taking me from behind while the dress and shoes indeed stayed on. Then he showered us, and took me again. We got up early to attend the goodbye breakfast, therefore the rest of the day I dragged, dog-assed tired.

Last night wasn't much better. I'm not sure what had gotten into Brice—not that I complained at the time, though I was feeling it that morning, trying to function on very little sleep. He'd attacked the second we'd made it through the front door. Hard, rough, and delicious. The second go around he took his time—lots of time—leaving no part of me untouched. The third time he'd woken me up in the middle of the night and taken me somewhere between the first and second. It was slow and sweet, but still frantic. I couldn't get enough.

Between all of the sex in the last twenty-four hours, lack of sleep, and general laziness, I didn't get out of bed when Brice left for work. Therefore I fell back to sleep and I was now thirty minutes late to work.

Oops.

My phone rang from somewhere in the depths of my purse, likely my dad asking me where the hell I was. Of all days for me to be late. Normally no one would know, but I'd stupidly scheduled a meeting with my dad on a Monday morning.

Shit, fuck, he was gonna be pissed.

I beeped the locks to my car still five feet away and was deep in thought trying to come up with an excuse for my tardiness. The endeavor was fruitless because my dad could sniff out a lie a mile away.

Damn!

"Quinn Walker?"

I rocked to a stop and looked at the man who'd called my name.

Then my insides turned to ice.

There was no time to scream.

No time to run.

No time to breathe.

I heard it first—the gunshot—it pierced through the quiet before the pain registered.

And when the pain hit my chest, it was excruciating.

When the second blast went off, I heard it but didn't feel it.

Overwhelming. Unbelievable.

Unbearable.

There were no last thoughts before I closed my eyes. I only wanted escape from the agony.

26

I pocketed my phone after leaving Quinn a voice-mail, surprised to see Jackson cruising into the station bay on his day off but even more surprised he wasn't glaring at me like he was ready to go a few rounds.

Just because he and Quinn had made amends didn't mean Jackson had given me an inch. He'd come into work as I was leaving, and as annoying as it was that he was avoiding me, I didn't push. I'd said what I had to say and though it was killing me inside that I'd lost a good friend, it was more important he and Quinn had worked things out.

"You gotta minute?"

I braced before I answered in the affirmative—

just because Jackson didn't look pissed didn't mean he wasn't simmering on the inside.

"Heard you took Quinn to Savannah to meet your parents," he started.

"You heard correct."

"How'd that go?"

My brows drew together, not understanding his question. "I assume Quinn told you we went, she didn't tell you if she had a good time or not?"

"Heard what she had to say, but I'm asking *you* how it went."

I thought back over our amazing weekend, other than my fucking uncle being a prick and some random chick from my past being a bitch. Quinn not only handled Wendy in a way that was amusing instead of letting it fuck up our whole night, she'd also waved off any concern my family had about my uncle.

Something new about Quinn I'd learned—besides being gracious and classy, she also rolled with the tide and didn't let anything stop her from having a good time. Which surprised me. I'd heard stories about the Walker girls and their legendary grudges; it was good to know that drunk, handsy uncles and bitches didn't register on the grudge list.

"My parents love her, but that was never in question. Seth got drunk and acted like a fucking dick. No big surprise. My dad was thoroughly pissed, but that's nothing new when his brother embarrasses him. Adam and Bryan are on my shit list, since both of them repeatedly told her she'd picked the wrong brother and battled it out about which of them was a better fit for her."

Jackson was fighting back a grin and shaking his head. "Good time then."

"It's always a good time when I'm with Quinn," I told him and watched his grin turn into a scowl. "Why are you here?"

"Got a few things I need to say."

"I'm not gonna lie, Jack, fucking sucks this rift between us, but now's not the time to piss me off. We had a good weekend and I worked hard to keep Quinn's mind occupied and off having to testify. My family helped with that. But as soon as we got back, all that effort went to shit. Quinn's nervous, I'm annoyed as fuck I'm at work knowing my woman's home alone lying through her teeth telling me she's fine. I have until tomorrow five a.m. before I can go home to her and help her relax. With all of that, I'm fresh out of patience. So if what you need to say will make me lose my mind, I'd appreciate you keep it to yourself until after I get Quinn through the trial."

"I know I was a dick," Jack said. "I've apologized to Quinn and now I'm apologizing to you. I was pissed for selfish reasons. After all this shit with the trial is over, we'll grab a beer and I'll explain, but for now all I wanted to say was, I'm sorry."

An apology from Jackson Clark? That was not what I'd been expecting. I couldn't say it was unwelcomed but now wasn't the time to get into a lengthy discussion, not when my mind was full of Quinn and her upcoming testimony.

"Neither of us handled the situation the way we should've," I told him. "I lied to you, I get why you're pissed at me. I'll gladly take you up on the beer as long as you understand I won't apologize for falling in love with her. Sucks the way it happened only because it meant I was lying to you, but the rest of it? I'm not sorry for a single second I've spent with her."

"I'm seeing things a little clearer now. I'm happy for you both. Happier for her because she deserves a good man."

Fuck, that felt good. I had no idea how badly I needed to hear Jackson say that.

"Tuesday wants you and Quinn over for dinner," Jackson continued.

He was so full of shit—*he* wanted us over for dinner and he was blaming it on his wife.

"Right. I'll tell Quinn. But you and I are working opposite shifts now, so it might take a few weeks before we find a time."

Even saying that was a kick in my gut and it may've made me a pussy, but losing Jackson as my partner hurt. Hurt even worse Jackson went to such extremes to put distance between us.

The tone sounded and both Jackson and I cocked our heads to listen to dispatch call out orders.

"Catch ya later," I told Jackson and headed back into the bay, joining the rest of the crew.

I stepped into my turnout gear, shrugged on my coat, slapped the Station 57 insignia on the side of the truck, and swung into the jump seat. The rest of the crew piled in, Mike climbed into the driver's seat, Captain Casey in the front passenger, and Louis, Mark, Pete, and Joanne followed.

Without delay, Mike flipped the lights and followed the ambo out of the bay.

Street signs and buildings blurred as Mike raced to an accident scene. My head was full of Jackson, his unexpected visit, and the possibility we could go back to being friends. I checked my phone and smiled, either Quinn was still asleep or she was at work, meaning she was in a meeting with her dad and Carter, therefore she wouldn't have answered my message. The smile wasn't because of what time it was or the meeting she was likely in. Hell no, the grin was from remembering the soft, satisfied, sleepy form I'd left in bed this morning, and her sweet kiss goodbye.

My plans to ask Quinn to marry me while we were in Savannah got shot to shit. No matter how hard I tried, I couldn't stop thinking about the shit Seth pulled but even if I could've found a way to bury the disgust, I couldn't ditch my goddamned brothers. Both had stayed until we left. However, on the drive home, I was thinking my inability to propose may've been a good thing. I didn't want memories of our engagement to be tangled with the trial.

Now I had a huge ass diamond ring burning a hole in my pocket.

As soon as the hearing was over, I was asking.

"Two minutes out," Captain Casey cut through my thoughts. "Single vic. GSW to the chest."

Christ.

I thought about who was on duty today—Kendall and Lance, both experienced medics. Lance had medical and field training from the Army. Kendall had ten years under her belt as a trauma nurse. A gunshot wound to the chest would require their combined skills to ensure the victim's survival.

What felt like seconds later, ambulance thirty-one skidded to a halt and Mike angled the beast of a fire engine to block traffic. The morning traffic had already started migrating, funneling into the lane nearest the double yellow lines. I quickly scanned the area, a red BMW with its hazards flashing was parked half in the right-hand traffic lane, half in the narrow emergency lane.

Louis, Mark, and Pete waved looky-loos on. Joanne grabbed her med-kit and rushed to help with the victim. Captain Casey immediately made his way to two uniformed officers.

The scene was buzzing, heartrates pumped, and our training took over. I yanked the second kit free and started in the direction of the victim.

"Fuck!" Joanne shouted and I quickened my pace.

If the calmest of the crew was cursing then it had to be bad. Before I made it to the sidewalk where the victim lay, Mike stepped in front of me. His hands went to my chest and he shoved me back.

"Back in the truck," he barked.

"What the fuck?"

Before I could blink, Captain Casey was at my side while an officer jogged in my direction.

"Lancaster! Truck," Casey demanded.

I looked over Mike's shoulder. Kendall shifted to pull something from an open med kit and I froze.

From one beat of my heart to the next, the organ seized.

A shock of black hair blanketed the dirty concrete.

Impossible.

I pushed past Mike and was in a dead sprint before either man could stop me.

It couldn't be her.

There was a flurry of commotion as Lance, Joanne, and Kendall worked diligently to resuscitate the victim.

Bile rose fast and furious.

Not the *victim*—Quinn.

"Step back, son, let them work." Cap's hand grabbed my bicep and I wrenched free. I took the last two steps and went to my knees.

"Quinn, baby," I choked.

Words were spoken, hands were moving, clothes were being torn away, leads were being connected. Not a goddamn thing penetrated I was so focused on processing that it was Quinn with a hole in her chest, blood oozing, leaking onto the sidewalk. It bubbled from her mouth, down her chin, staining her beautiful flesh.

Impossible.

"No breath sounds…"

Fuck. Jesus fuck.

"Come on, Quinn, stay with me, baby," I demanded.

"…move her now."

No, *no*, fuck, no.

"Fight, Quinn!"

Then she was up, the gurney squealed as they extended it, and Lance was on the move.

I however was staring at my woman's blood—too much blood—so much blood I was in shock.

"Let's go!" Kendall shook me out of my stupor. "Now, Brice!"

They loaded the ambulance and I barely made it in time to jump in before Lance slammed the door. A second later, the rig shot forward and Kendall went back to work.

"I need you to put a line in, are you steady enough?"

"No," I answered honestly.

Kendall's blue eyes snapped to mine and I wished I was looking in emerald ones.

"You need to be, right now, Brice. Snap the fuck out of it. We have no choice. She needs you, right damn now, to get your shit sorted and help me."

I took the gloves she offered and shoved all my fear, all the panic, every ounce of emotion I was feeling aside and got to work.

The next five minutes were a blur as we worked on Quinn. Machines beeped, Kendall called in our ETA, my hands stanched the flow of blood.

There was not one hole, there were two.

Two fucking holes in my woman's chest.

Two angry, puckered *holes* threatening to take her away from me.

Tears formed and spilled down my cheeks, rolled off my chin, and fell, mixing with the blood drying on Quinn's chest.

Then there was silence—deafening, soul-crushing silence.

"Goddammit. Start compressions," Kendall ordered.

"Come on, baby. Fight, Quinn!" I clenched my jaw and I counted aloud with each downward push.

I hadn't made it to ten before the back door to the rig flew open and Lance was pulling the stretcher out. My feet went to the roller platform, not stopping my bone-crushing attempt to force much-needed oxygen into Quinn's lungs.

I heard nothing until I felt someone shoving me aside to take over. Then Kendall was yelling at me to move.

I didn't. I couldn't. Not until I was forcibly pulled away.

Then the ache in my soul turned into more—terror—as I helplessly watched Quinn being rushed down the hall surrounded by a team of doctors and nurses. When I took a step to follow, Captain Casey was there shoving me against the wall.

"Best chance she has is going up now. You do not want to slow that, son."

Best chance.

The gravity hit. All of the weight I pushed aside in the ambulance bore down, so much weight I was dizzy with it. So heavy I couldn't bear it.

My ass landed on the floor, my head went between my bent knees, and part of me died.

"Someone call in Jackson," Captain ordered, and my head popped up.

"No! I need to call him."

"Don't think you're—"

"It has to be me. I need a phone."

Joanne was there pushing a phone into my hand

and I woodenly dialed to make a call I never in my life thought I'd make.

"Hello?" Jackson greeted, sounding upbeat.

Fucking shit.

"Hello?" he repeated.

"Brother," I croaked.

"Brice?"

"Fuck—"

"Where are you?"

"County," I choked. "I need you here now. Call your dad, tell him to get Levi and Lenox and lock down Jasper."

"The fuck?"

"It's Quinn, brother. You need to get here but Jasper needs to be locked down first."

"How bad?"

"Ba...bad."

"Motherfuck! Was she in an accident?"

"I'll explain when you get here." My head dropped and my eyes closed. "Might not.. might not..."

Jesus fuck, I couldn't say the words. Couldn't think them.

"Brice," Jackson whispered, and there was no missing the anguish.

"Just...get here."

Joanne reached down and peeled the phone out of my hands. The soft murmur of her voice did nothing to soothe my ravished soul.

IT COULD'VE BEEN ten minutes, it could've been ten hours. I'd lost track of time as I sat on the floor of the ER. Not a single person dared to tell me to move.

Even with all of my focus on the bloody gloves I still hadn't removed, I felt his presence. Pain that matched my own—so thick, so heavy, it was crippling.

My head came up, our eyes locked, and then there were no words necessary.

"No!" Jasper roared.

Levi and Lenox flanked him when his knees gave way.

There were only a few things in this life that would bring Jasper Walker to his knees, all of those things revolved around his family.

I had nothing left inside of me to give.

No reassurances.

No words.

Nothing.

I was hollow.

And with every second that passed I died a little more.

Clark stood next to Jackson, both looking at me wide-eyed.

Jackson broke away and crouched in front of me.

"Brother?"

"Two GSWs to the chest."

Jackson sucked in a breath and I forged on, needing to purge the images of a lifeless Quinn being wheeled away.

"We...um...fuck." I swallowed a sob but couldn't stop the wetness from pooling in my eyes. "We lost her right before we pulled in," I whispered. "We started CPR, then she was wheeled up to the OR."

Jackson shot to his feet and I went back to ignoring everything and everyone. I knew I needed to get up off my ass and talk to Jasper. Offer him something, fuck if I knew what that something was, and fuck if I had anything in me.

I was debating how I was going to stand—and once I got to my feet, if I'd be able to stay upright—when Jasper stepped in front of me offering me his hand.

I shook my head, not wanting to transfer his daughter's blood but also not wanting to take off my gloves.

It was morbid but I had to keep something of hers with me.

He yanked me to my feet, then Jasper's arms went around me and pounded my back with an earthshaking thud.

"I...fuck..."

Nothing, I had no words.

I felt Jasper's body convulse and his breath hitch.

Jesus fuck.

27

Two hours later, I walked out of the restroom. Cap had gone to the station, grabbed me a change of clothes, then perched his ass in the waiting room along with the rest of Quinn's family. The rest of the crew had been in and out, offering what they could— soft words to Emily and Jasper. Checking on Jackson and staring at me with concern.

I shoved my hand in my pocket, feeling the inside-out balled-up pair of gloves I was still keeping ahold of.

Two hours of pure torture.

I was turning the corner when Kendall stepped in front of me and stopped.

"I asked a lot of you in the ambulance and I wasn't very kind about it," she started.

Pure Kendall. Tough as nails when she was in work mode, soft as a kitten when she wasn't.

"I fucked up," I admitted. "Totally froze and couldn't see past that the victim was Quinn."

"Not Quinn," she whispered. "The woman you love. I just wanted you to know I'm sorry for snapping at you."

I noticed she offered no platitudes—she didn't tell me not to worry, or that Quinn would pull through. Kendall may've been soft and kind but she was no liar.

It would be a miracle if Quinn survived.

"'Preciate everything you did for her."

She nodded and gave me a tight smile. "I won't keep you from your family. Lance and I are heading back. You stay strong."

Strong? Right.

If nothing else, today had proved just how weak I was. There was not a damn thing strong about me, not when it came to Quinn.

I made my way back to the waiting room and forced myself to swallow down the ugly shit churning in my gut.

Before I could take two steps into the room, Jackson was there pushing me back out, his dad right behind him.

349

Fuck.

"Jack, I'm not in the mood—"

"Enough," Jackson snapped.

"Enough? What the fuck does that mean?"

"I know you." He leaned in and barked straight into my face. "I know you so well, I know you're beating yourself up for something. Stop. Quinn doesn't need this—"

"Quinn's not fucking here!" I bit out.

"She sure as shit is. Right fucking here." Jackson balled his fist and socked me in the chest. I stumbled backward, but before I could punch the asshole back, his dad stepped into the way.

"What happened to Quinn isn't your fault. Fuck! None of us saw it coming. Ethan was keeping his ear to the ground. Jason called in every favor he had keeping tabs on everyone in Allen's gang."

I rocked back. This information was new to me.

"Come again?"

"What I'm telling you is, they were smart. They kept their shit tight and carried out the hit internally."

Christ, a hit.

"I shouldn't've—"

"This is not on you," Clark semi-repeated.

I closed my eyes thinking about the ways today

would've gone different if I'd just called in more vacation days. Or if I'd asked Quinn to go stay with her parents. Or if I'd—

"She needs you," Jackson growled. "She needs you to believe she's gonna make it. Fuck, brother, *I* need you to believe it."

My eyes opened and I stared at my friend, Quinn's cousin. Quinn's childhood playmate. The agony shone clear as day. His eyes blazed with it.

"I fucked up," I admitted.

"You—"

"I did. I fucked up so bad. I couldn't fucking breathe. I saw her. First thing I saw was all that beautiful black hair. Christ. Then when I got to her, so much blood." I let out a strangled grunt but I was so lost in my grief I didn't stop. "Fuck, it was pourin' out of her. My woman's blood was seeping from her body and I couldn't move. I couldn't think, I couldn't even comprehend what was going on. I left her in bed this morning smiling at me then she's bleeding out on a goddamned sidewalk. I froze. So damn paralyzed with fear I couldn't move. Weak, goddamned weak. The woman I love was dying and all I could do was fucking stare at her. Who the fuck does that? Jesus Christ."

"A man who left the woman he loves lying in bed

smiling," Jasper said. "A man who went to work thinking his woman was safe. A man who loves her down to his soul and was dying right along with my daughter."

Jasper's words sounded choked as he of all people tried to console me. "Remember the day Jason was taken like it was yesterday. I was so fuckin' scared I couldn't see straight. That's something a man never forgets. He also never forgets walking into a hospital room after his daughter's been kidnapped and beaten. Delaney's battered face is seared into my brain, the fear of Jason being taken forever tattooed on my soul. Both of those times my life crashed around me. But neither of those times did I witness what you did. We're all feeling this, Brice, and when I say that, I'm telling you terror like I've never known is eating at my gut while I'm praying my daughter pulls through. But none of us *saw* it. None of us were stopping the flow of blood. None of us were in that ambulance saving her life. That was you. Only you. I'll say this once—if I walked up on that, no way I'd be able to do what you did. So get that shit out of your head."

"Jasper—"

"Quinn Walker's family?" A doctor walked to us.

"Yes," Jasper returned.

Clark crowded Jasper and I felt Jackson doing the same to me.

"Quinn's out of surgery. Both gunshot wounds were through and through. We repaired the lung and we performed a procedure called a thoracostomy. What that means is, we inserted a chest tube to drain the blood from the pleural cavity." The doctor stopped, his Adam's apple visibly bobbing before his forehead furrowed and my heart nearly stopped. "I won't lie to you, Quinn's condition is grave. When she arrived she was in hypovolemic shock. That's a forty percent loss of blood. Right now, the hemothorax is the least of our concerns and the next hour will be crucial. From there, we'll go hour to hour."

Hour by hour.

Christ.

I could feel my will to live drain away.

"Where is she now?" Clark asked.

"Being moved to the cardiac care unit."

"When can her parents and fiancé see her?"

Fiancé. Fuck, I wish that were true. I wished that when we were in Savannah I would've slipped my ring on her finger.

"In about thirty minutes. One person at a time, for five minutes. She hasn't regained consciousness and I don't expect her to for a few days."

"Thank you," Clark muttered.

The doctor took that as his leave, but before any of us could recover from the news, Ethan and Brady approached. Ethan had been the only family not to stay at the hospital, and that was on orders from his father, Lenox, to go to the station and find out what had happened.

"That the doctor?" Ethan asked.

Clark quickly ran down what the doctor had told us and I silently watched as Ethan's features turned to stone.

"Update," Clark demanded, still the only one capable of speech.

Ethan glanced at Jasper before he began.

"Nine-one-one call came in that shots were fired at the apartment complex. Five minutes after that, another nine-one-one call came in from a woman saying a body was thrown out of a moving vehicle. The caller pulled over and when she saw Quinn was bleeding she immediately started life-saving measures. A bloody miracle our good Samaritan is a vet, only thing better would've been a doctor. But she was not afraid to step in and help, and by the sound of it, her medical knowledge assisted in saving Quinn's life. The vet is being questioned at the station. She had a vehicle description and a partial plate, but didn't see who was in the car."

"Find. Them." Jasper's hate-filled demand wasn't directed to his nephew who was a police officer. Quinn's father was staring at a former Delta Force operator.

Brady said not a word, the only acknowledgement to the order was the jerk of his chin.

"Uncle Jasper—"

Ethan clamped his mouth shut when Jasper's eyes sliced to him.

"Need to talk to Em." Jasper took two steps before he stopped and looked at me. "You get the first five minutes."

Fuck, that sounded painful but I'd take it.

Then Jasper was gone.

28

"I swear, baby, you'd be laughing your ass off." I heard. The sounds were muffled and far away but I could still make out the words. "The nurses don't know if they should run away every time they see your dad or if they should bow to him before they carry out his orders. If you don't wake up soon, he might be banned for life."

Wake up?

"Love you, baby. I can't wait for you to open your pretty green eyes. I miss you."

"YOUR SISTER IS CRAZY. Today she brought the

nurses cupcakes to bribe them into letting her bring in baby Emma. She swears you'll wake up if you hear your niece babbling."

I am awake.

"At this point I'm willing to try anything. Damn, I miss you so much."

"JACKSON IS DRIVING me up the wall. Baby, if you do not want me to strangle him before I throw him off the roof of the hospital you better open your eyes."

Jeez, what did Jackson do now? And why off a hospital roof?

"Tuesday might be pissed if I kill her husband but I'm out of patience."

"Why? What'd he do?" I croaked.

"Quinn?"

"I feel like I'm floating."

"Jesus fuck. Quinn, baby, open your eyes!"

I opened my eyes and everything was hazy and bright.

"Fucking hell, I missed those pretty eyes."

Missed me? Why would Brice miss me?

I squinted, trying to bring Brice into focus but the fog was too thick. I blinked and tried again. When I finally could see clearly I was shocked. Brice looked like hell. Tired eyes, messy hair, days' worth of stubble on his face.

"What's wrong?"

He frowned and gave me a sad smile.

"Quinn, do you know where you are?"

What kind of question was that?

"Baby," he whispered. "You're in the hospital. You were shot."

Then like a freight train everything came rushing back. Everything! The fear. The excruciating pain. The darkness. Only now I wasn't feeling anything.

"I can't feel my legs," I whispered.

Brice's gaze slid away from mine and looked at something over my shoulder. "She's awake."

"Good news," a bubbly voice announced, and suddenly a very chipper blonde woman stood at the foot of my bed. "Hi, Quinn. I'm Dr. Graham."

"I can't feel my legs," I repeated.

The doctor's smile did nothing to calm my rising panic. I could not feel my legs, as a matter of fact, I couldn't feel much of anything. I tried to lift my arm but it was too heavy. Then I felt Brice's fingers tighten on mine and I thought that was a good sign. But I still couldn't move.

Nothing was working.

"Are you in pain?"

"No."

"Good. You're on a high dose of pain meds. Give me a few minutes to examine you then we'll sit and chat and I'll answer all of your questions."

"But my legs."

To say I was freaked out was an understatement. Maybe I should've been more concerned about being shot in the chest, which I remembered, or asking Brice to fill in the gaps of what happened after I passed out from the pain. But all I could think about was not being able to move my extremities. And I was trying, but there was a disconnect—no matter how hard I tried I couldn't get my feet to move.

"Quinn, baby, calm down and let Dr. Graham check you over."

"I am calm," I lied.

Brice looked at a bank of beeping monitors and smiled. "As much as I love to see that wave on your EKG—and I watched it for hours over the last three days, reminding myself your heart is beating—baby, it's telling me you are not calm. Your heartrate is elevated, and right now, that is not a good thing. Relax."

"How can I relax—"

"Baby, breathe. Just breathe and trust me." Brice leaned forward, his handsome, albeit scruffy face filled my vision. "Damn, I missed you. Prettiest girl I've ever seen. Breathe with me, Quinn."

I took a deep breath and pain seared through my chest.

"That hurt," I complained and Brice's mouth twisted.

Suddenly I felt pressure on my foot and my eyes widened.

"I felt that," I whispered. Then something tickled the bottom of my foot. "And that, too."

"Good," Brice whispered back and pressed a kiss to my forehead before sitting back down. "I'm going to step into the hall and make a few calls. I'll be right outside your door."

"Okay."

Brice stood, but before he moved, he stared down at me. A look of pure love crossed his face, mixed with something that looked like wonder. As if it was the first time he'd ever seen me.

His eyes fluttered closed and when they opened they were glassy. "Scared the shit out of me. Every second that passed I felt my life slipping away."

And with that he walked out of the room, leaving me speechless.

"You're very lucky," Dr. Graham said.

"Was it that bad?"

"I'm not talking about your injuries, though yes, they were life-threatening. I'm talking about Brice. That man hasn't left and it wasn't for lack of trying on your family's part. They all told him to go home, eat, rest, shower, but he refused to leave your side. No one is supposed to stay the night in CCU, but the nurses gave up trying to kick him out. He hasn't left your side since you got out of surgery."

I didn't know what to do with any of that. I knew Brice loved me, he told me. But the truth was, he showed it more than he said it. So instead of thinking about Brice sitting vigil at my bedside, which warmed me from the inside out—and if I continued to think on it too hard I would burst into tears—I focused on what wouldn't turn me into a babbling fool.

"How long was I out for?"

"Three days."

"Three?"

"Three days that felt like an eternity. I've been a

doctor a long time. Never seen more love surrounding one of my patients. You're blessed."

"I am."

For the next twenty minutes, Dr. Graham did her examination. The good news was, I could feel my legs, feet, arms, and hands. I couldn't move them because of the pain medication, which she told me they would be tapering down but would continue to administer so that I was comfortable. She also informed me that depending how my vitals looked over the next twenty-four hours, I would be moved to a step-down unit.

Then she sat next to my bed and told me about my injuries. She did this softly and with kindness though she didn't sugarcoat it. When they brought me in I was near-dead. Brice performed CPR because my heart stopped in the ambulance. I also flatlined during surgery. The knowledge that I basically died twice was something I couldn't begin to process. Sure, it was a terrifying thought, but obviously I was alive so the doctor was able to resuscitate me. What I couldn't stop thinking about was Brice and my family and what they must've been going through. All of them, but most especially Brice. He was the one who had saved me and I couldn't imagine what he'd been through.

He'd said I'd scared the shit out of him, and I figured that was the truth. But there was more he wasn't telling me. And my heart ached for him. I hated that my strong man had been scared. But even more, I hated that he saw me shot and left for dead.

"Do you know what happened? I mean, who did it or how I was found?" I asked.

"I think the police would prefer to speak to you about that." Dr. Graham patted my arm and stood. "And please remember you still need to rest."

She'd explained that, too. I was still recuperating and the chest tube would remain in a few more days, as well as another very unpleasant tube that was inserted in a place I didn't want to think about. I could deal with all the sticky pads placed over my chest, the blood pressure cuff that was annoying but not intrusive, the machines beeping, the dressings that covered my wounds, the hospital stay, but what I didn't want to think about was the catheter and the fact that Brice had been sitting next to my bed with a bag full of...gah...I couldn't even think about it.

I knew it was stupid, immature, and the least of my worries, but it was embarrassing as fuck.

"I will," I promised.

Brice entered and the doctor exited, giving him a pat on the shoulder as she passed.

"Thank you," I murmured when he sat down next to me.

"For what?" His head tilted and he held my gaze. So much pain lingered on his face.

"For saving my life. For staying with me."

"I didn't—"

"I know what you did in the ambulance. I'm sorry you had to go through that."

"Quinn—"

"We have to talk about it."

"Can't," he choked. "Not now. Maybe not ever."

"We need to," I pressed. "You can't bottle it up."

A knock at the door interrupted our conversation. And for the next two hours every member of my family came to visit. Their time was limited to five minutes a person but as soon as someone walked out the door someone new walked in.

I'd done a good job holding it together until my mom and dad came in together. That was when I lost it.

My dad looked ravaged with grief and my mom was no better. Tears flowed freely down my mom's cheeks and while my dad tried to hide his—I saw them.

All the fear I had instantly turned to anger. I was so damn angry at the world. Furious at the man who shot me. My heart shattered seeing the strongest man I knew reduced to tears. I fucking hated that everyone was in pain because of me.

"I'm fine," I told them.

My mom muffled her sob into my dad's chest and I wished I could leave this stupid freaking hospital bed and kill the asshole who put me here.

"You need to rest," my dad told me. "We'll be back after dinner to say goodnight."

His tone was gruff and full of carefully harnessed fury. Brice must've heard it, too, because his hand tightened in mine.

"Daddy..." My dad's eyes slammed shut and his face screwed into something ugly before he locked it down and looked at me. "I really am okay." He jerked his chin and I continued. "Promise. But I'm worried about all of you. I was sleeping while all of you were going out of your minds. I'm sorry I—"

"Don't you apologize," my dad admonished. "You didn't do a damn thing wrong." He paused and took a few deep breaths. "Won't lie to you, the last three days have been hell. Pure *fucking* hell. It's going to take more than a five-minute visit to ease the knot. You get some rest and we'll be back."

I nodded and said, "I love you. Both of you. So, *so* much. I hope you know that."

"We do," my mom answered. "And we love you so, *so* much, sweet girl."

"Brice. A word before I leave," my dad said.

Brice got up, leaned forward, and brushed his lips against mine. "I'll be right back."

"Okay. I'll be here."

Brice's face got tight at my attempt to lighten the mood.

Damn.

"I'm fine. Go talk to my dad."

With another press of his mouth to mine, he straightened and headed to the door.

"Mom?" She paused and turned to look at me. "Please come here."

She untangled herself from my dad and motioned for him to leave. She gently clicked the door closed behind Brice and my dad before she made her way to the side of my bed.

Her hand went to my forehead and she brushed my hair behind my ear. Something she used to do all the time when I was a kid.

"Wanna tell me how are you really doing?" she asked.

Pure Emily Walker.

"I'm scared."

"Of?"

My mom's hand rested on my arm and I wasn't ashamed to admit I was drawing all the strength I could from her.

"For Dad and Brice mostly. But I'm also worried about you and Delaney, Hadley, Adalynn, and Jason. Everyone, really."

Mom nodded her head in understanding and smiled. "My sweet girl, always worried about those she loves and never afraid to show it. This family of ours has been through some tough stuff. Painful, scary stuff, and we always pull through it and come out stronger on the other side."

"I know we have but—"

"Let me finish." She grazed her hand down my arm and threaded our fingers together. "Do you know why we only get stronger?" I shook my head in the negative. "Because when one of our own stumbles, the rest of the clan closes ranks. We come together. We fight. When your dad and I had nothing left because our girl was literally fighting for her life, they lifted us up. They gave us all their strength."

"And Brice? Who gave him strength?"

"You did."

I sucked in a painful lungful of oxygen.

"But I was—"

"You did, Quinn. And he soaked it in, he never left you."

"What now? How do I help him and Dad and the rest of you get over what happened?"

"You heal and be patient. Your dad is the best man I know. The fiercest, the most loyal, and most protective. For a man like him, having his child's life threatened and all of his control stripped away? That's going to take a long time to repair. But I'll handle your dad."

"And Brice?"

"Give him a few days. If he doesn't open up, I'll set your dad on him."

"I don't think that's a good idea. Dad can be...Dad is..."

"He'll know how to handle it."

"Okay," I agreed.

"I know it was only three days, but it felt like a lifetime." My mom gave me a sad smile. "I love you."

"I love you, Mama."

"He loves you, Quinn," my mom said and squeezed my hand. "I've had the pleasure of seeing what true love looks like. And Brice? He wears it well. Give him time, sweetie."

My throat clogged and I nodded. I loved that my mom saw how much Brice loved me. I liked it for me,

I liked it for Brice, but mostly I liked it for my parents. I knew they'd always worried about me. Dad had called me his wild child for as long as I could remember. If Dad seeing me settled and loved could bring him peace, I was happy about that.

Lethargy hit and I closed my eyes but I couldn't find sleep. I was too worried about Brice.

29

"Brice!" I heard Jackson call as I was opening the door to Quinn's hospital room. "Glad I caught you. I need to give you these."

Jackson held out a set of keys and I gladly took them.

"Everything moved?"

"Yeah."

It had been two weeks since Quinn opened her eyes. Two weeks of ups and downs, fears of secondary complications, but mostly Quinn getting stronger. Two weeks of me planning her release. And Jackson delivering the keys to our new house was perfect timing. Dr. Graham would be around in the next hour to discharge Quinn.

I'd argued against the discharge. Fourteen days

seemed like it was pushing it. I thought she could use at least another week, something Quinn was vehemently against. Jasper pulled me aside and made me see it from Quinn's point of view, then I relented. Although I did it under duress. I still wanted her in there under medical supervision.

She had no idea I'd rented a house and had all of our belongings moved. She was never going back to the place where someone almost took her life. And neither would I force her family to go there to visit her.

"'Preciate all your help."

I did have a moment of guilt that it was Jackson, Tuesday, Nick, and Meadow who had to pack and move everything, meaning they had to face what had happened there. However, Jackson and Nick had assured me they wanted to do it instead of me hiring movers.

"Not something you need to thank me for. I told you I'd do anything for you and I meant it."

"Know you did. Still, you have my gratitude."

"How ya doing?"

I shifted uncomfortably, not wanting to talk about how I was. I could easily talk about Quinn and her recovery. How she was mentally handling everything. But what I didn't want to talk about was me.

"I'll be fine when she's settled in at the new house."

"Not what I was talking about."

"Well, that's all you're gonna get."

"You need to—"

"Jackson, leave it."

"No. It's been two weeks."

"You think I don't know how fuckin' long it's been since my hands were covered in my woman's blood?"

Jackson flinched and I felt like shit.

Fuck, but I didn't want to talk about this.

"I'm sorry. That was shitty."

"If you're sorry, then talk."

My head dropped and I studied the gleaming linoleum floor. I fought to push back the memory of Quinn's hair on the sidewalk, her chest oozing blood. Every image stayed fresh in my mind. Each one seared there for life. Every second burned into my soul. Every minute of agony.

"I can't. I can't talk about it. Every time I think about it, it feels like my insides are being ripped out of me. So close. We were all so close to losing her. I... just...can't."

"Brother." Jackson stepped closer, his boots now in my field of vision. Then his hand went to the back of my neck. "We are talking about this. You can't let it eat at you. You need help and we're gonna get it for you."

Jackson stepped away and muttered his goodbye. It took me awhile to gather my thoughts before I headed back into Quinn's room.

And the moment I saw her sitting on the edge of the bed, feet dangling over the side, a wide bright smile on her face, the knot in my chest tightened.

So fucking close to losing that sight forever.

"Are you ready to take me home?" She beamed and I returned her smile.

So damn beautiful.

"About that." I lifted my hand and showed her the keys. "We moved."

"We...we...moved?"

"Yep. Found us a house two blocks from your parents. We're all moved in."

"Found us a house?"

"I wanted to buy something, but there wasn't time," I explained. "When your mom told me she saw the 'for rent' sign, I called and the house was vacant and ready for immediate move-in. Jackson and Nick did the heavy lifting while Tuesday and Meadow packed us up."

"I don't know what to say."

Shit, Quinn didn't look happy.

"Baby, I thought—"

"I can guess what you were thinking. And I love how much you want to protect me, but I'm going to have to face it, you know? The police told me where I was dumped." Her eyes came to mine and I rocked back like she'd punched me. Reminding me all over again that I wanted to beat the holy fuck out of the cop who'd given her that information.

"Quinn," I growled.

"What? I was thrown out of a moving car. That is the very definition of being dumped. We have to face it."

"Stop—"

"No. I know it's hard, honey, God, do I know. But please stop hiding from me. I see it every time you look at me, I see the pain. We have to let it go."

Fuck if she wasn't right, but I wasn't ready. And I was beginning to think I never would be. I was a damn coward.

Dr. Graham strolled through the door, smiling. "Ready to go home?"

"So ready," Quinn told her.

Barely ten minutes later Dr. Graham had finished with all of her instructions, which I didn't think was comprehensive enough, but I wisely kept my mouth shut and added looking up 'wound care' to my mental to-do list.

Then much to my dismay, a chipper candy-striper pushed a wheelchair into the room.

Fuck goddamn.

I wanted to rage that Quinn needed more time but I held my tongue and grabbed her bags from the bed and followed the gabbing women down the hall.

The only good thing about taking Quinn home was...well, fuck...I couldn't think of anything other than I could shower without having to leave her bedside. I could also get her whatever she wanted to eat or drink without having to go down four floors, which meant I had to leave her to get her what she needed.

But the flip side was, I would lose the nurses coming in once an hour to check on her.

"Wow." Quinn's eyes widened when I pulled into the driveway of our new home. I wasn't sure if it was because of all the cars lining the street alerting us to the fact we had company—and not a little bit of it, but by the looks of it the whole family—or if it was because she liked the house.

The fifteen-minute drive home had been done in comfortable silence. Quinn was pleased as shit she'd been sprung from the hospital and I didn't have it in me to spoil her good mood.

"Do you like it?" I asked, pulling her car into the garage next to my truck.

"Yes. I've been in this house. My friend Leslie lived here when I was in elementary school. I remember it being awesome but I was also nine, so..."

"I only signed a six-month lease so if you hate it—"

"Stop. I won't hate it. And I don't think I said this earlier—thank you. I appreciate you taking care of me. I just wish you'd let me take care of you."

"Baby—"

"Not now. We'll talk later when we don't have a house full of people. But I mean it, I love you and thank you for everything."

"I love you, too."

"By the way." Quinn grabbed my arm before I could get out of the car. "If you tell me to go in and sit on the couch, I'll castrate you. Straight up, I've been flat on my back for two weeks. I'm over it."

Damn if she didn't know me.

"I like you flat on your back." I smiled.

"You also like me up on my knees and bent over.

Which means you want to keep your balls intact—and to keep them in tip-top shape, you better not baby me."

"Can't promise you more than two hours."

"Brice—"

"Two hours, then I'm putting on a cup and wading in."

"Fine. Two hours."

That was too easy, which meant she knew by the time her two hours were up, she'd be exhausted and ready to sit.

"Well-played."

Her gorgeous smile told me I was right. It also reminded me she was alive.

I DIPPED out into the backyard to check out the new patio furniture Jasper and Emily had bought us when I heard the sliding glass door open, and Jackson, followed by Lenox, Levi, Clark, Nick, and Jasper stepped out onto the brick pavers.

I was trying to come up with something to say that would curtail this conversation but I wasn't fast enough. Therefore I was unprepared when Nick spoke.

"When Meadow was taken, I died a thousand deaths." He launched right in and my chest started to burn. "Then we found her in a dirty alley with a psychotic serial killer. Meadow was duct taped and she'd already been stabbed. I had so much guilt about how that played out I couldn't even stay in the room while they fixed Meadow up." Nick stopped and shook his head. "I called the one person I knew who could help and first thing he told me was he was proud of me—then he told me I had my head up my ass. A few hours later I had my uncles surrounding me and they refused to allow me to give up. And it's a damn good thing I didn't. So I'm gonna tell you the same thing my uncle told me—get your head out of your ass, go to your woman, and hold on tight."

"Nick. I'm damn sorry—"

"Do you know what happened to my wife?" Clark cut me off. "Do you know she lost a kidney because I was too busy denying I was in love with her. That when I found my woman, not only had she lost a goddamn organ but she was being prepped so the motherfucking bastards could take her eyes." I jerked at the ferocity in his tone. "Her eyes, Brice. The sick fucks were gonna slice up and take what they could from her body to sell, then leave her for dead. You wanna talk about a mindfuck? A monumental screw-up on my part? Yeah, I know a thing or two about guilt. You know what I repeated to myself a million times? As long as Reagan was breathin' I could love her through anything. Thank fuck, Quinn's alive and breathin'—love her through it."

Jesus fuck! I had no idea Reagan had gone through any of that. There wasn't a damn thing I could say so I said nothing. Clark's words only made me feel like more of a pussy for not helping Quinn sooner.

"I wasted twelve years with Lily. Twelve miserable years, then when I finally got her back, she was kidnapped and almost taken from me—permanently. And considering she was pregnant with Carter, I would've lost him, too." Lenox stopped, crossed his arms over his chest, and leveled me with a hard stare. "We all know how much you love Quinn. So what's the problem?"

"There is no problem," I grunted.

"Didn't take you for a liar," Levi interjected and my back snapped straight. "You think we don't see it? You think we haven't felt it? Man, that shit is tattooed on your forehead. It's etched into your eyes. Each of us, every one of us standing before you have felt the guilt. We've tasted it, we've gagged on it. Something you haven't figured out yet, but you will—

in this family we don't let shit fester. We will not stand idly by as you blame yourself for something you couldn't stop, that none of us knew. And as much as I never thought you to be a liar, I never took you as stupid, which means you gotta know Quinn's feeling this. She knows you're bottling shit up and she's knocking herself out to make it better for you."

"You're not weak," Jasper boomed.

"The fuck I'm not," I growled. "I fucking stood there, Jasper. Told you that. Her goddamned hair..." Why my mind kept focusing on that, I didn't know. But I couldn't get it out of my head. "Christ. I shut down. I couldn't move. She needed help and what did I do, I stood like a motherfucking idiot while the woman I love bled out."

My chest heaved and I figured I was moments away from passing out.

"Goddamn idiot." Jackson stepped closer and I braced; he looked like he was getting ready to take a swing at me. Jack knew I'd acted like a pansy-assed bitch.

"I didn't—"

"Shut up for a second and think about what you're saying. Is your ego so big you think you're some sort of superhero? That, what, it makes you less than because you love Quinn so deeply that seeing her on a sidewalk bleeding would stop you cold? Seriously? You think loving her that much is weak? I keep telling you this but you don't wanna listen. You did nothing wrong."

"I can't stop seeing it. Every fucking time I close my eyes, I see it," I told Jackson.

"See what?"

"I'm not talking about this with you. With any of you."

Five men grunted and all of them closed in.

"Why's that?" Nick asked.

"Because you all love her as much as I do. And I'm especially not talking about this with Jasper. None of you need this shit."

"You got something to say, spit it out. You think you can shock us, you are wrong," Levi offered.

Fucking hell, I didn't want to do this. My molars were grinding to the point of pain. My temples throbbed and I could swear my throat was closing, making it hard to breathe.

"What do you see?" Jasper asked.

I shook my head and dropped it forward.

"What do you see?" he repeated. "Besides her bleeding?"

Wasn't that enough? Her blood spilling onto the pavement. Fucking everywhere.

"Brice!" Jasper snapped.

"I see her fucking eyes looking at me like, fuck, like she found something beautiful. Her pretty emerald eyes, soft and so full of love. When I was frozen in place all I could think about was how I was never gonna get that look again. How I was never gonna hear her voice. Brush her hair off her neck so I could kiss her there. Years I wasted running from her. Years I'd never get to make up to her. So many regrets. Rivers of fucking blood all around her, bubbling out of her mouth and all I could fucking think about was me. How I should've asked her to marry me. How I was never gonna see that again. Goddamn, I'm a selfish prick. A weak, selfish moth-erfucker."

After my outburst, silence fell. Damn, why did I tell them that? Why the hell did I admit what an asshole I was?

"You think that's selfish?" Jasper whispered. "Then, son, I'm standing next to you telling you I'm just as selfish. The whole time my daughter was in surgery, all I could think about was how much it was going to kill me if I never heard her call me Daddy again. I couldn't begin to comprehend how I was going to continue to live if she was gone. How would I console my wife and our other children when I knew I'd never recover from the loss? For the first time in my life, I'd resigned myself to failure because if Quinn hadn't've made it, I wouldn't have been strong enough to hold my family together."

"That's not selfishness," Levi added. "That's real. That's love."

I heard feet shuffling and felt a few pounds on the back, then the slider opened and closed. I still kept staring at the patio bricks.

"I need you to look at me," Jasper called, and I reluctantly lifted my gaze to meet his. "I'll tell you this as many times as you need until you let this go. I appreciate you loving my daughter the way you do. And I think you know me well enough to know, if I had a sliver of hesitation I'd make it known. I also think you know I don't blow sunshine, I don't sugar-coat shit, I don't lie, and I never fuck around about my children's happiness. A few weeks ago I welcomed you into the family and I see you don't understand the full meaning of that. You're more than Quinn's man. You're more than Jackson's friend who hangs around. You're family. You're my son, you're Levi, Clark, and Lenox's nephew. Being one of us means you'll never be left behind to sort yourself alone. We will always have your back. I'll repeat that as many times as you need, as will they. One last thing before we go inside—tell Quinn what you told me tonight. Tell her what you were thinking. She deserves to know."

"What?" I mumbled, still stuck on the part where Jasper called me his son.

"You take a second to think on it. What you think is selfishness, she will not. She'll see the beauty in it and my daughter deserves every moment of happiness you can give her."

Jasper headed back inside, leaving me alone with my jumbled-up thoughts. There was so much to sift through, so many feelings I needed to sort, but they'd have to wait because while Quinn's cousins and uncles were outside handing me my ass, she'd been inside pushing herself to entertain.

Her two hours were up.

30

I was in the kitchen actively trying to ignore what I saw. When my dad, Nick, Jackson, and uncles all cornered Brice on the patio, my mom stopped me from going outside. Her tone may've been gentle but her words were resolute. She'd told me in no uncertain terms I was to stay in the house and trust my dad.

I did trust my dad, but Brice was twisting himself in knots and I hated he wouldn't talk to me. Further, I was worried that Jackson would push until Brice snapped and the two of them would go back to being mad at each other.

So now I was looking around, searching cupboards, checking out where Meadow and Tuesday had blended my stuff and Brice's together in the cabinets. It was obvious I'd had more than him because there weren't many new pots and pans added to what I had.

I felt my hair brushed over one shoulder right before lips pressed to the back of my neck. "I'm wearing my cup, sweetheart." My body started shaking at the matter-of-fact way Brice had made his announcement. "I love feeling you laugh."

Damn, I'd missed this—missed Brice just being Brice. Sweet and funny instead of wound so tight I was afraid he'd snap if someone breathed in his direction.

I turned in his arms for reasons other than I wanted to see his face. When our eyes locked and his were soft and gentle, I shoved my face in his throat and I pinched my lips together as hard as I could and willed the tears away.

"I love you," I reminded him.

Brice gave me a swift but gentle hug, ever so careful not to cause me any pain. It's worth noting bullet holes to the chest were a pain in the ass. I had yet to look at them, and carefully kept my eyes diverted when the nurse changed the dressings. I also knew Brice hadn't seen them. Something we were going to have to face together.

I was ready. I had a feeling Brice was not.

"Now that my balls are safe from injury," Brice said as he rested his chin on the top of my head, "it's time to sit down."

I nodded the best I could and Brice stilled.

"What's wrong?"

"What do you mean?" I asked.

"You agreed. Are you in pain? Do you need a pill?"

Of course he'd notice I wasn't putting up a fight. The truth was I wasn't in pain, but I was overdoing it and I knew because it was still hard for me to breathe. Something the doctor had explained would take months to heal. It didn't hurt, but the shortness of breath was obvious. I figured I was better off sitting down and relaxing before I did something stupid like pass out.

That would send every family member currently milling around my new house right over the edge. So far they'd kept the babying to a minimum, but I wasn't dumb enough to think that they'd all decided to leave me be. No, it was because they knew Brice was there and he'd lord over me until I behaved.

"No to the pain pill. I'm fine. We agreed on two hours. Is it so hard to believe I'd keep my end of the deal?"

"Yes. I know you."

"I'm wounded," I feigned insult.

"Right."

"But since I'm behaving and all, do you think you could talk Delaney into letting me hold Emma?"

"No."

"Damn. It was worth a shot."

I heard Brice chuckle and my heart soared. I hadn't heard that sound since the morning before I'd been shot. A sound I greatly missed.

"You may like *feeling* me laugh, but I love hearing yours."

Brice's body locked and I wanted to kick my own ass for making such a stupid comment.

"Brice—"

"Shh, baby. We got some stuff to talk about. But not with your family here. Let's get you on the couch."

With patience I normally didn't have—somehow I'd managed to channel Emily Walker—I nodded and followed him to the living room.

Thirty minutes later, I yawned and that started a mass exodus. Everyone said their goodbyes and Brice locked up the house, leaving me to wander back to the bedroom.

Even though I'd already taken a tour of our new house, I was still taken aback when I saw the room.

Tuesday and Meadow had unpacked and put all my clothes back in the dresser, or maybe they moved it over without taking anything out of the drawers.

When Brice came in, I was still pondering how awesome my family was. They'd dropped everything to take care of Brice and me. *God, I loved them.*

"Everything okay?"

"They even hung the pictures up," I told him something he obviously knew considering he had eyes and could see just fine.

"I told Jackson I'd handle the unpacking, but Tuesday and Meadow insisted."

"Sounds like them." I nodded.

"I hope—"

I turned and found Brice leaning against the doorjamb, hands in his pockets, one ankle crossed over the other, his expression unreadable.

"It's perfect. All of it. I know I was...bitchy when you first told me we'd moved. But honestly I didn't want to go back there. I was too afraid to admit it."

"Seems there's a lot both of us are afraid to admit."

"What are you afraid of?" I whispered, praying he wouldn't shut down like he'd been doing the last two weeks.

"Of losing you."

I sucked in a sharp breath and immediately regretted it when the burn in my chest bloomed, leaving me winded and in pain.

"Come on, let's get you changed and in bed."

I didn't argue, mainly because I knew I'd lose but also because I was exhausted. I went about rummaging through my drawers, finding what I wanted. Then a great battle raged in my mind. I had two choices, go into the bathroom and hide or change in front of Brice.

Quite frankly I was tired of being scared. Neither of us was going to get past what happened if we kept bottling everything up and locking it away. *I* was never going to get over it unless I made myself.

It was easy to lie to everyone and say I was fine when really I wasn't. It was easy to go into the other room to change so Brice wouldn't see what I was left with. It was easy not to look at the bandages. It was easy to look away so I didn't have to see the scars. It would be far too easy to pretend that I wasn't affected by what had happened when I damn well was.

Fuck it.

Fuck the fear.

Fuck the lying.

Fuck the asshole who tried to kill me so I couldn't testify.

Fuck them all.

I was stronger than this. Brice was, too. *We* were stronger and we *would* move on.

I carefully slipped off my sweats and traded them for a clean pair, then started to unbutton my flannel. Delaney had gone out and bought me a bunch of bandeau style bras so I could step into it and slide it up over my hips. It was so much easier than trying to lift my arms, and forget a regular bra— the seams had rubbed and hurt like a bitch.

With half of the buttons undone, my courage started to wane. Brice was busy fluffing and stacking pillows, making me a soft nest in the bed and not paying attention to what I was doing. That made it a little easier to continue. I shrugged the material off my shoulders and paused.

"Babe?"

"Huh?"

"Open your eyes."

Damn, I hadn't realized in a moment of panic I'd closed them.

"No."

Heat hit my back and warm breath fanned over my shoulder. "Baby. Open them."

I didn't answer. I couldn't. All of my good intentions had vanished. Gone. And all I was left with was a knot in my stomach. Stupid. I was so damn stupid thinking I was brave.

Brice's hand went to my hip, his thumb glided over my exposed skin.

"So damn pretty."

I tried to hold them back but tears pooled then spilled down my cheeks. Slowly at first until they were a steady stream and my body bucked.

So much for my *fuck it all* courage.

"Baby, open your eyes."

Begrudgingly, my lids fluttered open, and much to my discomfort, Brice had twisted us to face the mirror over the dresser.

"Prettiest girl, ever."

I started to shake my head, maybe in denial, maybe to stop him from saying anything else, but Brice didn't give me a moment to collect myself—he went on.

Brice's hand on my hip remained but his other one moved—feather-light, his fingertips skated up my belly, until he reached a lock of my hair. He twisted it around his hand then let it fall back over my breast.

"I used to think it was your green eyes that captured my attention. But I was wrong. The first time I saw you, it was your hair. Thick, shiny midnight black that is so shocking against your complexion it's hard to believe it's real." Brice's gaze came to mine in the mirror and I was unable to look away. "So soft. Sometimes I wake up and it's fanned out over your pillow and I can't stop myself from running my fingers through it. That's what I saw, the day you were shot. All this thick, soft, shiny, black hair." Brice played with the ends of my hair, his fingers brushing over my breasts, and for the first time since the attempt on my life, my libido woke up. "Only it was all wrong. So fucking wrong seeing it on the dirty sidewalk."

I didn't know what to say. I knew he'd been at the scene, I could begin to imagine what he saw, but he'd never told me.

"I was so scared I couldn't move, couldn't breathe, I couldn't even believe what I was seeing. None of it seemed real, yet there you were, and I couldn't do *anything*. When I say it was the worst day of my life, that with every drop of blood that was leaking from your body, what I'm saying is, I wanted to die. I did not want to live without you. And the whole time I stood there watching my crew work on you, all I could think about was me. How it wouldn't be possible to go on without you.

How much *I* would miss your laugh. How *I'd* never get to see your smile again. How *I'd* never hear you tell me you love me." His body tensed behind mine and my heart squeezed. "I'm so sorry I was so selfish."

"Thank you," I wheezed, finding it hard to breathe. It had nothing to do with recovering from a lung injury.

"What?"

"Thank you for loving me like that."

"Fuck," he muttered and closed his eyes.

"Is that what you've been so worried about? You seriously thought I'd think you were selfish for not wanting to go on without me? You thought I'd be upset because you were in shock and thought I was going to die? Honey, I'm the one that's sorry you had to see that. I wish more than anything it wasn't your station that got the call. If I could change one thing it would be that you never saw me on that sidewalk. I'd take the bullets again and again if it meant I could erase you finding me."

"Don't say that," he growled, the force of his words wafting over my skin. "Don't *ever* say that again."

"But it's true. You don't think I love you that much? That I'd take that pain again if it meant you didn't have to." Brice didn't respond so I rushed to continue. "We're gonna get through this."

"Of course we are."

Strong.

Resolute.

Final.

My stomach started to untwist until Brice's gaze dropped to the bandages.

"I'm not ready to see them," I admitted.

"The dressings don't need to be changed until tomorrow. You don't have to look."

"I'm not ready for you to see them."

"Why?"

"I'm gonna...they're gonna be ugly."

Something changed. I couldn't say if it was coming off of Brice or if it was rolling off of me because Brice was looking at me funny. What I did know was the air crackled and whatever that some-thing was, it made my belly pitch.

"My head may've been filled with a bunch of shit the last few weeks, most of it guilt, a lot of it fear, but not once, not even for a second, did I doubt how much I loved you. Never did I think we wouldn't come out of this stronger. I just needed to pull my head out of my ass."

My heart pumped so fast it hammered. My lungs

were on fire as I tried to pull in enough oxygen.

"I'm sorry if that made you think I was pulling back. I love you, Quinn. Straight up, you are gorgeous, with or without scars." His hand still on my hip flexed and he lowered his chin to rest on my shoulder. "You are the sexiest woman I've ever laid eyes on. All of this." He trailed a finger from my throat down over the white gauze taped to my skin. "All of you, baby, every inch of you is mine. There's nothing ugly about you."

I nodded even though I didn't believe him. I hadn't seen them, and I didn't need to, to know how ugly they'd be.

"I know you don't believe me now, but you will."

There it was again.

Strong.

Resolute.

Final.

Brice led me to the bed, helped me settle—partly sitting up so I could breathe—then he went about his business of getting undressed.

And for the first time since we started sleeping together, he put on a pair of sweats before he slid in next to me.

I clenched my jaw and remained quiet. This sucked. All of it. I couldn't lie flat, I couldn't cuddle into him, he couldn't hold me close and pull my leg over his thigh.

"In a few more weeks everything will be back to normal," he muttered and tangled our legs together.

That was the best I was going to get.

And it sucked—big time.

THE NEXT MORNING, Brice changed my bandages.

I didn't look.

I'D BEEN out of the hospital three days. I couldn't say that there was anything wrong—*per se*. Brice had opened up, we were talking about what happened and what each of us was feeling. That part was great. We tinkered around the house and rearranged things here and there. It felt natural and easy—the two of us moving in together, blending our lives.

Brice was attentive, maybe a little too much, but I didn't complain and let him do what he needed to do.

Each night we slept together, the same way we had the first night—feet tangled, holding hands.

We cooked together. We watched TV. We laughed.

Things were good—kind of.

I wasn't even freaked-out Brice's parents were coming over in a few days and they planned on staying with us for the weekend. I was looking forward to seeing them again and my parents were eager to meet Bonnie and Bryan.

But there was something—a nagging in the back of my mind that wouldn't go away, a ball of unease—unanswered questions about the man who shot me and who had helped him dump me on the side of the road. And my questions didn't go unanswered because I hadn't asked—I had, lots of times. But every time I did, Brice told me he didn't know what was going on. I somewhat believed him because he'd been with me, therefore not involved in the manhunt.

However, when I asked my dad, his face turned to granite, he grunted evasively, then flat out told me not to worry about it.

So of course I was worried about it. My dad did me no favors keeping me in the dark, instead it fueled my fear.

Now we were in my car—Brice still wouldn't let me climb up into his truck even though my legs were fine and his truck wasn't that difficult to heft myself into. Yet another thing I gave him his way about—mainly because it wasn't worth the energy it would take to argue about it. No, I was conserving that energy for the discussion I vowed to have with my dad this afternoon.

We were headed to my parents' house for the first time since I'd been released. Brice and I were going to them rather than them coming to our house, only because I told Brice I was going stir crazy and needed to get out. He agreed although he'd done it begrudgingly. But as I said, he was catering to my every whim so he gave in.

It must be said, it wasn't lost on me that Brice was on edge. The entire drive to my parents'—which was only a few blocks, we could've walked to their house almost as fast—Brice had been hyper-alert. His eyes never stopped scanning the street, the sidewalks, the cars we passed, even the houses.

This only strengthened my resolve to have it out with my dad. We were not leaving my parents' house until I got answers.

Little did I know, I wouldn't get any of my questions answered. Instead, I'd get something else, and it would happen immediately.

I heard shouting before I opened the door. Brice

tried to stop us from entering but I wasn't having it. Not bothering to knock, not that my dad would be able to hear it over the yelling, I walked in and stopped dead when I heard his angry words.

"She will not be testifying!"

Oh, fuck.

That's what I'd forgotten about. That right there was what the niggling in the back of my mind was about. Fear slithered down my spine and Brice wrapped his arm around me.

My dad shouted into the phone. "You think I give two fucks what it does to the case, Ethan? This family's been through enough. Quinn has been through enough. Not gonna fucking happen."

I barely had a moment to feel bad for my cousin for being on the receiving end of my dad's ire when he turned—stone-faced, eyes wounded, mouth tight.

Rage took over. I couldn't stand seeing my dad look like that. I'd seen it enough since I'd been shot. I'd seen the same look coming from Brice.

I was done.

D.O.N.E.

"I'm testifying!"

Brice stiffened beside me and my dad's expression went hard.

"Gotta call you back," my dad said to Ethan.

I launched right in, not waiting for my dad to end his call.

"Tell Ethan," I demanded. "Tell him I'm testifying."

"Quinn—"

"No! No more. I took two bullets to my chest because Kenneth Allen wanted me silenced. He doesn't get to win. He doesn't get to silence me. I'm testifying."

"Quinn—"

"Fuck, no. I'm alive and I'm testifying. And I can't believe *you* of all people would expect me to cower. *I am a goddamn Walker.* We do not cower. We don't run and hide. We stand and fight. We do what's right. We protect people." My chest burned from exertion and it pissed me right the hell off I couldn't even rant without losing my breath. "Don't make me the coward of the family, Dad. Don't make me be the one who hides. Don't make me be the one that allows a murderer to walk. You know it's not right."

"Goddammit!" my dad roared and I vaguely wondered where my mom was and hoped the neighbors were all at work.

"Tell him, Dad. Tell him I'll do it," I begged.

It went without saying I hated Kenneth Allen,

but watching my big, strong, larger-than-life father struggling turned that hate into homicidal thoughts. I was testifying no matter what. Kenneth Allen was going to prison, and once he was locked away, I hoped he found himself on the receiving end of a shank made from a plastic fork and I hoped it was a painful way to die.

Then there was Brice. He'd gone statue-still yet he managed to vibrate with anger. That was when I wished I had prison connections—someone on the inside who could make the asshole's death slow and torturous.

"Baby," Brice muttered.

My gaze moved from my dad to Brice and I braced for his censure.

"Yeah?"

"Proud of you." My eyes widened in shock and my body locked as I waited for him to continue. "So strong. So brave. Walker through and through."

He nodded his approval and my heart soared.

I was too busy basking in the light of Brice's praise to pay attention to what my father was doing. My eyes stung, my throat was clogged, but my heart floated somewhere in the stratosphere, delighting in the knowledge Brice believed in me.

That ball of unease was gone.

31

The judge presiding over Kenneth Allen's case hadn't been happy with the delay and he'd let his displeasure show in a multitude of ways. None of them were good for the defense.

That morning as Quinn got ready for court, she'd pretended to be calm and cool and I let her have that play. She needed it. She'd remained calm until five minutes before they called her to testify. Then all pretense slid away and she was jumpier than a jackrabbit.

Every member of the Walker, Clark, Lenox, and McCoy clans—sans Liberty McCoy who was deployed—were in attendance. Once again they'd closed ranks with the addition of my parents who'd stayed an extra day to support Quinn.

The weekend had gone great—we had a huge gathering at our house, family came and went the whole day Saturday. Quinn was in heaven. Something I realized about her, it didn't take much to make her happy. As long as the people she loved were around and smiling, all was right in her world.

Sunday had been low-key. Just her parents and mine. The women sorted through the boxes stored in one of the extra bedrooms, making piles for me to toss out. Jasper, my dad, and I sat out on the back deck and shot the shit.

For the most part, Jasper had done a good job at hiding his concern over Quinn testifying. Though I did catch him staring at her with more than apprehension—he was proud of her, even if he was worried.

Now we were all in the hall waiting for Quinn to be called. Jasper and my dad hung off to the side, giving me a moment alone with my woman before she went in, and the rest of the family were already seated in the gallery.

"Baby, look at me." I squeezed her hand and waited for her gaze to come up from staring at the marble floor, something she'd been studying for the last two minutes.

"I'm okay," she whispered.

"I know you are. I just wanted to see your beautiful eyes."

Her lips started to twitch and the first sign of a smile started to appear.

"You know you don't have to sweet-talk me, right? I'm a sure thing."

"Not sweet-talk when it's the truth."

Quinn's mouth curved up into a fucking beautiful smile then she leaned forward and rested her forehead against mine.

"I'm scared."

"I know you are."

"I can do this."

"Damn right, you can."

"You'll be there."

It wasn't a question. And just like every time she showed me she trusted me, it burned. A sweet, warm burn that scorched my chest. The most beautiful pain.

"Always."

"Always," she returned.

"Quinn Walker?"

She jolted at the sound of her name, then settled.

"I'm so proud of you," I reminded her.

"I'm ready."

"Fuck, yeah, you are."

We stood and walked into the courtroom, only separating when the bailiff escorted her to the stand.

My dad took his seat, Jasper followed, then I pulled up the rear and sat in the aisle.

I felt eyes boring into me and turned to look at Jasper. Sharp, hard green eyes full of anxiety pinned me in place as the man worked through his emotions. Jasper's body jolted when Quinn's firm, strong "I do" rang out in the courtroom. It was then his gaze turned warm and full of approval.

Quinn was strong. She was ready. She was a Walker and no one was going to keep her down. Not gangster trash, not two bullets to the chest, not even her own father.

Quinn Walker was fierce.

Throughout her testimony, Quinn's voice never wavered. She was precise, to the point, and matter-of-fact as she answered the questions presented. Kenneth Allen's attorney tried his best to get her to stumble, however he'd greatly underestimated Quinn. The harder he went at her, the calmer she became until the attorney looked like a bumbling idiot.

She was spectacular.

Before Quinn left the stand, even though the prosecution had already asked her to do so, the judge asked if she would one more time "for the court" point to the man who stabbed and killed Homer Wallace. Quinn lifted her steady hand and pointed to Kenneth Allen. She did not flinch, she did not shake, she did not cower.

"One hundred percent, Your Honor. Kenneth Allen."

Quinn was dismissed, the bailiff escorted her back to the gallery, I took her hand, and my beautiful, brave woman walked out of the courtroom with her head held high.

The family followed, and once we were in the hall, each of them accosted Quinn, giving her hugs and words of praise.

And through it all, Quinn never let go of my hand.

Jasper and Emily followed us back to our house. My parents and the rest of her family went their separate ways, with Ethan promising to call as soon as he got word a verdict was reached.

It could be hours, it could be days. Either way, I didn't give a fuck. Quinn had done her part and it was over—almost.

Jasper had been cagey on the details about the investigation into who shot Quinn. I needed answers two weeks ago, but hadn't pushed. Today I was going to push.

Emily took Quinn into our room to help her change into something comfortable, leaving me in the living room with Jasper.

"I need a word," I told Jasper. Not bothering to wait, I opened the sliding glass door and went out to the patio.

He silently followed me outside and didn't make me wait. "The man who shot Quinn, his name is Rey Patel. The driver's name is Oscar Patel."

"They affiliated with Allen's gang?" I asked.

"Yes."

Well, that answered a few questions but not all of them.

"Go on," I prompted.

"We've discussed this and think it's better if—"

"Who's *we*?"

"Levi, Clark, Lenox, and me."

"Whatever you've discussed is bullshit. I need to know."

"No, Brice. You stay clean. All you need to know is it's being taken care of."

"That's not good enough."

"It's gonna—"

"Respect, Jasper, but I'm telling you, it's not good enough. I didn't say I wanted to know. I'm telling you I *need* to know." Jasper examined me silently—our eyes were locked, his mouth was tight, but he was close to giving in. "If we were talking about Emily, you wouldn't let this shit slide. No way would you accept the bullshit you just fed me. I don't give two fucks about staying clean. I've had one job in the last few weeks and that was making sure Quinn pulled through. But you don't think that I wasn't pissed the fuck off I couldn't go out and look for this guy myself? You don't think that it didn't eat my gut that while I was taking care of my woman, the motherfucker who shot her was out there roaming the streets and there wasn't a damn thing I could do about it? Quinn needed all of my time and attention. She got it. The trial's over, she's healin', and now I get something I need. Tell me, Jasper, what the fuck is going on?"

"Brady found the brothers," Jasper told me.

"Go on." Fucking Christ, it was like pulling teeth.

"It's unlikely either of them will be turned over to the police."

Fuck.

"Quinn's gonna be real unhappy she has to visit

her dad or uncles behind glass for the next twenty years."

Jasper's mouth twitched and he shook his head. "Then it's good she won't have to."

"She likes Brady, she won't be pleased to have to visit him, either."

"Brady put the word out, we have them. He's also made it known that the brothers like to talk, and what they're saying is making more than a few people uncomfortable. Brady's negotiating a deal. When he's happy with the terms, he'll turn the Patels over."

"And Quinn?"

"That's part of the deal. They forget she exists."

"They're fucking gangbangers. You really think they'll keep their word?"

"With what Brady got out of the brothers? Yes."

Thank fuck. Quinn would be in the clear, and even better, she wouldn't have to identify the man who shot her, and she wouldn't have to see the inside of a courtroom again. We could finally put all of this behind us.

"When is he delivering the brothers?"

"Tonight."

"Before they're turned over, I want my shot."

Jasper tensed and started to shake his head. "You get your shot?"

"Brice—"

"Did Lenox? Levi? Clark?" Jasper remained silent and his gaze slid from mine.

Yeah, they all took their shots. All of them.

"She's mine, Jasper. *Mine*. And that fucker almost took her from me. I get my turn."

His eyes came back to me, and he nodded.

"Hey." Emily poked her head out the sliding glass door. "We're gonna order lunch."

"Brice and I have an errand to run, sweets," Jasper told Emily. "You and Quinn go ahead and order lunch without us."

"We can wait..." Emily paused and must've read something in Jasper's stare because her smile faded and she gave in. "Okay. We'll order without you."

Jasper and I followed Emily into the house, Quinn was standing in the kitchen and I took a moment to study her. She looked relaxed—no tension, no anxiety, no fidgeting. She'd faced her fears head on, and damn if she wasn't stronger for it.

I quietly explained Jasper and I were going out for a bit and I watched for any unease, but it never came. She smiled sweetly and kissed me goodbye.

It was almost over.

JASPER SILENTLY DROVE us to a shit neighborhood not too far from where Quinn had watched Kenneth Allen murder a man. He pulled in front of a rundown house and parked.

When we entered the house, it was no better inside than it was outside. The place was a shithole, blankets covered the windows blacking out all outside light, old dirty shag rugs carpeted the floors, but I only had eyes for the filth handcuffed to the lone chair in the middle of the room. Brady leaned against the wall, face set to stone, and stared at me.

"This him?"

Brady grunted in the affirmative and I looked back to Rey Patel.

They'd worked him over pretty damn well. Both eyes blackened and almost swollen shut, dried blood caked on his face from either his nose or the gash on his left cheek, and a busted lip.

I felt nothing.

"Uncuff him." When Brady didn't make a move, I repeated myself. "Uncuff the fucker."

Brady pushed off the wall and Jasper nodded his approval. Once Brady removed the handcuffs, Rey stood.

"Can you see me?" I asked as I walked closer to the man who nearly took Quinn's life.

"Fuck you," he grumbled.

"Answer me, I want to make sure you can see me."

"I see you, motherfucker," Rey snarled.

"Good."

"Shoulda made sure the bitch was dead."

That was all I needed. Any lingering guilt I had about taking my shot after he'd obviously been worked over evaporated.

My fist connected with his jaw, then my elbow swung back, splitting open a new gash on his left side. The sight of his blood spurred me on. Over and over. My knuckles ached and my chest burned with hatred. I no longer saw Rey Patel standing in front of me. My vision blurred with images of Quinn's lifeless body on the sidewalk, then it flashed to her on a gurney, her heart not beating. By the time Jasper pulled me back, I was so lost in the memories I was numb.

"Enough!" Jasper shouted, pulling me from my nightmare.

It took a moment for me to focus on the room, my eyes finally hitting the man crumpled at my feet.

With one last savage kick to his stomach, I

walked to the door and waited for Jasper. He said something to Brady then opened the door and led us back to his SUV.

We were on the road a few minutes when I finally started paying attention. "Where are we going?"

"My house so you can clean up."

I glanced down at my hands and winced. I spent the rest of the drive to Jasper's searching my mind, trying to sift through my thoughts and process what I'd done.

Nothing.

I felt not a damn thing. Not guilt, not joy, not even a hint of remorse.

Rey Patel's blood coated my hands and the only thing I could summon up was relief.

It was over.

Quinn was free.

Jasper pulled into his driveway. But before we went in, I had to tell him something.

"I'm doing it tonight," I said and Jasper looked at me. "I wanted to wait until she was healed, until the trial was over. You all right with that?"

"Already told you I was."

"No, I mean now." I held up my hands, not sure what I was really asking or even showing him.

"Especially now." I nodded and started to open the door when Jasper continued. "When a father gives his daughter to a man, he does so with the hope that the man he's giving her to will love and protect her the way you would. Delaney found that in Carter. Wouldn't have thought less of you. Didn't even want you too near the situation. But I have to say, I'll be goddamn proud to walk my daughter to you."

There was nothing left to say, not that I could've spoken if there was.

32

Brice came home wearing my dad's shirt, his knuckles torn to hell, but otherwise uninjured. I wanted to ask where they'd been and what happened, but I didn't. Not when Brice looked at me and smiled.

Peace.

That was the word that came to mind when Brice pulled me into his arms and kissed the top of my head. All the questions I had seemed to flit away, leaving me with nothing but calm. Something I hadn't felt in a long time.

My parents had left shortly after Brice and my dad had returned and I still didn't ask. Wherever Brice had gone, whatever he'd done, he obviously needed it. If he wanted to tell me I had to trust he'd do so—in his own time. Something I'd learned about Brice—he liked to mull things over, sort them out in his mind before he talked about it.

I was okay with that. What we had, our bond, was unbreakable. It was far from superficial.

I was in our bedroom looking at the laundry basket full of clean clothes my mom had insisted on folding. Mine and Brice's. Something about that made me smile. Even our clothes looked good mixed together.

I heard him doing something in the living room and I knew it was time.

Today was the beginning of a new chapter.

Today marked the end of me being afraid.

The trial was over—I'd faced the monster. I'd sat on the witness stand and looked Kenneth Allen in the eye as I drove home the nails that would bury him. The verdict wasn't in yet, but I had no doubt he was going down. I watched the jury as I told my story, I saw the flinches when I described in detail what I saw as Kenneth Allen plunged his blade into Homer Wallace's throat.

I'd faced a lot of fears today but there was one more I needed to conquer.

Before I could chicken out, I made my way into the bathroom and gently pulled my t-shirt over my head. I was still sore but had vowed to push through the lingering pain. I couldn't have Brice or Mom helping me dress for the rest of my life.

I dropped the shirt on the floor, pulled the bandeau down, settled it around my waist, and stared at myself in the mirror. Two white bandages covered my wounds—mocking me, reminding me what a wimp I'd been.

Not anymore.

I looked down at my chest and peeled away the tape quickly and efficiently but didn't linger on the scar. I moved to the second one, repeated the process, tossed the bandages into the sink, and closed my eyes.

Come on, Quinn. It's now or never. Buck up and open your eyes.

I took a deep breath—luckily it was getting less painful each day—and opened my eyes.

I winced as two angry, puckered marks marring my flesh came into focus. Ugly greenish-blue bruising surrounded both wounds. My gaze flicked back and forth from the scar damn near in the center of my chest to the second one just over my right breast.

I was damn lucky both bullets had gone right through me. Neither of them had hit my heart.

Movement caught my eye and I glanced to the door. I found Brice standing there staring at me, his face tight, expression unreadable. He'd seen them of course; since I'd been home, he'd been cleaning and changing the dressings.

Each time I'd kept my gaze adverted. I'd been too afraid to watch him even though he'd already told me I was beautiful—no matter what.

Now there was no hiding.

"They're not as bad as I thought," I admitted, and they weren't.

In my mind, I conjured up all sorts of grotesque and gruesome images. But I didn't even have stitches, just red, irritated, creased skin, and a bruise.

Brice moved farther into the bathroom and came to a stop behind me.

"Beautiful," he whispered.

"Touch me."

"Quinn—"

"Please, Brice. I need to feel you touch me."

His hands went around me, one palm rested on my belly, the other went higher and he cupped my left breast. I watched in the mirror as his thumb grazed my pebbled nipple.

"More."

"Prettiest girl I've ever seen," he whispered

against my neck right before Brice nipped my shoulder.

My hands had already started to push down my shorts when his head came up and his gaze caught my movement.

"Baby—"

"More, Brice."

"Not—"

"I have the all-clear. So unless you no longer—"

My words were cut short when he turned me in his arms and I was suddenly face-to-face with a very pissed-off male.

"Mine!" was all Brice said before he gently picked me up and carried me to the bed.

His clothes were gone in a flash and he was climbing on the bed before I even had a moment to enjoy the sight of him naked.

Then he stopped, reached into the nightstand, after a second of fumbling, he rolled to his back, gingerly taking me with him so I was sitting astride him. My knees were pressed to his sides, my palms resting on his chest, but the only thing that I registered was his pounding heart.

"Are you—"

"I wanted to do this later. Hell, I've wanted to do this a hundred times. I wanted it to be special, something you'd look back on and smile. But I can't wait," he said bizarrely.

Brice pulled my hand off his chest and kissed my palm before he slid something down my finger.

"Marry me."

My lips tipped up and I smiled so wide I was sure I looked like a loon.

"Was that a question?"

Brice returned my smile, only he did it better. He didn't look like a loon, he looked hot. Then his smile faded into a sexy smirk and I knew I had my answer —he wasn't asking.

My gaze left his lips, moved down the column of his throat, hit his bare chest, then slid to my left hand resting on his chest. And I got my first look at my new, sparkling diamond.

Holy shit, I'm gonna marry Brice Lancaster.

"Make love to me," I croaked through the lump in my throat.

"Was that a question?"

I leaned forward, brushed my lips against his, and whispered, "Hurry, honey."

Brice didn't hurry. He took his time. Slow, gentle, and unbelievably sweet. When I was close, he knifed up, slammed his mouth on mine, and we fell off the edge together. Both of us moaning our pleasure.

It was perfect.

It was sublime.

Brice was all mine.

After we came down, Brice settled me on my side. My left hand rested over his heart, my leg hitched over his thigh, his hand was on my hip, and just like he'd done hundreds of times, his fingertips gently grazed my skin.

"Are you happy?" he asked.

"I'm dizzy with it."

His fingers stopped moving and he squeezed my hip.

"Good," he returned.

"Are you happy?"

"No, baby. Happy doesn't begin to cover it. This is bliss."

I lifted my head off his shoulder, looked down at his handsome face, and I saw it.

Bliss.

It would be much later that night, when my eyes were closed and I was near sleep, when I heard it.

"Mrs. Quinn Lancaster."

That's when I realized what Brice had called bliss was really heaven, and it was a really great place to be.

33

Levi McCoy

"We need to start recruiting," Jasper said, and Levi looked up from the case file in front of him.

Jasper was not wrong.

"We need at least five," Carter agreed.

Levi looked around the conference room, and not for the first time, pride swelled in his chest.

They'd done it. What had started out as an idea jotted down on a cocktail napkin as he, Lenox, Clark, and Jasper were nearing the end of their Army career, had turned into more than they'd ever expected.

A legacy they'd pass down to their families.

"Jason ready to leave the DEA yet?" Clark asked Jasper.

"Not for a few years," Jasper returned, then asked, "What about Nick? Is he done with the FBI?"

"Soon," Clark told him. "Only so many years a man can take spending time in the minds of psychopaths before a career change is necessary."

"Then we need to start recruiting," Jasper reiterated. "I'll start making calls this afternoon."

"Sorry to interrupt," Lauren came to the door.

"What is it, Lauren?" Lenox asked, and the receptionist visibly shrank back.

"Sor...sorry to interrupt," she sputtered and Levi fought back the urge to remind her she'd already apologized. The woman was as skittish as a cat—something that Levi found mildly annoying—but Lauren's attention to detail more than made up for her nervous habit. "There's a gentleman here to see Mr. McCoy. He doesn't have an appointment but he says it's urgent."

"Did he give you his name?" Levi asked.

"Colonel Coffey," Lauren answered.

"Send him on back," Levi told her, and then closed the file in front of him.

He was barely to his feet when the colonel entered the room.

Levi couldn't stop the spasm in his chest.

Dress uniform. Official business.

Blank, assessing eyes took in the room and landed on Levi.

A chill slid up his spine.

"McCoy—"

"Tell me," Levi demanded.

Coffey glanced around the room a second time, and Lenox stepped closer to Levi's right, Clark positioned himself on the left, and Levi fucking knew.

"She's MIA."

His daughter.

Levi locked his knees as they started to tremble.

"Intel says she's being held by rebels."

His goddamn baby girl was a POW.

"We have a SEAL team en route to the region. ETA is two hours."

"Where?" Levi choked.

"That's classified."

"Where the fuck is she?" Levi roared.

"McCoy, you know. You know better than most, I cannot tell you."

The chill turned into fire and his heart threatened to explode.

His girl.

His daughter.

Taken.

Captured.

"Fuck!" The sound that emanated from the back of his throat sounded feral, tortured, savage.

Levi's legs buckled and Lenox was there to catch him before he went to his knees. Memories flashed in rapid fire. Liberty's beautiful gold eyes lit with excitement when she announced she was following her father and uncles' footsteps and joining the Army. The day she graduated from OCS. The day she pulled Levi aside to tell him she'd been chosen for RASP. The pride he'd felt when his only daughter explained why she wanted to be a Ranger.

Captured.

"Christ," he exhaled.

"Which team?" Carter asked.

"Yours," Coffey replied. "Drake says you know how to get in touch. I suggest you hurry."

Levi heard Carter leave the room. He knew he needed to focus, knew he needed to be strong. He took one last moment to allow his mind to wallow in fear before he shoved that emotion down and determination took over.

He found his bearings, steel infused his spine, and he looked at Coffey.

"We're gonna find her," the other man announced.

"Goddamn right, we are!"

"She's smart."

"Know that," Levi grunted.

"Toughest candidate I've ever seen. And I don't mean physically, though she is that, too. Mentally she's strong. A natural problem-solver. Best marksman in her class. She flew through land navigation like it was child's play. You did well preparing her, McCoy. You have to know that. Lieutenant McCoy was specifically chosen for this mission because she's smart, tough, and she's proved her fortitude is beyond compare. Liberty McCoy wears that beret with pride, she is battle-ready, and she knows surrender is not a Ranger word. Liberty McCoy will be coming home."

Goddamn right, his daughter was coming home.

It was then Levi prayed she wouldn't return in a flag-covered pine box.

Taking Liberty is up next

Thaddeus - Susan Stoker Universe

Kyle - Susan Stoker Universe

Maximus - Susan Stoker Universe

The 707 Freedom Series

Free

Freeing Jasper

Finally Free

Freedom

The Next Generation (707 spinoff)

Saving Meadow

Chasing Honor

Finding Mercy

Claiming Tuesday

Adoring Delaney

Keeping Quinn

Taking Liberty

The Collective

Unbroken

Trust

ABOUT THE AUTHOR

Riley Edwards is a bestselling multi-genre author, wife, and military mom. Riley was born and raised in Los Angeles but now resides on the east coast with her fantastic husband and children.

Riley writes heart-stopping romance with sexy alpha heroes and even stronger heroines. Riley's favorite genres to write are romantic suspense and military romance.

Don't forget to sign up for Riley's newsletter and never miss another release, sale, or exclusive bonus material. https://www.subscribepage.com/RRsignup

Facebook Fan Group

www.rileyedwardsromance.com

facebook.com/Novelist.Riley.Edwards

twitter.com/rileyedwardsrom

instagram.com/rileyedwardsromance

bookbub.com/authors/riley-edwards

amazon.com/author/rileyedwards

ACKNOWLEDGMENTS

To all of you – the readers: Thank you for picking up this book and giving me a few hours of your time. Whether this is the first book of mine you've read or you've been with me from the beginning, thank you for your support. It is because of you I have the coolest job in the world.